SIDETRACKED

David Harley

PART 1 – A VERY ENGLISH REVOLUTION

CHAPTER ONE

S o there he was, marching down Whitehall to discover his fate, prepared to fight for his life, at the head of a procession of half a million people stretching back to Hyde Park. In fifteen minutes they would arrive. His mouth was dry and he could hear his heartbeat. Striding relentlessly forward, he paid no attention to the growl and clatter of the helicopters overhead, or the rhythmic beating of the drums behind. Like an Orange march in reverse, he thought – after what had happened, he was no loyalist to the Crown. The only thing missing was the sound of flutes and the smell of burning tyres. The young volunteers in the armed trade-union militias, some masked, rifles slung from their shoulders, walked alongside. Bright-eyed and ready for action, they scanned the tops of buildings and side alleys as they moved down the street. They all knew the army was waiting for them in Parliament Square.

Matt shot Sam a sideways glance and their eyes briefly locked. The one person he could still trust. If anyone knew what was going on in his head, it was Sam. He hoped he looked fearless, but she would sense his gnawing nerves. He wanted to show her what he was capable of in the heat of battle. If they got through the day unscathed – stuff the burdens of office, they would find some time and a quiet place to talk. Away from the crowds and the razzmatazz, the ever-shifting doubts and certainties, the highs and lows of their fight together. She had never asked for anything more than he could give. He would tell her he owed her nearly everything.

'Have you spoken to our soldiers?' he asked her.

'They swear the plans are in place,' she replied. 'We'll only know for certain when we get there. '

They passed the Cenotaph, the Ministry of Defence, and then Downing Street on the other side, hidden from view behind the armoured vehicles and high concrete defences. Matt pictured James Crouch peering through his binoculars from the garret window, knowing the game was up but refusing to admit it, trapped in his bunker by his own doing. Once this absurd standstill was resolved, Matt would show no mercy. Crouch was guilty of treason. One could almost say the same of the King. His behaviour had been unforgiveable. Ten minutes left.

$$\Longleftarrow\mathord{+}\mathord{+}\Longrightarrow$$

The change in Matt had begun six months earlier, in the cocktail bar of the Mayfair Hotel.

He sat on the edge of the group, as the magnum of champagne arrived in a silver cooler, together with eight crystal flutes.

'To success!' said Justin Fishbourne, raising his glass. 'And to the man who knows how to work the system better than anyone in Westminster - Matt Barker!'

While everyone around him drank to his health, yaying and whooping, Matt stared at the pile carpet. Fishbourne leaned over and patted Matt on the thigh.

'You're an absolute genius. I honestly don't think we could have got this deal without you.'

'Thanks, Justin, but I was only doing my job.'

'Go on, accept a little praise. Why don't you loosen up and join the fun?'

'Everything's fine. The contract's signed, we're all happy, don't worry about me.'

After glancing at his watch, Matt looked across at the door leading out of the bar. He knew the compliments were a sideshow, and at the first sign of trouble they would disown him. The unspoken rule never varied: lobbyists provided cover when convenient and were eminently expendable.

He had been in the game for nearly ten years and could smell an emotionally vulnerable MP or civil servant at a hundred paces. He used to enjoy walking the high wire between what was probably legal and ethical, and what definitely wasn't. In this latest case, that sense of risk and danger had been missing. All he had done was convince an elderly backbencher to table a couple of amendments to the energy bill at committee stage, and play three games of squash with the permanent secretary, two of which he let him win.

This modest outlay had helped Western Energy to secure licences for fracking and shale gas production on Exmoor and in the Peak District. The potential profits were estimated in billions. Matt's employer, the public affairs agency Nightingale Booth, had charged a tidy fee of two million pounds for all his hard work. Matt himself cleared up a ten per cent commission, which would be a useful cushion over the next few months in case he ran into trouble.

'I've told the prime minister about you,' said Fishbourne, bending his head and leaning into Matt's ear. 'He asked me to tell you the government's very grateful.'

'No bullshit please, Justin. Flattery makes me suspicious. It gives me the feeling someone's trying to sell me something I don't want.'

'I'll be straight with you,' said Fishbourne. 'There's another small favour I'd like to ask. This time it's more of a personal matter: I need someone who's prepared to massage the media on a rather sensitive issue. Discreetly demolish a few reputations. Try a few diversionary tactics.'

'Get to the point. What's the issue and who's the client?'

'We've got a problem with some of our major shareholders. Some of them are drawing the wrong conclusions from the company accounts. To put it bluntly, they're accusing me of robbing the employees' pension fund.'

A wave of *ennui* swept over Matt.

'And did you?'

'How could anyone imagine I would do such a thing?'

Matt had spotted the gleam in his eye.

'You wouldn't be the first. If you want me to help you, you'd better start by telling me the truth.'

Fishbourne looked taken aback, even offended. Leaning forward, clasping his hands together, he lowered his voice.

'Of course, I wouldn't steal money from the fund. It would be disgracefully unfair on the staff. It's been badly managed for years, and I felt it my duty to obtain a better return on investment. So on one or two occasions I took out a small temporary advance. I'll pay everything back, naturally, once we've made a decent profit. There's no point in just leaving it there, year after year, earning nothing.'

Matt felt slightly nauseous but showed no emotion. It was all so cheap and predictable. The light from the table-lamp glinted on Fishbourne's gold cufflinks.

'What exactly do you want me to do?'

'Just dig around a bit. Plant a few stories questioning the moral probity of the shareholders leading the revolt – the usual thing, evidence of tax evasion, alleged involvement in white-collar fraud, lurid sex life – basically, whatever you can find that'll hurt their credibility. This pension fund's been a goldmine for me, I wouldn't want to lose it. I'll make it worth your while – just name your fee.'

Matt took a deep breath and blinked. His patience was seeping away.

'I'm afraid this may be rather difficult - '

Before he could finish, he heard someone call his name. He looked up and saw Felicity, Fishbourne's PA, waving at him from the other side of the room.

'Have you two got something to share with the rest of us?'

Fishbourne winced at the unwelcome interruption.

'Just business,' he growled back. 'Nothing for you to worry about.'

Felicity was not to be silenced.

'Why don't you say a few words, Matt?' she continued. 'Tell us your secret. How do you manage to get up the arse of so many politicians without any of them ever noticing?'

A silence fell over the room, as everyone stopped talking and waited for Matt's answer. With their uniformly silly grins, clearly impressed by Felicity's chutzpah, the others doubtless expected Matt to play the game and reply in the same vein. With Fishbourne's proposal still buzzing around his head, he slowly stood up to reply.

'You should know, Felicity. You and I have done it together often enough.'

It took two or three seconds of more mindless laughter before his words sank in, and their corner of the room fell perfectly silent.

Apart from Fishbourne, who looked puzzled, as though he was trying to recall a particularly complex mathematical formula, and Felicity, who had turned pink, the rest of them burst out laughing.

'No offence meant,' said Matt. 'Anyway, that's enough excitement for one night. You've been a great team. Goodnight guys!'

'You can't leave now,' Fishbourne spluttered. 'We've still got things to discuss.'

Matt waved him away with the back of his hand. All that was no longer his concern.

After downing his glass of champagne in a single gulp, he headed straight for the door and into the lobby. As he stepped outside into the damp winter night, the thought that he would never see any of them again cheered him immensely. He had just shouted goodnight to the concierge, when he heard the steps behind him and felt a hand gripping his arm.

'Will you help me?' asked Fishbourne, panting. 'I need to know now. If we don't sort this out in the next few days, I'll lose everything. My reputation, my directorships - '

Matt shook off Fishbourne's arm and pushed him away.

'Dream on! You've had your chance, you and people like you, and you've failed. You've done enough damage to the country. All those people whose lives you ruined are waking up. The party's over, Justin, you're on the way out.'

The next morning Matt handed in his notice. One week later, practical formalities completed, he said a final goodbye to his boss Alan Booth, CEO of the agency. Matt began explaining his ideas for setting up a new movement, but Alan clearly wasn't interested. Like most people in the PR business, Alan existed in a kind of ethical no-mans-land, where questions of moral principle were considered bad form. They shook hands and Matt left the office.

As he crossed Westminster Bridge on his way to Waterloo, to catch the train out to West London, he looked across at the Houses of Parliament. Through the drizzle, he could see the flag of St George flying from the top of the Victoria Tower, and the canvas awnings over the riverside terrace – green stripes for the Commons, red for the Lords. He thought of all the times he had sat there happily with MPs and peers, joshing and schmoozing, laughing at their jokes, while discreetly pressing the case of his client companies and dubious foreign governments.

For years the comfortable, easymoney world of PR had suited him perfectly. The pickings were greatest where politics met business – 'where the river met the sea', he used to call it. Money for old rope, really, if you were lucky enough. He turned to advantage his apparent modesty and deceptive air of innocence: tall and thin, approaching forty, with his brown wavy hair and square-framed glasses, he dressed smartly but never stood out. He knew when to stay in the shadows, and when to pounce and strike.

Only now, after his vanity had cost him his marriage and the pleasure of playing with his two young children, did he see that it had all been a game, a reality role-playing show. He had allowed himself to be seduced by the glamour, the drink and the parties. Those cheap glory days were nearly over – the markets were jittery and another crash was heading their way. He needed to position himself for when the system collapsed. His aim was to end up on the winning side.

Rob Griffiths was already waiting for him in the Taste of Marrakesh coffee shop, off Putney High Street. His long frame was squeezed on to the bench behind the corner table, amidst the musky smell of apple-flavoured shisha. The older men at the back of the room, all bearded, sucked their hookah pipes through a plume of smoke. Matt noticed that despite the fumes inside and the warm sunshine outside, Rob still wore his old beige raincoat.

They had known each other for some fifteen years, since their early twenties, when they had both played for the Sunday morning football team – Rob in goal and Matt as a roving attacker. Their paths crossed again, and favours were exchanged or traded, when Rob became general secretary of the transport workers union. As well as sharing a breezy outward cynicism, they were each convinced of the need to end rule by the plutocrats and the country's drift towards a one-party state. Rob's resources in money and members were vital to Matt's plans to turn the situation round.

Rob ordered a coffee and Matt a small measure of aniseed-flavoured arak.

'No second thoughts?' asked Rob. 'Do you realise what you're letting yourself in for? You can still pull out – today's your last chance.'

Matt gave him a stern look of mock disapproval.

'I know what I'm doing, and I'm aware of the risks,' he said. 'You trade unionists always like to play the hard men. But when things get difficult, you're often the first to cave in. You'd better deliver what you promised. What have you come up with ?'

Rob passed him a USB stick.

'It's all in there. Call me if you have any questions. We've got three weeks to get organised. The demo's not going to be like Trump or Iraq, but we should get a decent turnout. Then we can build on our first success. No one suspects anything unusual - we've told the police the protest's about workers' rights. In the meantime, it's your job to work on the donors and the media. I'll look after the rest. Once everyone's assembled in Trafalgar Square, you can make your speech. It'll be your moment of glory – thousands will be watching. If the first stage succeeds, we can set up the movement and go on to take the country.'

Rob stopped speaking, looking across the table at Matt.

'Seriously, why are you doing this?' Rob asked him. 'It's my job to squeeze the rich, yours was to make them even richer. It was your whole life - are you sure you want to leave all that behind? What made you change?'

A flicker of impatience crossed Matt's face.

'You'll have to trust me. If my children ever come back, I want the country to be in better shape than when they left it. I don't want them to ask me, in twenty years' time, why I didn't stand up to the nationalists and the fascists. We can't let the government get away with all the damage they're causing.'

Matt took off his glasses and polished them.

'It's taken you long enough to come round,' said Rob. 'I always said you were too good a person to be a lobbyist.'

'And I always replied that trade-unionists weren't much better.'

'So a fresh start then. Goodbye to the sleazebags – good for you. We'll tread carefully and see what happens. How long is it since the children left?'

'Only a couple of months. Don't worry, I'll get over it. Let's get down to business.'

'Getting rid of those nationalists won't be easy,' said Rob. 'Don't forget – our coup may not be bloodless. In this country the establishment always wins.'

CHAPTER TWO

M att stood on the steps of the Latvian Embassy, a redbrick Edwardian house behind Madame Tussauds, mentally re-hearsing his pitch. He had received an unexpected call from Alan two days earlier.

'Before you disappear, I've got one last favour to ask. Go round to the Latvians and see if they need any help – they must be feeling vulnerable. If it works out, we can split the proceeds, and I'll sort out some crowdfunding for your movement.'

'That's very generous,' Matt had replied. 'I'll see what I can do.'

Finding a way of helping Latvia, after the Russian occupation, was not quite mission impossible but certainly a challenge. Even by its own standards, the English government's equivocation had been pitiful. Matt had worked with the ambassador before and admired her courage. Some additional funding for the movement would also come in useful. With his new project in mind, any way of opposing and embarrassing the government was worth trying: Matt had nothing to lose.

After he had rung the bell, the embassy door opened and a young man in a shiny blue suit led him to the drawing room.

The ambassador sat in one of the two facing armchairs in front of the fireplace. Despite the flickering flames, the room felt cold. Still life paintings of unappetising fruit and vegetables hung sadly on the walls, alongside landscapes showing endless expanses of muddy fields. The upholstery on the sofa appeared worn and threadbare. A bronze bust of a bearded man's head looked across sternly from a small table under the window on the far side of the room.

Ilze Lukasevica stood up to greet Matt. She was over six foot tall with long brown hair tied messily in a ponytail, and her eyes were bloodshot.

'Your Excellency,' said Matt, ' it's very good of you –'

'Mr Barker, please, we know each other well enough. Take a seat.'

'Any news?' asked Matt.

'It's been over a year and nothing's changed. Every new day is a penance. They arrived in Latgale – the eastern capital – on our national day, the nineteenth of November. It obviously wasn't a coincidence. That's the way the Russians work.'

She took out a cigarette from the carved wooden box on the coffee table, and let it dangle from her fingers, her head lowered.

'It's when things get difficult that we find out who our real friends are,' said Matt.

Raising her head, she lit her cigarette and inhaled deeply.

'Is England our friend? Is the United States? How much longer must we wait?'

'They're still making the same old excuses,' Matt replied. 'You know the litany – "we must respect international law, military conflict is not the answer, we need to find a political solution". Meanwhile, two years have gone by and one-third of your country remains under foreign occupation.'

'Mr Barker, your analysis is spot on, but you're too polite about your compatriots. I can't take any more of all this hypocrisy. What's happened to you Brits? What sort of a country have you become? The Latvian economy's at a standstill, the people are starving, and our so-called friends don't lift a finger. My nephew in Riga, who's eight years old, told me yesterday that the gas has been cut off again and they can only heat his school for two hours a day. You used to be true to your word and respected all over the world – when you made a promise, we believed you. Now you flirt with dictators and act as though we don't exist.'

'You know I'm on your side, Ambassador. That's why I asked to see you – so we could consider ways of ending this shameful stand-off. Up to now you haven't had a fair hearing in the media – we can help you change that.'

She turned away her head and blew out a large cloud of smoke.

'You mean more of your famous "stakeholder mapping" and pictures on TV of starving children? Despite your fine words, I suppose you'd make us pay through the nose as usual? Bloody lob-byists! Always ready to screw us, even in our hour of need.'

'"Consultant" might be a better word, Ambassador,' said Matt. 'More importantly, we want to help. We've done so before, and we won't give up now.'

'Who are you exactly, Mr Barker? What are your special quali-ties? Tell me why I should believe you're any more likely to succeed than all the others.'

Matt appreciated the ambassador's directness. Hoping he looked suitably deferential, he sat up in his chair, placing his hands on his knees.

'You're right to be sceptical, after the way you've been treated. Only you can judge whether I'm the right person for the job. If there's someone else that you prefer, I'd quite understand. What I can offer you is this: my personal commitment, a strategy for mobilising the media and public opinion, and some leverage over the foreign secretary. I'll spare you the details, but we know how to shame him politically and embarrass him personally.'

The ambassador threw back her head and laughed.

'Leverage! Over that unprincipled idiot! What on earth do you mean? We have a mutual interest to act against the Russians, can't you see that? You're under threat and we've got the intelligence. I heard the other day they've already infiltrated the heart of Downing Street, yet your government pretends nothing has changed. I can even give you the name of their agent – they say she's won over the prime minister. Anyway, we can't afford to pay you this time.'

Matt made a mental note of the remark about the PM. It was probably nonsense, but he would check it out. Despite the usual mixture of melodrama and paranoia, Matt was still determined to help her.

'The issue of payment shouldn't stop us from working together. How can anyone put a price on freedom, or on peace and security? We've got several options – we know one or two Ukrainian oligarchs who'd be happy to embarrass the Russians. Even the Chinese are starting to show interest. We can find someone to meet the cost – but we can't move without your go-ahead.'

'What you get up to with Watson is your business – I don't want to know. For the rest … you have my support.'

The ambassador stubbed out her cigarette and walked over to the table by the window. Against the amber evening sun streaming softly in behind her, she laid her hand on the bronze head.

'This is Oskar Kalpaks,' she said. 'Every Latvian child knows the story of his life. He was a national hero, who fought against the Bolsheviks and was killed by the Germans. There are only two million of us and we've been through desperate times before. We won't let the Russians snuff out our culture and our identity.'

She took Matt by the elbow and guided him into the hallway. They stood together in the half-light, facing each other, saying nothing. Taking a handkerchief from the sleeve of her dress, the ambassador dabbed her eyes and opened the front door.

A long crocodile of schoolgirls in grey uniform were walking two by two along the pavement in front of the embassy, chattering noisily and skipping over puddles. The ambassador forced a smile.

'Don't let my country disappear. Do whatever you can.'

CHAPTER THREE

It was a bright, fresh day in early March. Matt walked across St James's Park, through the last of the daffodils, towards Whitehall. The prospect of another meeting with his nemesis Alexander Watson, the foreign secretary, depressed him. He would keep his promise with Ilze Lukasevica and defend Latvia's interests, but shifting the government's position on relations with Russia would not be easy.

Although Matt and Watson had been in the same group of friends at Oxford, they had never been close. Matt didn't begrudge Watson's success – it was the mean-spirited arrogance that wore him down. He had grown tired of the pretentious verbal jousting that was a preliminary to every encounter. Matt knew the surface buffoonery was all an act, and when provoked Watson could reveal a furious temper. If Watson proved uncooperative, Matt had one or two inconvenient truths in reserve that might knock him off balance and make him more conciliatory. Coming away with nothing to show for his pains was inconceivable.

He walked up the steps at the bottom of King Charles Street and presented himself to the security guard. After a brief phone call upstairs, he was escorted across the quadrangle and up the cream marble staircase to the foreign secretary's immodest office – 'its size in inverse proportion to the influence of its occupant', an American ambassador had waspishly put it. As Matt waited in the anteroom, he noticed a newly hung picture, placed next to the door, depicting Napoleon's surrender to the Duke of Wellington at the Battle of Waterloo. A buzzer announced that the foreign secretary was free to see him.

'Ah there you are,' said Watson from behind his mahogany desk. 'Always a pleasure to see an old friend. How's Penny?'

'It's Jenny. We got divorced six months ago and she's living in Australia, with the children.'

Matt wasn't going to allow Watson to throw him off course. He helped himself to a chair.

'You seem to get about a bit yourself, from what one hears. How's your long-suffering wife?'

Watson switched on his poker face and snorted.

'This had better be important,' he said. 'If you hadn't done me a few favours over the years, I'd never have agreed to see you. Now you've cashed in your chips, you won't get in so easily next time. You've got ten minutes.'

Despite all the bluster, there was something comical about Watson's unusually large head and small hands.

'Why don't you slow down for a moment, and we can try to be a little more civilised,' Matt replied. 'We're old friends after all – even if I can't compete with your dazzling career. You look tired. Something keeping you awake at night? Too many fancy receptions – or is it those phone calls from the Pentagon at four in the morning telling you what to do?'

'You're the one who should have a bad conscience, given all your dodgy clients. Which corrupt country are you representing today? North Korea perhaps, or Uzbekistan?'

'I suppose you still pride yourself on never reading your briefs. You've got yourself quite a reputation in Whitehall for being a master of improvisation. I'm here to ask for justice for a small defence-less country that's occupied by a foreign power and that we seem to have abandoned.'

'Don't expect me to break down and cry – I was vaccinated long ago.'

'Doubtless you know about the NATO principle of collective defence – "An attack against one ally is considered as an attack against all allies". Article 5 of the Treaty – '

'Lecturing me won't get you anywhere.'

Watson leaned back in his chair with a pained expression, scratching his paunch.

'Matthew, I understand you have to do this for a living. I've always found your naïve side rather touching, but it's time you returned to reality. You really shouldn't believe everything they tell you – I suppose you've fallen for their usual sob story. The Latvian Government's hardly a champion of democracy. The native Russian speakers – a quarter of a million of them – aren't allowed out of the country and have no civil rights. What's more, your Latvian chums supported Hitler during the war.'

'Moscow would be proud of you, Alexander. You've learned your lines perfectly.'

A muscle twitched on Watson's left cheek.

'Nice try, Matthew. You may think that sounds clever, but you're way out of your depth on this one. Anyway, Latvia's a piffling little country of no importance to NATO. We should never have let them join in the first place – the Russians were bound to see it as pure provocation. There's nothing I can do to help you. Nothing. You've done what was asked of you – now you can go back to your Baltic friends and claim your fat cheque. Time's up I think – good talking to you. Are we done?'

Matt stretched out his legs and settled comfortably in his chair.

'You're not getting rid of me that easily – there's something else you need to hear. I think you'll agree it's in your interest.'

'If you really have to – keep it short.'

Matt took his time before he languidly resumed talking, with a quiet deliberateness.

'Wasn't Oxford a wonderful time? I've brought some photos in my briefcase of those happy days – would you like to take a look?'

Watson frowned.

'I'm already running late. Call my secretary and let's arrange lunch one day – '

'You remember that alcoholic picnic we had on Christ Church Meadow after our finals? And that pretty blonde boy you started chatting to? I never knew what he saw in you. The two of you went for a swim in the river, if I remember rightly, and you stayed friends for months afterwards. I bumped into him the other day – Miles, I think his name was – and he remembered it all vividly. Asked after you warmly. You were always an expert in the art of seduction – I suppose that must be helpful in your current job? I've got some photos where you and Miles look quite charming together.'

The foreign secretary stood up. Matt saw that Watson's hands were trembling as he stuffed them in his pockets.

'You're taking the piss, and it's not funny. I don't know what you're talking about.'

'You've got nothing to be worried about – nobody cares any more,' Matt replied. 'I always found your gay side one of your most appealing features. Try telling the truth for once. Come out, and I'll be the first to support you. It won't make any difference when you throw your hat in the ring to become prime minister – it'll probably win you more votes. And from what I've heard, your wife has always shown great understanding, although I suppose you don't tell her everything. I've got a few more pictures in my collection if necessary, although I don't like playing games … unless I'm forced to.'

Watson frowned, and shot a glance towards the door.

'Can I tell Latvia you'll review your position?' asked Matt. 'Perhaps you could call in the Russian ambassador, then it would be on the record?'

The foreign secretary slumped back in his seat, chest heaving. Matt hoped he wasn't going to have some kind of seizure. Watson picked up a bronze paperweight from his desk and passed it from one hand to the other.

'I'll think carefully about what you've said,' he said, still breathing heavily. 'As it happens, the government decided this morning on a change of policy, at my suggestion. You can tell Latvia we'll honour our commitments. Now get out.'

The normally ebullient foreign secretary looked flattened.

'I'm glad we got that cleared up,' said Matt. 'Can I give them a specific date?'

'Don't push me any further,' said Watson. 'You look very pleased with yourself, but you've crossed a line with me today. You'll no longer benefit from my protection.'

'What do you mean? As if I cared – I don't need your protection.'

The foreign secretary's face had become less florid, and he was breathing regularly again. He pressed a red button on his desk.

'In case you don't realise it, they're on to you. Last week the home secretary called me about an intelligence report where your name was mentioned. The document alleged you were plotting with the far left to overthrow the government. I told her this couldn't possibly be true: you were a personal friend and perfectly harmless, although prone to occasional bouts of idealism, and they should call off the investigation. After what you've done today, you're on your own.'

Matt barely had time to register this unexpected threat, when the double doors to the office swung open, and two heavily built men wearing earpieces escorted him out of the building.

CHAPTER FOUR

He had exchanged a life of froth for a dangerous gamble. Matt's devotion to his new cause was unshakeable. Yet there were days when, underneath the façade of self-confidence, he was plagued by self-doubt and the fear of failure. What made it worse was that he had no one to talk to.

He needed to succeed in his new project if he was to stay sane and grounded. Forcing the foreign secretary to make a U-turn on Russia would hardly go down as a Sarajevo moment in history. Yet every blow that landed on the government, however small, was a battle won. Like Putin, Matt was in for the long haul, first destabilising his enemy by chipping away rather than launching a full-frontal assault. That might come later.

Ilze Lukasevica sent him a bottle of vodka by special courier, with a personal message of appreciation from the Latvian Prime Minister.

'What's your secret weapon?' she asked Matt on the phone, sounding more than usually cheerful, when he called to thank her. 'When this is all over, I'll invite you to my summer house outside Riga for a modest celebration.'

'It's early days,' replied Matt, 'but I'd be delighted. I've enjoyed working with you.'

He doubted he would ever see her again. The Latvian sideshow was over, at least for him, if not for the people of Latvia. He had done his best.

As for Watson's rather melodramatic threat at the end of their meeting, Matt found it hard to take seriously. The irony was that, while Watson's accusations were essentially true, Matt's plans barely existed. *Ergo,* no one could possibly have known about them. Either Watson was bluffing, or rather unsubtly trying to save face. Surely the Home Office had better things to do? Matt's past record was unblemished and he counted for nothing, an ex-lobbyist of little importance. The only people who knew about Matt's intentions were Rob and Alan: that either would pass on compromising information was unthinkable. If the security services were trying to flush him out, he would proclaim his innocence and show them he didn't care.

Unafraid of the risks, he drove himself forward, grabbing every opportunity to hit out on social media at the government's moral vacuity both at home and abroad. Painstakingly, he prepared for the launch of their movement, as the number of his Twitter followers grew by the day. James Crouch, the Prime Minister, and his corrupt cronies had gone unchallenged for too long. Across the nation, they trampled on the disadvantaged and made sure the rich got richer. In the wider world, they kowtowed to fascistic America and snuggled up to warmongering Russia. England's former allies in Europe looked on aghast. Never in the field of human relations had so many friends and principles been betrayed in such a short time as by the cowardly few who pretended to run the country.

'What a bunch of shysters! How do they get away with it?' asked Rob one evening in the White Swan. Earlier that day the government had announced yet another cut in disability benefits.

'Because no one stands up to them,' Matt replied. 'No one dares make a move on their own - and I don't blame them. Once they realise they're not alone, they'll be ready to come out and fight.'

Over those first two weeks, during the day, Matt was buzzing with optimism and confidence. As long as he kept himself busy, all was well. Only the loneliness that enveloped him at the end of each day made him wonder if he was strong enough to succeed and survive on his own.

He told himself he didn't miss Jenny, but he hated himself for losing his children. He hadn't anticipated it would happen that way, that she would rip them away from him, his own flesh and blood. He had made a terrible miscalculation. The previous Sunday had been Jack's sixth birthday, the first one he had missed. Glued to his computer screen, fighting the tears, he had watched Jack blow out his candles on the other side of the world, and Sophie, who was two years older, try to boss her brother about as he opened his presents. Matt wasn't yet used to such pain.

What he found most difficult to put up with was his own company. He had forgotten what it was like to live on his own. His sparsely furnished two-bedroom flat was cold and impersonal. Apart from the photos on the mantelpiece, he still hadn't got round to furnishing it properly. A shot or two of a peaty malt before he went to bed helped him to wipe clean his doubts and send him to sleep, hanging on to the picture in his mind's eye of two tousled-haired children playing in the sun, or sleeping in the bunk beds he had seen on the videos, Jack with his striped tiger and Sophie with her rag doll. If only one day he would wake up and find them asleep in the next room.

Despite his protestations to himself that Jenny no longer meant anything to him, after particularly stressful days – or a few malts too many - she regularly popped up in his head in the middle of the night. As if to tease him, she always had on the emerald green dress that she had worn the night they decided to end it all.

In the midst of his troubled, muddled dreams, her image shone a harsh and glaring light. Over and over again, she mercilessly recalled their honeymoon in Italy, throwing the full works at him in a fast-shaking kaleidoscope of disjointed yet vivid snatches of long-buried memories – when they took the boat out in the middle of the night, diving off high cliffs, swimming out to hidden caves by the light of the moon, the sun and the light on the warm cobalt-blue sea, the hidden path where they clambered down to their secret bay.

After nights like this, his mind felt sliced up. Matt would wake drenched in sweat, vaguely aware from the ache in his head that his subconscious had taken a hard pummelling. Bleary-eyed, he would stumble to the bathroom, still chased at the back of his mind by the mocking vision in the emerald dress, who never made it clear if she wanted him back or to make him suffer. To his relief, as each week went by, these nocturnal visits from Jenny became less frequent. He would soon get over her, once and for all. The harder he worked, the further she receded.

He didn't realise until later the danger that laid in the other kind of day, the ones that held not the slightest trace of melancholy or worry, when the world around him positively glowed with promise. Rob had spotted the warning signs.

'Don't get ahead of yourself,' Rob told him. 'This is just the start. Focus on the work, not on the prize.'

These were the days when Matt felt euphoric and intoxicated by his project. He knew he shouldn't let it go to his head, but still … he had no idea what alchemy or rare conjuncture of stars had brought him, of all people, to this place at this time. He heard the warning voices, but could no longer avoid that clash with destiny… don't get above yourself, too full of yourself, keep your feet on the ground, organise, organise, build a trustworthy praetorian guard, you can't do it alone, but you can do it … He could feel the mounting mix of personal pride and faith in the cause starting to prey on his powers of reason, but he couldn't resist the excitement. Already there were times when indisputably nothing else mattered.

He was now working from early morning to midnight every day, preparing the official launch of the movement with Rob, as the date of the planned demonstration in Trafalgar Square drew closer. There were times late at night in the flat, immersed in charts and spreadsheets, media grids and bank statements, when he rubbed his eyes and shook his head and marvelled at the sheer improbability of what they were doing. Did they seriously believe they had a chance of making this work? Yet the first results showed there was a mass of potential support to be tapped: Alan's crowd-funding had brought in sizeable donations; people from different walks of life had responded positively to Rob's targeted online appeal for 'Help to save our country.' They included trade unions of course, and contacts from Matt's years in government relations, but also students, faith organisations and charities, a few enlightened business leaders, and a new group calling itself 'Soldiers For Democracy'. It was as though the country was slowly waking up after a long, drugged sleep and starting to feel hungry. Would those pledges of support turn into practical action when the crunch came? The governing class's reaction would be brutal, and he and Rob would be in the front line. Their disparate support base would need strong leadership. Matt was impatient for the action to begin.

Matt's faith in the justice of the cause they were fighting for never wavered. He shared the classic progressive analysis that one-third of the population suffered from poverty and oppression. Millions of people all over the country had seen their lives wrecked by the nationalist government and their repressive policies. As soon as his campaign kicked off, he would visit the regions worst affected – the North East, the eastern coastal regions, the many pockets of urban deprivation in towns and cities all over England - and listen to the people who suffered and struggled – however much they might not want to admit it. People who were paid a pittance for working long hours with no job security, who relied on public services which had been decimated, young people who had no prospect of ever buying their own home, communities where infant mortality and life expectancy were the worst in Western Europe. At first they had believed the nationalists' cynical promises of a better future based on fantasy economics and fabricated figures, and responded to the whipping up of xenophobia and prejudice, dressed up as an appeal to national pride. Now they knew they had been duped.

One day Rob put it to him that even if all that were true, liberal values and good intentions would not be enough to defeat the enemy.

'Once our campaign gets under way, the first reaction of the very people we want to help will be to tell us bluntly where to go. Precisely because they've been so screwed, they'll treat any new political movement with deep suspicion. They'll think we're just the same as all the others. They've had enough of being patronised.'

He knew that Rob was right – the old idealism was no longer a match for the new populism. He would need all his former lobbyist's combination of low cunning and emotional intelligence to put together a set of radical, practicable policies that resonated with the people's hopes and needs, and to convince them to stand up the nationalists.

While in London's moneyed mews and terraces the elites continued to enjoy their life of plenty, across the rest of the country nothing worked. Food shortages and power cuts were commonplace.

Schools were full to bursting point, hospitals closing, railways and roads no longer maintained. The country - or what was left of it, since Scotland and Northern Ireland had decided to go their own way, and Wales still hadn't made up its mind - was edging towards a bloody crossroads. There wasn't much time left.

CHAPTER FIVE

The Right Honourable James Maxwell Crouch, Prime Minister of England and First Lord of the Treasury, often complained to his closest advisers that people outside government didn't begin to understand the complexity of running the country. Every time he was called upon to take a decision, he had to weigh up a series of complex and competing considerations, including the national interest, the effect on his poll ratings, the cost, and how it would play in the media; as well as the assessment of the whips, the likely reaction of the party, how much support the decision would receive in cabinet, whether or not it was a manifesto commitment from the last general election or might figure in the next one, and – a factor to which Crouch attached particular importance - whether it would screw his enemies, above all those in his own party.

If he thought too hard about all these criteria, he'd never take any decisions at all. Fortunately, Crouch's political instincts never failed him. He had that special quality bestowed only on the greatest political leaders: when faced with a difficult problem, he always knew the right thing to do. He allowed no disagreement or dissent around the cabinet table. Questioning his views and decisions clogged up the process of government and was a waste of time, for Crouch had never been known to change his mind.

So when the home secretary, the prim and conscientious Martha Hunt, had seemed to balk at Crouch's instruction to crack down on their political opponents, the prime minister had not been amused. As she rambled on about civil rights and freedom of expression and even the United Nations Charter, Crouch had become increasingly impatient.

'Home Secretary, your job is to keep the country safe, not run an NGO,' he told her. 'We live in troubled times, and the people are rightly looking to us for firm leadership. If they feel we're getting soft, they won't vote for us.'

'With respect, Prime Minister – '

Crouch cut her off.

'There's no point, I know what you're going to say. I've heard it all before. You believe it's your duty to raise obscure points of law and refer to our international obligations. All that was fine when we didn't have rioting in the streets and anarchist movements funded by the Russians who are hell-bent on bringing down the government. Given the current unrest, our objective is to hunt down every potential terrorist and enemy of the state, and show no mercy. If you have to cut a few corners, don't worry, you'll have my full backing. Is that clear?'

Heads nodded around the cabinet table.

'Very well said, Prime Minister,' whispered Sir Christopher Jenks, the cabinet secretary, covering his mouth with his hand. Jenks always sat on Crouch's right at these meetings and was unfailingly loyal – or sycophantic, depending on one's point of view. At the very least, he knew which side his bread was buttered.

'Understood, Prime Minister,' said Hunt, a little flushed. She gathered her papers together in a tidy pile and laid her hands flat on the table in front of her.

'Before you disappear,' said Crouch, 'why don't you tell us what sort of people are on your list. Are they just the usual suspects – a fair sprinkling of radical clerics and clapped-out trots, I suppose – or are there any new categories we ought to know about?'

The home secretary cleared her throat.

'I don't know if that would be wholly appropriate. Could it wait until – '

'Just get on with it. The cabinet should know the kind of people we're dealing with.'

'As you wish. There's been one disturbing new development. Our services have picked up some traffic coming from the union leader Rob Griffiths.'

'That's not unusual – I thought he was one of ours.'

Hunt pursed her lips.

'We're not supposed to know that, Prime Minister. We believe that Mr Griffiths is no longer entirely reliable. What's more, he seems to have a surprising new friend.'

'Who is?'

'Matt Barker, the lobbyist. We have evidence to suggest he may be changing sides. Some of you may know him socially.'

Martha Hunt gave the foreign secretary a trenchant look.

The prime minister laughed.

'Is that the best you can come up with? I don't know him well, but I always thought Matt Barker was quite reasonable... a bit earnest and full of himself, but hardly likely to join the revolution. If there's the slightest doubt, make sure they give him the full treatment. The meeting's closed.'

As the members of the cabinet shuffled out of the room, Crouch thought he saw the foreign secretary wink at Martha Hunt.

Well, there's an unlikely alliance, he thought. I'll have Jenks intercept a few more phones. The trouble with this job is you can never relax.

CHAPTER SIX

'Delightful spot, isn't it?' said Giles Penfold, tossing the lettuce and tomato salad.

They were sitting outside the bungalow, under a faded yellow parasol, on a small decking area. Having consulted Google Maps on the way down, Matt knew that the derelict village of Pagham Beach was five miles west of Bognor Regis.

'It's quite a suntrap in the summer,' Penfold went on. 'So peaceful. Helps to get things back in perspective. Would you care for some more vinaigrette?'

Although he was still wondering what he was doing there, Matt had to admit it was a pleasant scene. In normal circumstances, he would have half closed his eyes and given himself over to the sensation of the breeze in his face and the sound of the sea. He might have even taken a stroll over the shingle and put a toe in the water. Not today.

Their end of the beach was deserted. The houses next to Penfold's – although Matt doubted he was the real owner – were empty and boarded up.

'They've suffered terribly round here from coastal erosion,' Penfold explained. 'Nobody comes any more, and the houses are worth nothing. The government's refused to put up any money for defences, which sounds cruel but I suppose it's understandable. Sooner or later there'll be one of those storm surges combined with a spring tide, and there'll be nothing left of the place. Then they can turn it into a nature reserve. At least, until that happens, we've got the beach to ourselves and we won't be disturbed.'

A man with a shaven head and a gold chain round his neck stuck his head out of the kitchen window behind them. After picking Matt up from the station in Bognor, he had prepared their lunch.

'Everything in order, sir?' he asked.

'Thanks, Logan. Delicious salad,' Penfold replied. 'I'll give you a shout if we need anything.'

They ate in silence for a few minutes. The whole place - the view that stretched out for miles in front of them, the abandoned houses on each side with their chipped paint and broken windows, the makeshift terrace where they were sitting – seemed cut off from everyday life. Barely twenty yards away, the sea lapped noiselessly on the shore. Every so often a few rays of weak sunshine would pierce the overcast sky and then disappear again. Just below the horizon, Matt could pick out the spindly masts of wind farms through the haze. In the middle distance, two giant container ships, one behind the other, were sailing imperiously towards Portsmouth, their stately progress barely perceptible. At the water's edge a small crowd of seagulls were arguing loudly over a rotten fish.

'Thank you for coming all this way,' said Penfold. 'I presume you didn't tell anybody? Let's have some fruit.'

'You made it clear I didn't have much choice. Nobody knows I'm here.'

Logan came out to clear away the plates, and laid two bowls of fruit salad on the table, with a jug of cream.

'Oh dear, I hope I didn't sound too rude. I felt it was one of those situations where it's better to come straight to the point. Your situation's become rather difficult, and I had to speak to you in person. I'm not sure I can keep them at bay much longer. The good news is there's still time to save you. Whether you survive depends largely on you.'

'I thought I'd come here to help you, not the other way round.'

'Sorry if I told a little white lie - I couldn't afford the risk of you turning me down. I knew I could count on your better nature. People like you are too good for this world.'

Penfold picked up a large scallop shell and lobbed it towards the seagulls who, after flapping their wings and squawking their annoyance, went on pecking the fish.

He had known at once that the call the previous day, so soon after Watson's warning, could hardly be a coincidence.

Matt had known Giles Penfold for several years as a senior civil servant in the Home Office, with the ostensible responsibility of facilitating visas for prospective investors from China and the Gulf States in London's commercial property market. Some of those high net worth individuals had been Matt's clients. Penfold had always been helpful and efficient, if rather taciturn, with a veneer of excessive politeness that Matt found both amusing and vaguely unsettling. He had occasionally wondered what Penfold did when he wasn't overseeing visa applications, but asked no questions.

'I know this may sound strange,' Penfold had begun. 'I've got a new job - I'm working at Number Ten - and I urgently need your advice. I didn't know who else to turn to. I need to speak to you in person.'

Matt felt cornered.

'How could I possibly help? We barely know each other.'

'I'll explain once we meet. I know your political skills, and what's more, you've got the contacts. We always got on so well when we worked together, don't you think? I've got a little place on the West Sussex coast – could you make it for lunch tomorrow?'

'This is a bit sudden – '

'Trust me, Matthew. I'll make sure you won't regret it. There are excellent train connections. Tell me when you'll arrive in Bognor and I'll send someone to pick you up.'

Reluctantly, Matt had accepted the invitation, on the grounds that it was probably better to know the precise nature of his fate before trying to resist it. He was confident that they didn't have any hard evidence against him, and he could easily out-bluff Penfold.

Penfold pulled his chair forward, closer to the table. He sat up straight and flexed his fingers.

'They say you've changed sides. If true, that would be regrettable. I'd be grateful for an explanation. Do help yourself to cream and sugar.'

Taking his time, Matt poured some cream from the jug over his fruit.

'Nothing's changed, I assure you,' said Matt. 'I'm still the same person you've always known. Now we've got over that misunderstanding, perhaps you could tell me about your new job – I'm curious.'

'The PM took me on as his security adviser to keep an eye on the home secretary. She sometimes allows her admirable principles to complicate government policy. When she's too soft, my job is to provide some steel behind the scenes. So I try and gently steer her in the right direction, preferably without her noticing. Let's get back to why we're here. I've told you what I'm doing; now it's your turn. Why are you acting against the state?'

Matt replaced his spoon in his bowl and reached for a glass of water. Penfold's gaze hardened. Logan came out of the house and stood in the doorway behind them, arms crossed, staring out to sea.

'I'm doing no such thing – '

'The facts are there, I'm afraid. We've intercepted a lot of compromising material recently – your emails and text messages, phone calls and various movements recorded on your Android. You seem to have discovered a new passion for good causes, but we take a rather different view. We've already got enough evidence to detain you indefinitely under the counter-terrorism act, although I hope that won't be necessary.'

'You're making this up. Just because I might disagree with the government on one or two issues, that's my right - it doesn't make me a terrorist. You've got the wrong man.'

Penfold smiled benevolently.

'The rules have changed. Since you're such a champion of democracy, I'm surprised you haven't noticed. Defending those in need is no longer our priority, quite the opposite in fact. We punish minorities now, whenever they step out of line and start creating trouble. It's what the vast majority of English people ex-pect from their government. They want to be protected from criminals and terrorists – and foreigners. Why are you doing this, Matt? If you make a full confession, we could probably still salvage the situation. Shall we go for a little walk – it'll help the digestion.'

'I've got nothing to confess,' said Matt, sounding too loud, fol-lowing Penfold towards the sea. Logan walked a few paces behind.

'What saddens me,' Penfold began,' is that we trusted you - we always saw you as one of us. That's why we made sure your lobbying career was such a glittering success, by giving you privileged access to government information and senior ministers. Surely you didn't think that you won all those contracts because of your own excep-tional abilities? No, Matt, it was because we saw a mutual interest. You did very well out of our unwavering support. Why have you turned against us?'

Matt saw no point in replying. They were walking side-by-side along the beach, each avoiding any eye contact. The attempt to needle him had been a little too obvious. He fixed his gaze on the silhouette of Bognor Regis pier protruding into the sea two or three miles ahead.

'I genuinely want to help,' Penfold went on. 'We can all take a wrong turning in our lives. The ultimate test of any man's integrity is to be able to recognise his own mistakes. Tell me everything, and we can still sort this out.'

He pointed to an old wooden bench at the foot of a nearby dune. They clambered up the sand and sat down. Looking around, Matt saw no sign of Logan.

'What makes you think I'm a threat? It doesn't make sense,' he said. 'Why are you making all this fuss?'

'It's time you dropped that air of false innocence – you're not fooling anyone. You've got more influence than you realise – you know too many people and you understand how the system operates. That makes you a potential threat. The prime minister believes that if our country is to survive, it has to be united. Those who stand in his way must be neutralised. No exceptions.'

'You make it sound very dramatic,' said Matt. 'Suppose I don't take your advice – what would happen than?

Penfold narrowed his eyes and scanned the sea, as if searching for a rare bird or a school of dolphins.

'That would be unfortunate. We hardly ever use physical violence nowadays – there are so many other ways we can destroy people's lives. Empty all your bank accounts, drop some bacteria into your weekly shop, plaster nasty-looking photos all over the Internet … the possibilities are endless. We operate in Australia too. I suggest you disappear, take a few months off, go and see the children. We can even help with the airfare. You'll come back feeling a whole lot better.'

Matt felt his stomach tighten. He got up from the bench and stood in front of Penfold, looking down on him with a mixture of pity and contempt.

'You've also got a choice - we all do,' said Matt. 'Can't you see what's really happening to our country, away from the rarefied groupthink of Downing Street? Propping up a failed state isn't being loyal to your country, quite the opposite. While the country's falling apart and the economy's collapsing, Crouch's only concern is staying in power – and protecting his fortune. The people have seen through him, they're demanding change, and I'm on their side. If I was you, I'd get out before it's too late.'

Penfold stood up, brushing some imaginary sand off his trousers.

'You're making a terrible mistake, and it's all so unnecessary,' he said. 'If you don't pull back, you're finished. Don't underestimate the consequences for you and your family. Wherever you go, we'll be watching your every move. We can make you suffer in ways you've never dreamed of. You'll soon find out the real meaning of pain. We can get inside your head and stay there until you scream to be released. You've had your chance and you've turned it down – you're in a different category now. You'd better make your own way home.'

Matt was no longer listening to Penfold's cheap histrionics. A dark raincloud scudded across the sky, blotting out the sun, and he shuddered at the sudden drop in temperature. He strode off along the beach in the direction of Bognor Regis, hoping to get there before the downpour, and looking forward to catching the first train home.

'I've spoken to him, Prime Minister. He got the message. I don't expect him to give us any more trouble.'

'Keep him under surveillance all the same. Lay off for a couple of weeks, until he feels secure again. Then send him a little reminder. Let Griffiths know what we've decided.'

CHAPTER SEVEN

Entering the warm fug of the White Swan was like stumbling across a mountain refuge in a blizzard. Relief swept all over him. Matt stood in the doorway and took in the scene: everything was in its usual place – the dark wooden chairs and tables, the pile of logs in the grate, the pub dog asleep under the coat-stand. After waving at Dexter the landlord, he looked over at their usual table in the corner, where he saw Rob deep in conversation with a young woman with short black hair. They hadn't yet noticed him. He wasn't too pleased at the thought of having to talk to someone he'd never met before.

The slow train back had stopped at every station. In his carriage, every seat was taken. He observed the other passengers - young and old, smart and shabby, sad and cheerful – and wondered who they were. There was no chance he was already being followed, but he should stay alert. He remembered the poster they used to put in buses: "Transport police officers are easy to recognise. They look like everyone else." Extra vigilance would doubtless soon become second nature.

He faced the danger head on. When he got home to his flat, he changed all the passwords on his computer, smartphone and bank accounts, and arranged for a locksmith to come round the following day to change the locks on the front door and windows. Even though these precautions wouldn't stop anyone determined to break in, they helped him to believe he still had some control over his life. His thoughts went back to the deserted beach, the noiseless waves, and the oily monotone of Penfold's voice, dripping with malice and evil intent.

He needed to know that Sophie and Jack were safe, and no one had tried to pick them up from school or frighten or molest them. She wouldn't thank him for it, but he would never forgive himself if something had happened to them, so he rang Jenny immediately. She replied tersely … didn't he realise it was late and she was busy and could he please call on Sundays as they had agreed … yes, yes, the children were fine …no, nothing unusual. The line went dead.

Nothing seemed to have changed inside the flat. His limited number of personal possessions – photos of the children, a few books – mainly historical biographies, his collection of glass birds on the shelves in the alcove by the fireplace – were all where he had left them. He peered nervously in all the cupboards, under his bed and even in the fridge, but saw no signs of any intrusion. Thank goodness he was meeting up with Rob later for a drink.

Matt walked over to where the others were seated. They both looked up and greeted him warmly, the woman with an expression of cheerful curiosity.

'Meet Sam,' said Rob. 'I've asked her to come and work for us - if you agree, of course. I know her from her time as a press officer in the union. She can handle the media for us, and help you organise your life. I'll get some drinks, and you can get to know each other.'

Matt sat down opposite Sam. She was small and slight, with black curly hair and piercing blue eyes. She gave off a freshness and directness that threw him off balance. He had come for a quiet pint - he didn't want anyone to organise his life, although he could do with some help in sharing his workload.

He studied the blackboard over Sam's shoulder with the day's specials. Then he glanced around the room, to see if there was anyone there he knew and hadn't noticed.

'Rob gave me an idea of what you're planning,' she said. 'I'd really like to contribute. What sort of person are you looking for?'

Matt turned his head to face her. Again, he felt the rush of her enthusiasm. He didn't have a ready-made job description in mind. If Rob vouched for her, he had to rely on his judgement. He took it as given that she could perform the basic tasks required - writing press statements, monitoring social media, helping to define messages and holding the line under siege. More importantly, how would they fit together? Would she be loyal?

'How much has Rob already told you?' he asked.

'That you're setting up a new political movement to overthrow the government. First of all, people join together in their local communities, to campaign on local issues, and then the movement builds upwards and outwards to take power nationally. If all goes well - that's the plan anyway. You've got a lot to do and not much time.'

It was a reasonable summary of the situation. This time he looked at her straight in the eye, in a not unfriendly way, but insistently.

'Why do you want to get involved? You may be putting your life in danger – are you sure you're ready for this?'

She returned his gaze, unwavering.

'Because I support what you're trying to do,' she said. 'I understand the risks, and I'm capable of making up my own mind. If you take me on, we'll have plenty of time to talk about what brought me here. In the meantime, you'll have to trust me. There's one thing I'd ask from you.'

'What's that?'

'No patronising. Ever. '

Matt raised an eyebrow.

'I didn't then and I never will.'

'So we have a deal?'

As Rob arrived with the drinks, Matt mouthed "yes" and he and Sam both smiled.

'Have you sorted everything out?' said Rob. 'She's the hardest working press officer I've ever met – '

'Not exactly the greatest compliment I've received in my life,' said Sam. 'But then with Rob, you have to take what you can get. He's a miserable bastard, haven't you noticed?'

'Don't I know it,' said Matt.

The three of them clinked glasses.

'Now down to work,' said Matt. 'I suggest Sam starts immediately. We've got just over a week to tell the country who we are and what we stand for. Sam, you and I will come up with some key messages. Rob, you'll keep us posted on the likely numbers of participants. The first time is bound to be difficult. We need a name and some brand recognition - how about the Save Our Country Alliance?'

'I can live with that,' said Sam. Rob nodded his agreement. With the minimum of fanfare, SOCA was born.

Matt offered to buy another round, but Sam said she'd better not and had to get home. She and Matt exchanged numbers and agreed to contact each other the next day.

'Sam seems very smart,' said Matt, after she'd left, as he brought back a pint for Rob and a double malt for himself. 'Thanks for the introduction.'

'You won't be disappointed. How was your trip to the coast?'

Matt stopped for a moment before replying, momentarily distracted.

'I was interrogated by a man I used to know from the security services. He claimed they knew about us, but I find that hard to believe. Now tell me what we should do after the demonstration, assuming it goes off well. How do we stay one step ahead of Crouch and the government in the weeks ahead? How can we take them by surprise?'

Before going to bed, after two stiff malts, Matt had a last look at his phone. There was a message on his voicemail from an unknown number. She didn't have to give her name – he immediately recognised Sam's husky voice.

'We need to organise a meeting to launch SOCA. I thought we'd do it the evening before Trafalgar Square. I'll try and bring in a few hundred people from all over the country. Leave it to me.'

Impressive. She had made a good start.

A question was gnawing at the back of his mind. He was sure he hadn't told Rob he was going to the coast.

Matt let out a long sigh. He put the bottle back in the cupboard, and ten minutes later he was asleep.

CHAPTER EIGHT

Martha Hunt was being particularly abstruse and holier-then-thou. She had only been in the prime minister's office for ten minutes, and she was already getting on Crouch's nerves. His back was playing up again. When he'd finished with Hunt, he would ask Valentina to give him a massage,

'Let me try once more to explain,' he said. 'I want to teach these people a lesson. We need to show the public we mean business. Preferably no fatalities, but baton charges, rubber bullets, Taser guns – all that's fine. Is that clear now?'

'With respect, Prime Minister, …'

Whenever he heard those four words, he knew he was about to be told the exact opposite of what he wanted to hear.

'…experience over the years has shown that using excessive force against political dissidents, while occasionally producing the desired result on the day, may prove counter-productive in the longer term, by creating an ideological underclass bent on undermining the institutions of a free democracy such as ours.'

'Did you learn that nonsense at the course you did at Hendon? They need to update the manual. I see the Met have got you round their little finger as they did with your predecessors. It's all empty theory, Martha. It's got nothing to do with the reality of the world we live in.'

'It's also contrary to established procedure, and possibly illegal, to decide in advance on the degree of force to be used at a peaceful protest,' the home secretary replied. 'We'd get crucified in the press and in the courts if anyone found out. We only use extreme measures if the demonstration gets out of control. Which we have no reason to believe will happen in this case. I'm only trying to protect you, Prime Minister. You'd be the first to complain, and rightly so, if I gave you erroneous advice. '

'Trying to protect me! Heaven forbid!' Crouch exclaimed.

Hunt was beyond belief. If he'd written her character into a work of fiction, no one would have taken it seriously.

He'd rarely met anyone so stubborn. So smug with it, as if she had a monopoly of virtue – which admittedly wasn't difficult given the current membership of the cabinet. She was so obsessed with doing everything by the book that he wondered if she didn't positively enjoy the rare occasions when he countermanded her. People were strange.

He slowly counted to ten in order to regain his composure and rediscover his inner peace. Perhaps it was time he played the flattery card.

'Martha, I've told you before how much I appreciate the fantastic job you're doing for my government. They say the Home Office is a graveyard of political reputations. In your case, it's the exact opposite: the longer you stay there, the more your reputation burns brightly, and the whole of Whitehall looks up to you for your diligence and vast experience.'

She was tapping her right foot, impervious and inscrutable. Oh well, at least he'd made an attempt to appeal to her softer side. Perhaps next time he'd try flicking her fanny with a feather duster – he quickly corrected himself. Anyway, it would probably produce the same result.

'You're absolutely right to point out the dangers implicit in transgressing the rule of law and the proper procedures. That's an important part of your responsibilities. My job is to decide what's best for the country, after weighing up the legal considerations and the political imperatives. Do we agree so far?'

Hunt nodded her assent, doubtless wondering where this was leading.

'Now what do we see in this particular case? What are the options before me, in deciding what's best for the country? It's quite simple, Home Secretary: next Saturday, several thousand trade unionists and extremists are holding a demonstration in the very centre of London, to shout abuse at you and me and incite revolt against the state. We know from our – sorry, your – intelligence that this is merely the first step in an orchestrated campaign to overthrow our democratically elected government.'

'Do we just stand by, and let them get on with it? Do we give their leader Mr Barker a free ride to create havoc and anarchy in our towns and villages?'

'Of course not, Prime Minister.'

'I'm glad we understand each other. This is what we'll do, Home Secretary. You'll tell the Met to show no mercy. We've got to stamp out this pathetic little movement before it has time to grow. Let the demonstrators listen to their leaders' boring speeches, have the police – the friendly bobbies – mingle with the crowd, putting them at their ease. Then when Barker comes on the podium, the police draw their truncheons and charge. No messing about. When this is over, I want to see pictures of bodies lying on the ground in the middle of Trafalgar Square covered in blood. Those images will go round the word, sending an unmistakeable message about who's running this country, and how we deal with those who question our values. That's what's best for the nation, Home Secretary, and that's what we're going to do. I expect you to inform the cabinet tomorrow. We've nothing more to discuss.'

Martha Hunt laboriously gathered up her pile of files and left the room, shoulders hunched, her heels clicking on the parquet floor.

⊨⊨⊨

Crouch switched on the intercom.

'Did you get that, Penfold?'

'Every word, Prime Minister. Couldn't have been clearer. I'll have a word with the Metropolitan Commissioner. He'll understand perfectly.'

CHAPTER NINE

The meeting to launch the Alliance the previous evening had attracted hundreds of people from all over the country. Over fifty thousand were now following Matt on Twitter. All in seven days, and everyone committed to support SOCA and fight for change.

'How did you find them?'

'Easy really – thanks to a loan from your old boss Alan, we bought some data. We accessed the voter files of those people most likely to support us, and sent them personalised messages on social media and by phone. Eighty per cent of those we contacted pledged support and gave donations, and half of them have turned up today. Now it's up to you to show them they're not wasting their time.'

Sam had booked the top floor of an old warehouse off Shoreditch High Street that had been converted into a pub, the Red Lion. After mingling with the crowd and thanking everyone he met for coming, Matt climbed on to a trestle table and Sam threw him a mike.

'We are living here tonight the very first minutes of a movement that we hope will soon sweep across our country. Not a political party, but a mass movement run by its members. We are literally giving power back to the people. Restoring their rights and their self-respect. No more centralised power structure, no more shameful inequality, no more diktats from on high – or from London.'

That one got him his first ripple of applause. Even the Londoners present laughed, if a little nervously.

'Our Alliance will help you campaign in the areas where you live and work on the issues that matter most to you. By organising with your communities, we can build support for the Alliance across the country, to win the next election and radically transform people's lives. From now on, nothing's impossible. Bring your families and your friends to Trafalgar Square tomorrow, and let's show the mainstream media and the world that together we can do it.'

He felt it and he meant it, as did everyone else in the room, he was sure. To loud cheers, he jumped off the table and found himself surrounded by his new friends and supporters. In turn listening to people's stories, answering questions as best he could, sharing jokes and laughter, the warmth flowed through him. He had never expected such an outpouring of energy and enthusiasm. He caught Sam's eye across the room, and guessed what she was thinking. The extraordinary journey had begun. He would not disappoint them.

The demonstration was the moment that Matt had been dreaming of for months, when everything was supposed to come together, and he would test his ideas and his speechifying against reality. He felt serenely confident and shit-scared at the same time.

When Matt and Sam came out of Charing Cross tube station, the top of the Strand was closed to traffic and packed with people walking towards Trafalgar Square. Surprised and impressed by the numbers, Matt stopped next to a newspaper stand, shuffling his thoughts, going through the bullet points of his speech. The last moment of solitary calm before diving into the crowd.

Looking left towards the square, he could see the top of Nelson's Column. The sky was cloudless and dark blue, with a sharp 9/11 luminosity. His mind scrambled back to that first unthinkable shattering of certainties. The origin of so many subsequent disasters could be traced to those two split seconds, the horrendous moment of impact on the eightieth and seventy-fifth floors, and the flames and carnage and bleak despair that resulted. The jumpers. His sister Sarah.

She had phoned him to say she was scared and the room she was in on the 106th floor was filling up with smoke. Eight minutes later the North Tower collapsed and she was dust. He never spoke of her; she was always with him.

What followed didn't help to assuage his grief. A nation first distraught, then swearing revenge. Hatred and fake patriotism feeding off each other. Intolerance and persecution let off the leash. Wars without reason, victors or spoils, just misery, maiming and death. The after-shocks hadn't stopped. From the Twin Towers to Trump Tower. Ignoble. Desecration.

'Bless you, Sarah,' he whispered to himself, turning his head away from Sam. 'Wish me luck.'

Matt shook himself and returned to the more mundane reality of the day that lay ahead. He should keep things in perspective. He was simply about to take a small step that was right for the country.

'Come on,' said Sam. 'Stop dreaming. It wouldn't look good if we were the last to arrive.'

She took his arm and gently pulled him forward, then let go as he broke into his stride.

In the forecourt outside the station, friends and supporters greeted each other noisily with much backslapping and high-fives, before unfurling their red SOCA banners. The crowd in the street moved slowly forward, to the accompanying rhythm of drum-beats and the blasting of klaxons and one or two vuvuzela horns. Children holding red balloons with the SOCA logo – a heart with an oak-tree in its centre – were carried high on parents' shoulders. Tourists standing in the doorways of souvenir shops waved and cheered in support.

When they finally reached Trafalgar Square, the supporters already occupied the entire central area south of the National Gallery. Led by half a dozen union stewards in hi-vis jackets, Matt and Sam forced their way through the crowd to the raised platform at the bottom end of the square, where they had arranged to meet Rob. On their way, they saw several pairs of policemen and women strolling around in their helmets and shirtsleeves, chatting to any young children they came across and discreetly making sure their presence was noted. The crowd was good-humoured, enjoying the day out, and occasionally lapsing into ribald jeers and fruity chants telling James Crouch where to go and where he could stuff his bunch of cronies.

'Your people have done a great job in publicising the event,' said Matt to Rob. 'Have you checked the sound?'

'Everything's working – we're ready to go. There's a lot of interest in your speech. Absolutely no pressure.'

'Do as we agreed and they'll love you,' said Sam, giving him a thumbs-up.

Rob and Sam took up position in the front row of the crowd, while Matt went round the back to the screened-off security area, waiting for his moment. After a few minutes the announcement came over the loudspeakers: 'Friends, ladies and gentlemen: let's give a warm welcome to the co-founder of the Save Our Country Alliance – Matt Barker!'

He heard the scattered cheers and took a deep breath. It was too late to worry about it now – either triumph or disaster lay in store, or anti-climactic mediocrity, the fates would decide. Clearing his head, he climbed the steps up to the platform and approached the microphone, to say a few words to the thousands of people that had poured into Trafalgar Square.

At first Matt had to speak over some low-level chatter and shuffling among the crowd, until the noise gradually died down.

'Thank you for coming,' he began. 'This is an important day.'

As the whole square fell silent, he saw the glow of anticipation on people's faces as they looked up at him. Expectations were high. The only sound now was the rumble of traffic and the squawking of pigeons.

'We stand here today, in our tens of thousands, with a simple message of change. We say to Mr Crouch and his autocratic nationalist government: the people's patience has run out. This country can do better. We demand fresh elections and a change of government.'

Encouraged by the first round of mild applause, Matt continued.

'Those who occupy the seats of power, only a few hundred yards away from here in Downing Street and Whitehall, have betrayed the people's trust. They had their chance and they've brought our country to its knees. The economy is broken, our institutions no longer function, and the England that we were once so proud of has become an object of pity and ridicule around the world. If Mr Crouch has any concern for our country's future, he should listen to the people's anger and draw the only possible conclusion: Crouch must resign from office immediately.'

The crowd had been unusually quiet up to now, unsure where Matt was taking them. His last words suddenly lifted the lid and a ear-splitting roar of approval engulfed Trafalgar Square. The chant began in one corner, quickly spreading, louder and louder - 'Crouch out! Crouch out!' – over and over again.

Their enthusiasm bowled him over. He had never imagined such strong support, so soon. Emboldened, Matt asked for silence and continued.

'From today, our Alliance will set up branches across the country, to defeat the nationalists by every peaceful means. This fight against hatred and intolerance is nothing less than our democratic and patriotic duty. We have one single aim and defining purpose - to save our country.'

As further deafening rounds of applause swept round the square, Matt looked over the heads of the crowd and noticed a dozen armoured vehicles drive slowly forward from the top of Northumberland Avenue. At first he scarcely paid attention. They came to a halt on the edge of the square, and out jumped several hundred police in full riot gear. Such a show of force was completely out of proportion. They must be on some kind of training exercise.

'I ask you to go back to your homes, your families, your friends and your workplace, and tell everyone you meet that the battle for England's future has begun.'

Surprised not to hear any reaction, Matt paused as he heard the collective gasp from the thousands in front of him. All eyes were focused on the police in their helmets and bulletproof vests. They were moving forward now towards the crowd, first in single file and then gradually fanning out, visors down, shields held up against their chests. Walking alongside them was the incongruous sight of a small group of men wearing balaclavas and carrying two red banners fixed to long wooden poles.

'Don't let them get away with this attack on our democracy,' Matt went on, in disbelief and desperation as he began to understand what was about to unfold. 'They know their days are nearly over. If we stay united, we'll be stronger and they'll be defeated ...'

He heard the sound of breaking glass. Turning to his right, he saw that the masked men had ripped off the banners from the poles, and begun smashing the windows of the bank and the bookshop on the corner of the street. Instead of trying to prevent the vandalism, the police drew their batons and waded into the crowd.

They began lashing out indiscriminately, beating whoever stood in their way, hitting or even kicking those on the ground as they passed, steadily advancing towards the platform where Matt was standing. To the dull repetitive thud of exploding tear gas grenades, and amid the crowd's screams of panic and pain, everyone began pushing and jostling to find a way out and away from the mayhem.

He tried calling for calm and yelled at the police to stop the violence, but no one was listening.

'Get down!' he heard Sam shout, as three policemen mounted the platform and ran towards him, twirling their batons.

The police dragged him down the steps and into the screened-off area behind the platform, out of public view. As Matt raised his arms to protect his face, he just had time to see they had no markings on their uniforms. Then he heard the crack of the truncheon on his head, raining blows, and his head shattered into a hundred fragments. The blackness engulfed him and he collapsed on to the ground.

PART 2 – THE CAMPAIGN GETS UNDERWAY

CHAPTER TEN

When he came round, he was lying on a hospital bed in St Thomas's A&E, with a nurse shining a light into his eyes and Sam standing next to her. The pain in his ribs and the pounding in his head were excruciating. With difficulty he tried to follow what Sam was saying.

'The doctors say you'll be fine after a few days' rest. Other people were not so lucky. Over thirty supporters were seriously injured and taken to hospital, two of them are in a critical condition.'

The throbbing became more acute. He cursed himself for his naivety in failing to foresee the violence. He was responsible for those innocent people being beaten up. Someone at the heart of government had tried to strangle his movement at birth. He would start the fightback as soon as he left the hospital.

The nurse gave Matt an injection and he drifted back to sleep.

Back at the flat the next day, nursing his aching skull and two cracked ribs, reading the media coverage did nothing to help Matt's recovery. As expected, the government press machine had taken full control. The largest-circulation tabloid, the Daily Standard, spoke of "a small minority of far-left agitators spewing bile and hate", and praised the police for their bravery in putting themselves in harm's way to protect the law-abiding public. Graphic photos of the bloody scenes were prominently displayed on the front pages of all the nationalist-supporting papers. Light relief was provided by the description of Matt as "a seedy lobbyist turned rabble-rouser in chief". He would print a copy of the article and frame it.

Matt's recovery was further endangered by a video on the London TV website showing James Crouch, described as "grim-faced and visibly moved", as he visited the injured in hospital and comforted their families. He promised that everything would be done to bring the perpetrators to justice. Asked about allegations of police brutality, Crouch announced his decision to set up an independent inquiry to reveal the full facts. He urged the home secretary "to get a grip" on her department.

The shameless hypocrisy of the man. Despite never having met Crouch, Matt detested everything he stood for – privilege and self-interest, corruption and cynicism. After his experience in Trafalgar Square, Matt's animosity towards the prime minister had become personal. The countdown to Crouch's exit from Downing Street had begun.

Matt wondered who had given the order to attack. Crouch himself would have been careful not to leave any fingerprints - anyway, such trifling matters were beneath him. The instructions probably came from some middle-ranking nationalist headbanger in the Met's counter-insurgency unit, acting without formal authority but knowing he had enough political cover. Then they sent in the special branch thugs, making sure the Met officers were kept well away. Who were these shadowy men in unmarked uniforms that had smashed his head with their truncheons and broken his ribs? Were did they come from, who paid them, where would they attack next?

A couple of days later, as Matt was beginning to feel himself again, Rob came round to visit him with a bunch of scraggy tulips. Matt was tempted to throw them back in his face.

'Is this some kind of joke? I'm not on my last legs you know. Where were you by the way - how come they didn't beat you up too?'

'Just kept my head down. At least you got some publicity. Good speech by the way, pity they cut you off just as you got going.'

After putting the flowers in water, in the hope it might resuscitate them, Matt sat down at the kitchen table and gestured to Rob to join him. He opened the window next to the sink to let in some air.

'That was the first skirmish – next time it may get bloodier,' said Matt. 'We've got to be better prepared. How can we defend ourselves?'

'First of all, whether you like it or not, you're going to need protection all round the clock.'

'That sounds a bit excessive.'

'You have to decide. Either we set up a professional organisation, with you as leader, or we're finished before we've even started.'

Matt had no wish to have his whole life turned upside down, but he knew Rob was right.

'Go on,' he said.

'Don't worry,' said Rob. 'Most of the time, you won't even notice them. We'll have a small number of armed stewards present at all public meetings. If things get rough, we've got enough light weapons and a few twenty-year-old machine guns to arm the trade-union militias – which officially don't exist, as you know – plus a small volunteer force we can set up.'

Rob seemed to enjoy the prospect of meeting force with force. Armed conflict had not been part of the original project. Matt had another idea.

'Let's hope we won't need any of that,' said Matt. 'We can only beat them by being quicker and smarter, and by mobilising enough public support. And we should use our strength among your members. How about organising a few selective strikes as a diversionary tactic? You could start next week with a blockade of the oil refineries. Do you think that would work?'

Matt saw Rob's eyes light up. Rob had once told him of his involvement, as a young union militant, in the blockade that over eight days in 2000 had nearly brought down the first Blair government. It was a good precedent.

'If that's what you want, consider it done,' Rob replied. 'You don't have to wait till next week. We can get the blockades in place at the main refineries – that's Ellesmere Port, Fawley and Humber – by tomorrow night, and from dawn the following day, nothing will go in or out. In less than a week, we'll bring the country to a standstill.'

'That's agreed then - I'll let you get on with it. Make it clear that this is exclusively union business, nothing to do with the Alliance,' said Matt. 'Don't hold back. We can't afford another defeat.'

Shortly after Rob had left, Matt was alone in his kitchen, a glass and a bottle of malt on the table in front of him, when his phone vibrated. The dial showed it was an unknown number. Tired and curious, he pressed Accept.

'Don't ring off, Matthew. You should know this conversation may be recorded,' said an oily voice. 'I'm sorry to hear you've been laid up, I hope you're feeling better – '

'You've got a nerve, Penfold. How did you get this number? I've got nothing to say to you – '

'It was all a terrible mistake, Matthew. Believe me. As you probably noticed, they were Special Forces, not policemen. The officer responsible will be severely reprimanded, and we'll offer you generous compensation, under certain conditions of course – '

Matt ended the call and switched off his phone. He downed the rest of his glass and poured himself another one.

CHAPTER ELEVEN

'I thought we'd abolished the unions – or at least watered down their rights so much they couldn't cause any trouble,' said the prime minister, glowering at Jeremy Burgess, the secretary of state for business and shared prosperity. 'We haven't heard a cheep from them for twenty years, and now all of a sudden they're creating chaos and holding the country to ransom. I'm told they've even formed some kind of alliance with our former friend Mr Barker. How do you explain that, Home Secretary? Surely Barker can't have any real influence?'

Martha Hunt looked him straight in the eye – unusually for her.

'My understanding was that, given its sensitivity, Number Ten was handling that particular case.'

So prim and up herself - he could have strangled her.

'Rather than playing the blame game, Home Secretary, the problem we have to deal with are the queues stretching for miles outside the few petrol stations that are still open. By tomorrow the shelves in most supermarkets will be empty. This situation has been going on for over a week, and the negotiations led by the oil companies are going nowhere. If we don't find a solution in the next forty-eight hours, we'll have to introduce rationing. Can someone tell me what's going on?'

Jeremy Burgess looked at his shoes, and Martha Hunt held up the page of a document, studying it intensely. The other ministers seated round the cabinet table looked straight ahead.

'Come on, be brave. We're all responsible for this mess. It's just that somebody must be more responsible than the others, and I'd like that person to have the honesty to own up.'

Eventually Burgess cleared his throat.

'The problem, Prime Minister, may be that the unions have been non-existent for so long, that nobody knows who's responsible for them.'

James Crouch was not impressed.

'That's an ingenious excuse, I'll hand it to you. Even if it was true, you wouldn't be absolved, nor would several other secretaries of state. The problem we face isn't only about the trade unions: the consequences of the blockade are felt right across government, affecting almost every department - business, naturally, but also energy, transport, security – even health and education.'

'Could I interrupt you there a moment, Prime Minister?' said Martha Hunt. 'I think there's something you've forgotten.'

Fuming, Crouch counted to ten, as slowly as possible.

'And what might that be?'

'You know full well, Prime Minister – because I sent you the file several days ago – that Barker's so-called movement is proving unexpectedly popular. There's no precedent for the level of support they've gained in such a short time. We told you it could quickly turn into a dangerous uprising if it's not stopped immediately. Frankly, the Home Office is surprised you haven't acted sooner.'

The icy silence spread all the way round the cabinet table. Hunt was the only one showing the hint of a smile. She must have been waiting a long time for this pathetic moment of satisfaction. Let her enjoy it while it lasted.

Looking around the table, but ignoring Hunt, Crouch gave his reply.

'We all know Martha's been under great strain recently, and she has all my sympathy. Now let's return to the grave challenges facing the country. I want each of you to listen carefully to what I have to say.'

The shuffling of papers ceased and all eyes were on him, showing varying degrees of nervousness.

'I've decided to end the blockade and crush any resistance by sending in the troops.'

His cabinet colleagues looked more horrified than impressed.

'Don't look so gloomy. This gives us a great opportunity. I'm surprised none of you has spotted it.'

Martha Hunt looked nervous.

'You're not thinking of a reshuffle, I hope, Prime Minister?'

'Quite the opposite, Martha,' said Crouch, his voice sounding unusually warm. 'If we play our cards right, we can stay in power forever. In five minutes you'll see what I mean. The press is waiting outside for me to make a statement. You're welcome to watch on the TV in the small drawing room. Now if you'll excuse me.'

The phalanx of cameras clicked and flashed as the door of Number Ten opened, and James Crouch strode out towards the lectern with the lion and unicorn crest, which stood in the street precisely four metres from the pavement.

Crouch enjoyed the company of journalists. The more deferential and sensible they were, the more he was inclined to give them privileged information. It was basic common sense. Whenever he had a go at the few remaining liberal members of the press corps, the other lobby correspondents would generally take Crouch's side and laugh at his jokes. Whether or not they were sincere was irrelevant: he had them where he wanted them.

Trying not to look too pleased with himself, Crouch began speaking.

'Good morning, everyone. Thank you for waiting.'

He held up his watch and looked at it.

'Five to twelve. Phew … it's still morning.'

On cue, he heard a few titters from the less hardened hacks.

'I will now make a short statement.'

Looking serious again, he started reading from the sheaf of paper that was placed in front of him on the lectern.

'This country faces the most serious threat to its democracy since the Second World War. As a nation whose constitution is based on the rule of law, we cannot allow a small minority to use violent means to prevent our citizens from going about their daily business. The primary duty of the government is to protect its citizens and maintain law and order.'

He paused, looked left and right, and continued.

'In view of the rapidly deteriorating situation concerning the availability of essential supplies of fuel and food, at its meeting this morning the Cabinet unanimously approved my proposal to send in the troops. The armed forces have been ordered to use whatever means they consider appropriate to restore order to England's transport, energy and food distribution systems, notably by ending all blockades of oil refineries and fuel depots by midnight tonight.'

The journalists were already frantically typing out and phoning through the story when Crouch held up his hand.

'I have one more important announcement.'

All eyes - and the TV cameras - were on him once again.

'Given the grave crisis in which our country finds itself, despite all the essential measures already taken by the government, I believe that further action is indispensable. I have therefore decided to seek a renewed mandate from the people, in order to defend our nation from the extremist and terrorist groups that are attempting, as we speak, to destroy the values we cherish and the very fabric of our society.'

'Earlier today, I proposed to His Majesty The King the dissolution of Parliament and the calling of a general election in three months' time. The King graciously agreed, subject to the usual constitutional requirements.'

Ignoring the instantaneous explosion of frenzy and the bombardment of questions, he folded the text of his statement and placed it in his inside jacket pocket. After standing for a moment for the cameras and photographers, with an expression of profound gravity and solemnity etched on his face, James Crouch turned and went back inside Number Ten.

He decided to avoid the inevitable hysteria that must have broken out among his cabinet colleagues in the small drawing room, and asked for a pot of tea to be taken up to the prime minister's private drawing room. His companion Valentina was out to lunch with a friend, and he had the flat to himself. He looked forward to curling up on the sofa and watching on catch-up, over and over again, the moment of history he had so artfully created. The delicious prospect of untrammelled power, for as long as he wanted. Not bad for a day's work.

CHAPTER TWELVE

Matt was chopping some vegetables, shortly before Sam was due to come round for supper, when he heard the news on the radio. The troops were on their way to the refineries.

His thoughts went out to the heroic men and women sleeping rough, or if they were lucky in tents, outside Ellesmere Port and the other main refineries. Spring had arrived, but at night the temperature fell to single figures. He pictured the army convoys driving through the night along the motorway, with orders to break the blockade, by force if necessary. The other questions stemming from Crouch's decision could wait. He phoned Rob.

'You're not going to like this, but you've got to call off the blockade. Immediately.'

There was silence, followed by an angry intake of breath.

'You can't be serious – there's no way I can stop them now. The reason Crouch has called an election is because we've got him on the run and he's trying to buy time - can't you see that? The government's lost all credibility. We've won the greatest trade-union victory in a generation. We can't just surrender and walk away.'

'It won't be a surrender. Crouch is panicking. Your people have been brilliant and they can be proud of what they've achieved. You can quote Churchill: "In defeat, defiance. In victory, magnanimity."'

'That's not going to help me much with my members. After all the nights they've spent outside in the cold, without any sleep, maintaining this blockade, I'm supposed to say thanks, but it's all over and by the way, we've won nothing.'

'We can't run the risk of having people shot and killed by the army. You know that's true. Tell them they've won the first battle in a war that's only just begun. The next challenge will be to kick out Crouch and the nationalists in the election.'

'Easier said than done, and I don't need you to write the script for me. I suppose I haven't got much choice.'

To Matt's relief, he could sense that Rob was coming round.

'I'm glad we agree. Now let's move on - we've got a million things to do and a very tight timetable. I'm calling a meeting for tomorrow morning, in our new campaign office, and I want you to be there. My former boss Alan's lent us a floor of his company's premises in Westminster. He said he won't charge any rent, provided we win the election. We move in tomorrow. Tonight may be your last chance for a long time to get a good night's sleep – make the most of it.'

'Okay, you win. I'll tell our people to lay off. See you in the morning.'

Matt filled a large casserole full of water and placed it on the gas ring. He hoped Sam would appreciate his cooking.

He had asked her round to his flat for a meal, to thank her for looking after him while he'd been recovering from his injuries. She'd been a great support during those difficult days, and he was looking forward to seeing her again. They were comrades-in-arms, and he wanted to show her his gratitude.

When he served up the *tagliatelle* with meatballs and leeks in a cream sauce, he was amused to see Sam tucking into the pasta with gusto, as if she hadn't eaten for a week.

'Delicious,' said Sam. 'I'd never seen you as a cook. I must come here more often.'

Matt shrugged off her praise.

'Really, it was nothing. It's a very simple dish. Your turn next time,' Matt replied, pouring her a glass of red wine.

They sat on opposite sides of the small square table in the living room, Sam facing the window and Matt with a view into the kitchen. He had repainted the walls the previous week, and bought a new lampshade that hung over the table, giving off a soft golden glow. He'd even dusted his collection of coloured glass birds that stood among the photos of Sophie and Jack on the shelf above the gas fire.

'Thanks for all your support,' he went on. 'I was in a bad way after Trafalgar Square. I don't know how I'd have got through that time without you. You were very kind and helpful.'

'Helpful?' said Sam, frowning, as if turning over the word in her mind. Perhaps she thought it sounded rather cold and formal. That wasn't what he meant - he hoped he hadn't offended her.

'You were a difficult patient,' Sam went on. 'Not very obedient. Are you always like that?'

She had this way of cocking her head on one side after she'd asked a question, with a faux-deadpan expression that flickered between ambivalence and mischief.

'I'm not quite sure what you mean,' he replied. 'Anyway, that's all over now. I'm fully recovered, and looking forward to getting down to work.'

Sam finished her pasta and carefully aligned her knife and fork on the plate. She poured them both another glass of wine.

'Let's not talk about work for once,' said Sam. 'How did you get into all this? Did you always want to start a revolution?'

He couldn't be sure, but the serious look on her face seemed sincere.

'No, I honestly never expected to end up in this situation. When things reached a new low point last year, I felt I had to do something about it. Most of the time I feel there's some force pushing me forward and there's no way I can turn back. Fate, I suppose. Not that I would want to change course.'

'Was the low point political or personal?'

'A bit of both, I suppose.'

'You said once you had a wife and two kids, and they're in Australia?'

Please God, he said to himself. Spare me the interrogation.

'That's right. What about you? When did you see the light?'

'When I met you, of course.'

Matt spluttered into his wine.

'Only joking.'

She reached across the table and patted his arm.

'Or half joking. I'll tell you about me some other time. Anyway, I'm pleased we're doing this together. I'll give it my all, I promise you.'

When the meal was over, Matt cleared away the dishes, and rinsed the plates before stacking them in the dishwasher. He was pleased to have asked Sam round, and everything seemed to be going well. He liked the way she was both strong-willed and quizzical. The two of them were on the same wavelength, and their partnership was essential to the success of the project.

He went back into the living room, carrying a tray with two cups of coffee, and they sat together on the sofa. Matt opened his laptop and began to show her the video footage of Crouch's statement announcing the election.

Sam looked uninterested and unimpressed.

'I don't need to see this all over again,' she said. 'I know it's asking a lot, but can't we forget about politics for a moment. Is there something else we could watch now?'

They agreed on *Under The Skin,* which they'd both seen before. When the first scary scene came along, Matt put his arm round Sam's shoulder. She snuggled up and they sat there, watching the screen intently.

All afternoon Matt had tried in vain to work out how he should react to the new situation created by the calling of an early election. That hint of a smirk on Crouch's face, caught on camera as he turned to go back inside Number Ten, gave Matt hope. In politics, complacency was so often the prelude to downfall, and everything came and went in cycles. The flummery and flattery that came with power had turned Crouch's head. The country had changed and Crouch hadn't noticed. His decision would backfire, by people seeing him as yesterday's man, up himself and out of touch. That was Matt's gamble.

Of course, he would take nothing for granted. Conventional wisdom would say that no rational person would launch a new political movement, and hope to win seats in Parliament, in the space of only three months. A respectable protest vote if they were lucky, but surely no seats. But these were exceptional times, when conventional wisdom counted for little. The challenge was to make the organisation of the Alliance's campaign strong enough to swim naturally with the prevailing political tide.

The more he succeeded, the greater the risks. He thought about Penfold, and the phone call enquiring after his health. The message was clear: they had him in their sights. If Matt didn't back away, hostilities would resume, but this time against the background of an election campaign, played for the highest possible stakes. The forces of the state would be ruthlessly employed, with a single aim: to ensure the continued exercise of power and pursuit of wealth by that part of the governing class that backed Crouch. They would brush aside anyone who stood in their way, without a second thought. They would come for him in the middle of the night, and extract his fingernails or slit his throat if they thought it would make any difference to the result. Without leaving any trace; no one would know. The great democratic celebration of the general election would continue as normal, while under the surface the parties' surrogates grappled and wrestled in the mud. "The dogs bark, but the caravan moves on."

It wasn't about pride. He would never tell anybody this, but he was infused by a sense of mission, bound up with the natural order of things and the cards he had been dealt.

The film was over and the bottle was empty. Matt had paid little attention to Scarlett Johansson's alien incursions into the back streets of Glasgow, his thoughts veering between his destiny and Sam. He sensed that Sam's thoughts had also been elsewhere. He could feel himself melting and hardening at the same time.

They watched the final credits roll, not saying anything, until she turned to face him. Her hair stuck up in places and her lips were moist.

When he leaned forward to kiss her, she took hold of both his hands and pushed him gently away.

'I've been thinking about what we were saying before the film, about fate and how we each got into this situation - there's something important we need to discuss,' she said.

'Go on,' said Matt.

She let go of his hands.

'What happened today changes everything. Not just for the Alliance, but for you. Surely you realise that?'

He shook his head, not getting it.

'You have to take him on. *Mano a mano*. In his seat. It'll be the perfect platform. You have to stand for parliament in James Crouch's constituency. The entire country and the whole world will be watching. You even live in the area. You'll never get another chance like this - go for it.'

'I'm not sure …'

His words were trailing, but his mind was racing. On the face of it, what she proposed was a suicide mission. But he was up for it.

There was no better way of guaranteeing massive media coverage and destabilising Crouch than to stand against him on his home territory. Like all the best ideas, the proposal was so crazy that it might actually work.

'You might be right.'

Their eyes locked. This time she let him kiss her.

Breathless, his head spinning and his heart pounding, he drew her towards him and held her tight.

At last. As the charge hit him, she felt so soft and luscious and inviting. He thought he had inoculated his weaker side against the risks of passion and pain, but apparently not. The timing and the context weren't perfect, but he wouldn't let that get in the way. Unbelievably smart and tender, all at once.

As they undressed in the bedroom he never took his eyes off her. He saw the reflection of their naked bodies and the dancing shadows across the room in the mirror behind her.

'Why did it take you so long?' she whispered as they lay next to each other in the bed.

'I must have always known,' he said.

'Well, we finally made it, that's all that matters,' Sam replied, head tilted on one side, giving him that look. 'We'd better make up for lost time.'

They started tentatively and then came together in an explosive, mind-and-body cleansing sense of release, unlike anything he had ever known. In the space of a couple of hours she had reset his life. As he stared in wonder at her sleeping face, he couldn't believe his luck.

Several hours later, he heard the sound of his phone vibrating from inside his trousers, which lay in a heap on the floor by his bed. At that time of night, it could only be Jenny. He stretched out his arm and managed to switch it off, without disturbing the rhythm of Sam's breathing beside him.

CHAPTER THIRTEEN

W hen he woke up shortly before six the following morning, feeling Sam's smooth warm skin alongside him, he gave a half-sigh, half-groan of pleasure. For a few semi-conscious seconds, the day was bursting with promise and he was at one with the world. Then he glimpsed in his mind the tidal wave of frenzy that was roaring down the hill towards him: once he had made his decision, there would be no escape. He would have to deal with whatever they threw at him. Sliding out of bed and padding to the bathroom that morning would be the last time for months that he did anything slowly and entirely of his own volition. From now on he would be living under the relentless glare of the prying press – as well as fending off the dark forces of the state. Goodbye to the world he had known all his life, hello to …what exactly?

He quickly showered and dressed, and whispered goodbye to Sam, stroking her hair and telling her there was no need to hurry. They would see each other later at the meeting. He left a spare set of keys on the kitchen table, and a note asking her to lock the front door. As he dodged round the bleary-eyed commuters on the way to the tube station, he wondered how long the light-headedness would last.

He was the first to arrive that morning in the new open-plan office, which occupied two thousand square feet of a converted attic in Tufton Street, with a partial view from the window of the two western towers of Westminster Abbey. By seven thirty, all the members of the campaign team had arrived and were hard at work, claiming desks, installing computers, experimenting with the printer and the coffee machine. Sam was one of the last to arrive, and brought Matt a coffee. When he looked up and thanked her, she raised a finger to her lips and sat down a short distance away.

Fifteen minutes later they were all seated around what Rob had already named the 'boardroom table', which they carried from where it stood against one of the side-walls to the middle of the room. As the team members took their seats, Matt greeted each of them in turn. He had invited the twenty people he relied on and trusted most. In addition to Rob and Sam, the participants represented the Alliance's core target groups – trade unions naturally, but also community action groups, small businesses, public service workers, students, IT start-ups, creative industries, NGOs, faith organisations and charities. They formed a credible coalition of interests from sectors of society that opposed the nationalists and all they stood for. They were all people who were known and respected in the communities where they lived and the areas where they worked.

Matt needed to have around him a team of people that wouldn't snap or snarl or panic when the crisis hit, and who believed in what they were doing. What they were planning to achieve together would be the greatest challenge that any of them, Matt included, had ever faced. The twenty stalwarts present that morning were the inner core, the backbone of the movement. He hoped he had chosen well.

Two of his favourites were Bernadette Poignant, who came from Brittany and had set up her own environmental NGO, and was both passionate and principled in everything she did, and Ahmed Khan, the leader of the students' union in the local university, who had the air of authenticity and easy charm of a natural networker. What Bernadette and Ahmed also had in common was that they were each brutally frank. Matt knew that any bullshitting on his part would be detected within seconds, and appreciated their readiness to challenge his ideas.

'You're wrong,' Bernadette had told him the other day, when they had been discussing ideas for a new housing policy. 'And you have a tendency to talk too much.'

Ahmed had just laughed, refusing to take sides.

'Don't worry about her,' he said eventually, noticing Matt's flicker of irritation. 'She means well, but she's not very diplomatic. Or modest. After all, she's French.' Ahmed ducked as Bernadette pretended to slap his face.

He looked around the table, checking that everyone had arrived, making eye contact with each of them. After calling the meeting to order, Matt gave each person present a series of tasks – setting up a legal structure, proposing a procedure for electing officers, organising a membership drive, fundraising, events planning, or buying advertising space. Matt himself would oversee policy; Rob would be responsible for general organisation, and Sam in charge of media and communications.

'Before you start work, there's something I want to tell you,' said Matt.

He felt twenty pairs of questioning eyes boring into him.

'I've decided to put myself forward to run against James Crouch in the general election, in the constituency of West Thameside, which he currently represents – hopefully for not much longer.'

As the news sank in, the initial expressions of surprise were cancelled out by a short burst of clapping, led by Ahmed. Rob sat stony-faced, the only one present that didn't join in.

'Obviously, like every other Alliance candidate, I expect to go through the proper selection procedure – which we have to adopt as soon as possible - so I'm not taking anything for granted. But my aim is to stand against Crouch on his home turf, so that our movement as a whole can benefit from the resulting publicity and media coverage. I wanted you to be the first to know.'

'You don't hang about,' said Rob, sitting down next to Matt, as the others went back to their desks. 'We need to talk about this – you've just signed up for a humiliating defeat. You should have consulted me first. Whoever gave you that idea?'

'It just felt like the obvious thing to do,' Matt replied. 'Anyway, my decision's made, and if I obtain the nomination, I'm going to fight to win.'

In the days and weeks that followed, whatever he did and wherever he went, the pace quickened and the pressure mounted. Incessantly buffeted about by the need for rapid-fire decisions and real-time reactions, continuously moving from one stage to the next, he had no time to question the purpose of it all. He was insane, he would tell himself after a particularly long day, completely insane, to be fighting on two fronts at the same time – the constituency battle against Crouch which he knew would soon become personal and venomous, and the nationwide campaign to win votes and seats for the Save Our Country Alliance. There were no bounds to his optimism and commitment to the cause, but the limits of his mental and physical resilience were being tested as never before. During those moments when the debilitating sensation swept over him that he was no longer in control of his life, he shuddered and forced himself to keep going.

In his mad dash for power and glory and against time, the precondition for success was setting up a dynamic and finely tuned organisation, comprising statutes, troops, resources, donors, advertising, a website, permanent media presence, airtime, policies – preferably costed – and a good measure of luck. The American politician Mario Cuomo had once said, "You campaign in poetry, you govern in prose". As he struggled to sort out all the essential practi-calities, Matt's new life was still short on poetry and emotion. Fired up and frustrated, he longed to reach out to the voters and start campaigning. He didn't dare think the prospect of power might be an illusion, or a threat to his sanity. He would soon find out.

CHAPTER FOURTEEN

His selection as parliamentary candidate could not be guaranteed in advance, and might backfire, but his better angels told him he had to accept the risk and lead by example. Two weeks later, scrupulously respecting the newly established procedure, a hustings meeting was held in the local adult education centre.

Each of the three candidates was asked to speak for ten minutes and then to answer questions. Matt's two fellow would-be nominees – Fran Williams, a shy history teacher and climate change activist, and George Simpson, a local businessman and former Labour moderate – gave performances that were solid but failed to set the room alight.

When it was Matt's turn to speak, he tried to move the proceedings up a gear, without sounding too full of himself. He stood behind the lectern, without any notes, his eyes scanning the hall as he tried to capture the audience's attention.

'What this constituency decides in this election will determine the future of our country. Change begins here in West Thameside. If you nominate me as your candidate, I promise we'll make history together. Voting to re-elect James Crouch will bring our country one step closer to becoming a dictatorship. Voting him out will send a message of hope all over England that it's time for a change. Over the past five years, he's betrayed his constituents time and time again by serving his own interests, instead of defending yours. He's out of touch and he has to go.'

As the applause began to grow, Matt reeled off a list of specific policy proposals for investment in local infrastructure – in schools and hospitals, care homes and transport; setting up community land trusts to build affordable housing with rents set at the average wage in the surrounding area; ending the abuse of property rights; promoting a sharing economy, based on mutualism and ethical practice, with new forms of finance and crowdfunding; reforming the tax system to make the local economy grow and create decent jobs for school leavers and apprentices with decent pay - everyone should receive at least the living wage.

He saw Rob at the back of the room flapping his right hand, as if to tell him to slow down or, more probably, to go easy on the uncosted promises. He had just begun to draw his speech to a close, confident that the nomination was in his grasp, when the trouble began.

A group of half a dozen well-built men, all in their late twenties or early thirties, stood up at the back of the room, and began shouting out a barrage of questions, without waiting for the chair to give them the floor. Matt guessed they were from the English Patriotic Front, and were playing the old Momentum trick of creating a disturbance to destabilise the meeting and then challenge its legitimacy. He would calmly wait to hear what they had to say, and then try to turn the incident to his advantage.

The questions and taunts came in quick succession, all directed at Matt, following by crude chants.

'What did you ever do for us? ... Why vote for a fucking lobbyist? ... Never done an honest days' work in his life ... Why should we trust you? '

Then in unison, pointing their fingers at Matt, they began chanting 'He's the same as all the rest - out, out, out', repeating the refrain over and over again. The chair of the meeting, a local GP called Richard French, told them to be quiet but they paid no attention. Gradually the rest of the room turned against them, and under a barrage of boos and jeers they finally stopped and sat down.

Unperturbed, Matt stepped forward. He addressed the hecklers directly.

'You've every right to express your views, and to be suspicious of politicians. They've had a bad record these past few years. The question you have to ask yourselves today is not whether I'll be any different from the others. The real question is "do you trust your own judgement?" Only you can answer that question. Now take a good look at the three candidates before you, think back to what we each said, and decide which of us would be best for you and your family and our community. Decide in your heart and your head what's best for your future. It's your free democratic choice. Don't waste it.'

The hecklers remained silent while the rest of the room applauded. When Richard French announced the result, Matt had received over eighty per cent of the votes cast by the three hundred SOCA members present, and was duly proclaimed parliamentary candidate. The public battle could now commence.

His first press statement as candidate, in which he branded Crouch as 'the symbol of everything that's wrong with English politics', had already been sent out. At the back of the hall, Sam was briefing three local journalists. Later that night, the first online articles would appear: even if Crouch remained the overwhelming favourite to win the seat and serve another term as MP, it was now clear he would not be re-elected unopposed or without a fight.

As people came up to congratulate him, the group of hecklers disappeared through the rear exit. After Matt had finished shaking hands and thanking his supporters, he went over to where Rob was standing with some of the union stewards.

'Where did that lot appear from?' Matt asked.

'No, idea. Not on our radar screen. Someone must have sent them – I expect they'll be back.'

As Matt walked home to his flat through the dark streets, he told himself he would take the rest of the evening off, after this first modest victory. He already pictured himself messing about about in the kitchen, and pouring himself a glass of wine. He would rustle up something that would pleasantly surprise Sam, and after supper they would analyse together the events of the day and plan their next success, before going to bed.

He looked up at his living-room window, and thought he saw a quickly passing shadow. Perhaps it was the reflection of the upper branches of the cherry tree that stood on the other side of the road, as they swayed in the wind. In any case, the shadow was no longer there. He saw two heads in the front of a grey Hyundai parked opposite, whom he assumed was his security detail. The arrangements had become more flexible as Trafalgar Square had receded into memory and there had been no further signs of danger. He went inside the main entrance and walked up the stairs to his flat on the second floor. He thought again of Sam's broad when the result of the vote was announced, as he rummaged in his jacket pockets, looking for his keys.

Then to his horror he saw that he didn't need them, because the door was wide open.

His heart thudding, he searched his mind for an explanation. Surely Sam must have closed and locked the door when she left that morning? If someone had entered during the day, might they still be there, waiting for him? The hallway in the flat was pitch dark, the only light coming from the landing outside. The inner doors to the living room, his room and the bathroom looked firmly closed. He stayed motionless and silent, straining to pick up a giveaway sound from inside, but could hear nothing. Without yet moving forward, from outside he extended his arm round the door to locate the light switch.

He pressed the switch and the narrow hallway, never particularly welcoming, was suddenly bathed in bright light. Still leaving the front door ajar, he gingerly opened the door to his bedroom: the cupboard was shut, the drawers closed, everything seemed as it should be. Nobody had broken in - there must have been a problem with the door. He would get it fixed in the morning. Relieved but still shaken, he went into the living room and turned on the light.

The glass birds were still in their place on the shelf above the fire, but something was missing. He took two paces forward, and then stopped. On the carpet in the middle of the room lay a little pile of shattered glass and empty frames, and on top of it the remains of his photos of Sophie and Jack. They were his favourites that he waved at every time he came home, and that made him feel a little less lonely even as he missed them. Simple childhood scenes: Sophie playing on the beach, Jack with his first cricket bat, the two of them together taken with Matt and their old dog Barney.

He knelt down and saw that each photo had been ripped in two: the children's eyes had been blacked out and the rest of their faces smeared with red paint.

Stunned and sickened, he ran to the window, but the car with the security guards was no longer there.

CHAPTER FIFTEEN

The prime minister had a pained expression. Penfold knew only too well what that look usually meant.

'I can't believe you let him become a candidate. And on my home turf – the cheek of it! If you're so keen on promoting Mr Barker's career, why don't you hand him the keys to Number Ten right away and be done with it.'

'But he's nobody, Prime Minister. Totally unknown in the constituency. No one will vote for him. Whereas you're universally admired and respected, with a long record of outstanding service. You'll win by a landslide, just like last time.'

'Just because you screwed up doesn't give you a licence to bullshit me. I don't take him seriously either, but I want to be spared any embarrassment. The point is that your friend Mr Barker – '

'- That's unfair, Prime Minister. He's not my friend, and we've been actively trying to prevent him from standing against you. Yesterday evening, immediately after his nomination, we organised a discreet break-in to unsettle him and make him think again.'

'Which from all accounts was a total failure. Next time you should be a little less discreet and a lot more effective. The point is that he's only been standing for one day, and he's already accused me of widespread corruption and abuse of power – not surprisingly, the press are lapping it up. I counted on you to protect my good name. I'm disappointed in you. What do you intend to do about it?'

'Would you like me to arrange an accident?'

'You know I don't reply to questions like that. I'd like to try a different approach. Give him enough rope and then stand back. Do nothing. Let him feel that everything's going his way. Send in a few more hecklers for credibility. Given his excessive idealism and lack of experience, his little bubble will probably burst without any help from us. If not, we can move in on his weak point, when he least expects it.'

Penfold's face beamed.

'The girl?'

'Precisely, Penfold. I'm pleased to see that you're still capable of rational thought – I'll grant you a temporary stay of execution. Just keep an eye on her for now. I thought she looked very fetching in bed with him last night – I wouldn't like him to have her all for himself. It's wonderful what modern technology can do nowadays. Don't take any action until I say the word. You'd better put Griffiths in the picture.'

'Understood, Prime Minister.'

Sam listened as Matt expressed all his frustration at the break-in and the damage to his children's photos. She had come round as soon as he had told her the news.

'How did they get in? That's what I want to know,' said Matt, as much to himself as to Sam. 'How are we supposed to set up a political movement, if our opponents can walk in and out of my flat whenever the mood takes them? I'll have to change the locks again, for the second time in a month. How can I lead a party in the general election, if I can't even be safe in my own home?'

'It's not a party, it's an alliance. But I know what you mean,' said Sam.

Matt called Rob, but there was no answer and he left a message demanding a full explanation. He wanted somebody to answer a simple question: was he or was he not supposed to be provided with protection? If Rob couldn't fix the problem through the union, they'd better find a better system, or hire a private company.

Rob eventually rang back. There had been an unfortunate misunderstanding. Round-the-clock protection had been reinstated. Matt waited for an apology, but none came.

He put the torn photos in a large envelope and placed it in the bottom drawer of his desk. He couldn't bear looking at them. The flat was empty without the children's smiling faces, and he felt bereft.

Sam took him in her arms and tried to console him, but his mind was elsewhere.

'That they broke in so easily is bad enough. But that they then started playing stupid mind games with the photos of my children, that's something I can't accept. If I find out who did this, I'll strangle them.'

'They're being deliberately provocative. It's a test to see how you react. Don't let them get to you – that's exactly what they want.'

Slowly the tension began to lift. They decided to order an Indian takeaway. As they tucked into the nans and papadams, sitting side by side on the sofa, Sam told him that his first press statement attacking Crouch was circulating all over social and online media, and the reactions were all favourable. Her phone hadn't stopped ringing all evening. He was already making a name for himself. They couldn't have hoped for a better start.

He slowly began to push the break-in to the back of his mind. He was sure he had some other photos of the children on his computer. They would soon be back in their usual place on the shelf. The next day would be his first as the official candidate. He would need to appear calm, self-confident and in control.

Although Matt's first days on the campaign trail began on a wave of enthusiasm, the clash of theory with reality soon produced a brutal shock. In their finely tuned strategy and careful messaging, he and Sam had disregarded two key factors: the people weren't interested, and they were afraid. The reactions on the street and on the doorstep were mostly friendly and polite, and Matt benefited at first from having a certain curiosity value. His principal opponent was less James Crouch than generalised apathy, mixed with fear and a desire to stay out of trouble. The majority of people they met were not so much hostile to politicians as profoundly indifferent. They had given up on the political class a long time ago. Besides, what was the point of being seen consorting with a would-be politician who came from nowhere, had no chance of being elected, and spent his time attacking the prime minister and local MP?

On the first Saturday morning since they had started campaigning, Matt and Sam were distributing flyers outside the Farmers' Market. As the rain came down in a slow drizzle and gave no sign of stopping, Matt estimated that their success rate in persuading people to take their material was about one in twenty.

'What's that about?' asked an elderly lady. 'More free offers?'

Matt did his best to look cheerful.

'We're a new political movement,' he said. 'I'm your candidate in the general election.'

The woman looked as though she felt moderately sorry for Matt, but realising there was nothing she could do to help someone in his condition, decided to move on quickly without another word.

'Do you want another five years of James Crouch, and his corrupt government?' Matt shouted after her.

She didn't look back. Other people in the street looked at Matt with incredulity. A smartly dressed man in a suit and carrying a briefcase crossed the road and began to harangue him.

'Who do you think you are?' he said. 'We don't attack the prime minister in public in this country. You should show a bit more respect. We live in a democracy, in case you hadn't noticed.'

A thick-set young man hurried by, carrying three wooden boxes of vegetables stacked on top of each other.

'What's the point in voting? Nothing ever changes,' he said. 'Crouch is the best of a bad bunch. Better the devil you know, I say.'

The more time went by, the less confident Matt felt that he would ever break through this point-blank refusal to challenge or even question the status quo and the sitting MP. The proud island race had lost its pride. Fear and grovelling submission had taken over instead.

'It's worse than indifference,' said Matt to Sam, a few days later.

They were sitting in a coffee shop, at the end of a long and unproductive day spend knocking on doors and leafleting in run-down housing estates on the edge of the constituency. In the last place they had visited, the lifts didn't work, and they had to climb up and down ten flights of stairs with no lighting and a strong smell of urine and chip-fat. In roughly one flat in three, they had been greeted with obscenities. One middle-aged man in his underpants had shouted that he was a nationalist and proud of it, before threatening Matt with a knife.

'It's what Rob warned me about when we first began. The very people that we're trying the hardest to help – the less well-off, the long-term unemployed, those dependent on benefits – are the least pleased to see us. As soon as they smell politics or politicians, they either run a mile or get abusive. They don't remotely see politics as a way of improving their lives. They've got other ways of doing that, often illegal. They see us as completely irrelevant. It's going to be hard work to make them change their minds.'

Sam tilted her head on one side and looked at him with a mixture of apparent affection and irony, as though she took pleasure in having to humour him in his periodic bouts of pessimism.

'Surely you knew that already?' said Sam. 'Getting soaked in the rain and spat at on the doorstep goes with the job, just as much as making inspiring speeches and dreaming up clever policies. They're not going to give you their trust overnight – you have to work for it. They've been screwed over and over again by the system. Don't blame them for not welcoming you with open arms. You have to show patience and understanding – hang your head in humility on behalf of the political class and take whatever they throw at you. You owe these people an apology, they owe you nothing. They're not under any obligation to take you on trust – it's the other way round. Why should they believe your airy-fairy promises? You've got to prove to them that you understand their concerns, and you're capable of changing things for the better. Keep plugging away, and they'll eventually start to listen. Slowly the mood will start to change, and some may even consider voting for you. In the end you'll see it's all been worthwhile. There's no other way.'

Matt knew she was right. He needed to focus more on specific local issues and less on general principles and finely honed policies. Perhaps Ahmed or Bernadette could come up with some ideas on how to put this shift into practice. If they didn't find a way quickly to relaunch the campaign, he would have to scale down his expectations.

The next day, the West Thameside News published the first opinion poll on voting intentions in the constituency. Matt's candidature was mentioned in a footnote as too recent to figure. James Crouch, who had always benefited from the paper's unswerving support, seemed unaffected by the bedrock of apathy encountered by Matt as he forged ahead of all the mainstream candidates. It was hardly surprising, given Crouch's strong name recognition and local links – and his hold over the media and mafia band of close supporters. His people were everywhere, watching and reporting back. There were still six weeks to go, but Crouch was twenty points in front, and looked unstoppable.

CHAPTER SIXTEEN

'There are some people I'd like you to meet,' said Ahmed to Matt. 'Twenty families on the Hancock Grove estate are threatened with eviction. They need our help – and I think you'll see it's a good issue.'

Matt immediately agreed, and the next day he found himself sitting in the Mukherjee family's living room with the other members of the residents' delegation. They didn't have enough chairs to go round, so Ahmed stood against the wall, chatting to the younger members of the families present.

The leader of the group was Harish Mukherjee, a small, nervous-looking Bengali in his early sixties. He stood up and explained their concerns. Matt already knew about the problem, but let him have his say.

'Now they've got the council's authorisation to develop the site for luxury houses and flats, the developers say they'll put up our rent by four or five times. We've been told that, legally, they're entitled to do this, and there's nothing we can do.'

'I'm not so sure about that,' said Matt. 'They should never have been allowed to build on land designated for social housing. It's yet another sordid affair involving Crouch, the council leader and their developer friends. They break all the rules, share the proceeds, and no one dares lift a finger against them. I think you've got a good case.'

'I'm not a lawyer,' said Harish, 'but I know my neighbours. There are twenty families in Hancock Grove, mainly Asians and workers of various nationalities – I prefer not to call them migrant workers, the term has lost its true meaning in recent years. After all, we're all migrants in one way or another, and we're all workers if we have the chance.'

Harish's wife, who was standing next to him in an orange sari and was even smaller than he was, tugged at his sleeve and told him to get on with it.

'We're all decent, hard-working people in Hancock Grove – except one or two hotheads in my wife Nita's family.'

On cue, Nita shook her head and wagged a finger in protest against this disgraceful slur.

'But we're not well off,' Harish went on, looking serious now. 'We can't afford to pay this massive increase in rent. So they'll wait until we can't pay any more and then they'll turf us out. What can we do to stop this? Can you help us?'

Matt wanted to help, but only if he was sure that he could obtain results. He didn't want to make any promises he couldn't later fulfil. All eyes were on him, waiting for his reply.

Nita took out a handkerchief from the folds of her sari.

'Can you imagine what it's like, Mr Barker, to be thrown out in the street through no fault of your own?' she said. 'How do we explain to our children and grandchildren that they have to leave their friends and their school and start their lives all over again? Help us, I beg you.'

Giving a little stamp of his foot, Harish turned to his wife.

'Get a hold of yourself. It's no use. I told you he would be no different than the others. Well, Mr Barker?'

Nita stared at the floor, dabbing her eyes.

Matt saw Ahmed looking at him. He smiled back – surely Ahmed didn't doubt his intentions – and got up from his chair, taking up position next to Harish.

'Of course, I'll help you. This is what we do in the Save Our Country Alliance – we help each other out. Tomorrow we'll deliver an ultimatum to Mr Crouch in the form of a public letter: either he condemns the council decision and publicly tells them to annul the authorisation, or we'll bring a legal action against the council. This isn't a threat, it's a statement of fact. Don't worry, we'll obtain the necessary funds for the legal proceedings if Crouch's cronies refuse to back down. I promise I'll do everything possible to ensure no one is evicted.'

As he finished speaking, he saw the pride in Ahmed's face. He and Harish shook hands, and Matt accepted Nita's offer of a slice of her butter cake.

He had meant what he said. He would do everything in his power to have the decision overturned. Twenty families were being thrown out into the street and made homeless, while at the same time a group of nameless sharks were making millions in profit. Forcing those currently in power to back down would send a powerful message throughout the constituency.

After telling Ahmed to take some photos of the residents and their children, he called Sam.

'I want to milk this story for all it's worth. It's a small but powerful symbol of everything that's wrong and pernicious about Crouch's system of government – the poor and defenceless being pushed out to make way for the rich. Give it everything you've got – I want to see pictures of those families, with close-ups of their frightened children and Mrs Mukherjee in tears, on the front page of every paper in the country. I'll go with Harish myself to Crouch's constituency office tomorrow to insist on a meeting, and call for the annulment of the decision. Try and get some cameras there. Our demand will be simple – fairness and justice for all. Is that understood? Sam … are you still there?'

She eventually came back on the line.

'I was just waiting for you to finish. I'll do my best.'

Giles Penfold took off his headphones and mopped his forehead. Even allowing for Matt Barker's over-excitement, this was all getting a little out of hand. The prime minister would not be at all pleased to hear of this development. Penfold would first have a word with one or two of his well-placed colleagues, to prevent any damaging leaks before they resolved the situation. Perhaps for once he would advise a tactical retreat, to allow the prime minister to reach out to the poor and underprivileged, and put the blame on the council. Making promises to the voters was surely what elections were all about. What the prime minister did after the election, when he was back in office, was not his concern.

CHAPTER SEVENTEEN

W hen Matt challenged Crouch to take part in a televised debate, he never thought he would accept. Crouch's relaxed
reply the following day, at a routine briefing for the local press,
caught Matt by surprise. The prime minister's remarks, clearly
aimed at a wider audience, were caught on camera.

'I'm a democrat,' he told the journalists. 'The beauty of the
system in this country is that every five years, we reset the clock.
Everyone's given an equal chance to stand for Parliament, whether
they're an outgoing prime minister with a solid record of achieve-
ment in the national interest, or someone completely unheard of
with no experience of politics or public service. I'd be more than
happy to defend my record in government, and my party's manifesto commitments for the future, with Mr Barker or any other
candidate.'

The two candidates and their respective camps agreed the
rules of engagement without too much difficulty. Discussions between Rob and his counterpart, Crouch's agent Stanley Baxter,
were unexpectedly civilised. The venue was a local church hall,

which could fit around three hundred people, and the moderator would be Caroline Bruce, a former BBC newsreader who lived in the constituency. The two candidates would toss a coin to decide the speaking order, and then each would take the floor for twenty minutes, followed by questions from the audience and five-minute closing statements. Although Rob was wary that Crouch would try and pack the room, they agreed that the meeting should be open to the public. Tickets could be reserved on a first come, first served basis, apart from a batch of fifty to be set aside and divided equally between the ENP and SOCA for distribution to their supporters.

Matt rehearsed every evening during the week before the debate. Rob played the part of Crouch, which he seemed to relish, much to everyone's amusement.

'I grew up in South London, the grandson of immigrants from Eastern Europe,' said Rob, as Crouch, in one of their more lively exchanges. 'Starting with nothing, I set up my own company and spent twenty years in business and public service, before becoming an MP. You've only ever been a squalid lobbyist. What makes you think you're qualified to serve the people of this constituency?'

Sam interrupted.

'I don't think he'd use the word "squalid". He'll try and play the statesman and experienced politician. The trick will be for Matt to get under his skin without looking aggressive, and make him lose his self-control and say something he'll regret, which we can quote against him afterwards. Remember that the audience we're targeting won't be the few hundred in the hall, but the hundreds of thousands watching at home on TV or on their computers and smartphones.'

'I'll stay calm, but I'm going to lay into him from the first minute, to throw him off guard. I need some dirt on him – Rob, you said you'd put an attack file together with a few stories and allegations from the past that we can keep in reserve if things turn ugly. I'll mix the dodgy bits – if you find any - with a series of objective criticisms and accusations. We'll need some hard evidence in case he pushes back. How about asking him to publish his tax returns - I can't believe he's always been straight about his financial affairs.'

'I thought you wanted to be Mr Clean, and would never descend into personal abuse,' said Rob, being himself now.

'That's exactly the image I want to project as candidate. That's why any dirty work will have to be done by someone else, with no trace of my fingerprints. I want to rile him by stealth. Asking the prime minister if he's ever committed tax fraud and evasion is a perfectly legitimate question. Particularly if we've got the evidence to back it up.'

'Crouch is bound to underestimate you,' said Sam. 'Let's reinforce that feeling by doing a few interviews to downplay expectations.'

On the day of the debate, the West Thameside News carried a short piece containing several direct quotes from Matt, such as *"Taking on someone of James Crouch's stature is a daunting challenge"*, and *"I'll be happy to get through the ninety minutes without committing a major gaffe"*. The paper had bought their rather simplistic strategy. However crudely, the battle-lines were being drawn.

Flanked by Rob and Sam, Matt led the way up the stone steps and through the double doors of the entrance to the church hall. The security guard on the door recognised him and greeted him politely. Matt and Rob were let through, but Sam was stopped as they checked her ticket.

'You two go on ahead, I'll catch up with you in a minute,' she said.

Inside the room was heaving and the noise deafening. All the seats were filling up fast. Matt turned round to see if Sam was coming but couldn't see her. He spotted Ahmed and Harish waving at them from among the small number of reserved seats near the front, and went to join them.

'Can you feel it?' said Ahmed. 'I've never seen any of these people before, yet they all seem to know each other.'

Matt looked around and saw that Ahmed was right. Most of those present exuded the unsubtle self-assurance of the comfortably off. The regular braying of laughter from all sides of the hall sounded false and even orchestrated. Matt's small band of faithful supporters were outnumbered.

Sam came up and joined him, sounding breathless. Her face was pale.

'They didn't want to let me in,' she said. 'They just stood there, laughing at me, and pretended my ticket wasn't valid. One of them asked what my new boyfriend was like in bed. He said he'd be waiting for me after the debate, mumbled a few more obscenities and let me through.'

Matt stared at her in disbelief.

'That's completely unacceptable - who do they think they are? Which was one was it? I'll go and speak to him – '

'Don't bother. They knew exactly what they were doing. I think you're needed on stage – we'll talk later. '

Matt turned round and saw that James Crouch and Caroline Bruce had already taken their seats on the platform and were chattering away to each other. Crouch was seated to her right, with an empty chair on her left. Trying not to look too conspicuous, Matt moved to the side of the hall to observe his opponent.

He'd never seen Crouch close up before. This was the man on whom his future hung. He was smaller than Matt had expected, and came over as self-contained, almost inoffensive. His jet-black hair was brushed back and kept in place by a few drops of shiny oil that made it shine and reflect the light, not a stray lock in sight. Impeccably groomed and turned out, nothing flashy or eye-catching. It was a clever and disarming look. He was smartly dressed, as one would expect from a prime minister, in a dark suit, white shirt and red tie. Matt wore a grey jacket and trousers and a light blue shirt, open-necked.

He and Sam had had a long discussion about the pros and cons of wearing a tie. He was in favour, in order to appear more states-manlike; she preferred informality, to highlight the age difference between Matt and Crouch and Matt's image as the outsider. Matt had eventually accepted Sam's advice.

He was still furious at the way she had been treated by the secu-rity guards. After the debate was over, he would demand an expla-nation and an apology, and make sure Sam would never be treated like that again. He tried to clear his head and focus on the debate. Patting the palms of his hands on his trousers, he stood up straight and strode on to the platform.

Although Matt's small group of diehard supporters applauded him lustily, Crouch paid him no attention and went on speaking to Caroline Bruce. Matt stood in front of him, waiting for him to react. Crouch let him wait a few seconds longer before looking up at him.

'So you're the famous Matthew Barker that no one's ever heard of.'

Crouch's grin was so broad, showing his gleaming white teeth, that for a moment it almost hid the traces of irony and mockery written all over his face. He appeared both affable and icy. On closer inspection, the malice and trickery were so transparent and writ so large that you could hardly fault him for it. Disconcerted, Matt found himself struggling not to warm to his enemy, as if he was being drawn in by some weird magnetic force. He thought back to all the pain and humiliation that Crouch and his hench-men had inflicted on him over the past few months. This was no time for sentiment or forgiveness - tonight was payback time. He would first lull Crouch into a sense of security – which shouldn't be too difficult, given his air of overweening arrogance - and then rip him apart piece by piece, but calmly and with a smile.

'Good evening, Mr Crouch. I look forward to our discussion.'

Matt sat down next to Caroline, who asked the audience to take their seats. Then she introduced the two candidates - "one of whom most of you have known for many years, and the other who has only recently arrived on the political scene" - and explained the ground rules for the debate. She spun a coin and Crouch won the toss.

To loud yells of support from the floor, Crouch slowly walked over to the podium. He stood for a moment, soaking up the applause, with his arms outstretched, in a Christ-the-Redeemer pose. After Caroline Bruce appealed for silence, the noise gradually died down as Crouch began to speak, quietly and in a low voice, forcing people to lean forward in their seats and listen.

'I stand before you once again, in all humility, to ask for your trust and support, and for the privilege to represent this constituency in Parliament. Many of you know my family story, how I was born in poverty and started with nothing. By hard work and sheer bloody-mindedness, I built a successful business and ended up running the country. What kept me going during those difficult, early years was my pride in being English. All through my life, and today more than ever, I have been a proud believer in the virtues and values of the nation of England.'

What a nerve – Matt guessed that Crouch didn't believe a word of what he was saying. But he had to admit that he spoke well, and was winning over most of those listening. Crouch's voice hardened as he began to speak more loudly and with greater intensity.

'Working together, sparing no effort, we've achieved a great deal for our country over the past five years. England has become free again from the dead weight of the Brussels bureaucracy, and from the constant drain on our public finances imposed by the never-ending handouts to Scotland and Northern Ireland. The sham union that held us back for so long is no more. We have finally regained control of our destiny. The clearly expressed will of the people was for England to become independent. Together we've made that happen. I've kept my promise to you. We're free again!'

The chant of "Free Again" reverberated round the room, until Crouch asked for silence.

'We've laid the foundations, but now we must build the house that will keep future generations safe, secure and prosperous. I ask you to give me the tools to finish the job, on your behalf. I ask you for five more years.'

As the applause rippled around the hall, Crouch stood leaning against the lectern, seemingly indifferent to the wave of emotion that he had unleashed.

'Before I finish, I'd like to say a couple of words about my opponent this evening.'

Matt wondered what was coming next. Perhaps Crouch would patronise him with some false flattery.

'Most of you had probably never heard of Matt Barker – I certainly hadn't. I'm told he wants to start a revolution. Let me give him a word of advice.'

Crouch turned away from the podium to look directly at Matt.

'You need to get real, Mr Barker. You're too late. The revolution's already happened, and your side lost. People like you – shady lobbyists, sleazebags, and profiteers - have no place in the new England that the rest of us have created with our blood and sweat. Go back to your liberal la-la-land – we don't want your sort here.'

As Crouch left the podium and went back to his seat, part of the crowd began chanting "Scum, scum, scum", fingers pointing at Matt. Some of Crouch's most vociferous supporters stood up, waving their fists.

If they didn't look so bitter and angry, their behaviour would be almost comical. The louder they shouted, the calmer Matt felt. Seeing the concern on the faces of Sam and Rob from their places in the front row, he gave an airy wave of the back of his hand to tell them not to worry.

Caroline Bruce called the room to order and gave Matt the floor. He approached the lectern, carrying a blue folder. For a few seconds he stood in front of the audience saying nothing, his eyes scanning the room, drawing the people in. Then he began to speak, softly, deliberately.

'I'll be frank with you: I don't recognise the mean-spirited England that James Crouch describes. He spoke about English values. I've no reason to doubt his sincerity. I'd simply ask for those values to be applied here today.'

He paused.

'I could suggest at least three. Tolerance. Respect for other faiths and cultures. Not descending into personal insults. All traditional English values.'

He could see the questioning looks around the room. Some of those who were aggressively chanting a few seconds earlier were now looking defensive.

'It's difficult, isn't it? When the outgoing prime minister sets the tone in the way he's done tonight. That was beneath you, Mr Crouch.'

Matt turned round and looked Crouch in the eye.

'I could go further. I would seriously suggest that, instead of giving Mr Crouch five more years, you let him take a long holiday. From his behaviour this evening, it's clear he needs a rest.'

From the amused expressions on one or two faces around the room, Matt could see that some of those present were settling down to enjoy the rare experience of ironic remarks made at Crouch's expense. He was just warming up.

'It's hardly surprising that he's feeling washed out, after spending five years running the country into the ground. By the way, don't be fooled by the self-made man shtick – he set up his company with a loan of three million pounds from his father. I've seen the evidence. I won't embarrass him with any details about his mother's profession, before she found herself a rich husband.'

He heard some kind of commotion coming from where Crouch was seated behind him, but didn't bother to look round. He assumed his words were having an effect.

'Instead, let's ask him why he hasn't paid any tax on his investments for the past ten years. Ask him why he keeps all his savings offshore, on a small island in the Caribbean …'

'Nonsense! That's slander. It's a complete fabrication – I've done nothing illegal,' Crouch shouted.

Matt turned to look at him, arms crossed, gently increasing the temperature.

'Which is it, Mr Crouch, slander or a fabrication? You'd better make up your mind, because after this election you'll no longer be protected. If you'd like to look at the evidence, it's all here.'

He picked up the large blue folder and waved it in the air.

Caroline Bruce was trying to impress upon Crouch that he would have a chance to respond once Matt had finished his twenty minutes.

Matt ignored them.

'It saddens me to say this, but the stakes for the country are too high. The people have to be told the truth. Mr Crouch's objective is to end democracy in this country, and turn it into a one-party state. He and most of the cabinet have illegally benefitted from million of pounds of taxpayers' money. His protectionist, isolationist policies are ruining England's economy and stealing our young people's future. Only one conclusion can be drawn from this deplorable record: James Crouch is unfit to stand for public office of any kind – '

It was as though a dam had been breached. The boos and jeers grew louder and louder. A few chairs were hurled in his direction from the side of the room but didn't reach the platform.

Caroline Bruce tried but failed to make herself heard above the pandemonium. Matt caught Sam's eye and made the sign of a square with the thumbs and forefingers of his two hands. She nodded back.

As he heard the screech of a chair scraping on the floor, he turned round and saw Crouch striding towards him across the stage. Matt took a sip of water, taking his time. He wasn't going to give way. The noise in the hall subsided, as the two men stood facing each other. Matt estimated he was a good four inches taller than his rival, and wondered if Crouch wore built-up shoes. Crouch's face had turned puce. The room fell quiet, as their terse exchange was amplified around the room.

'You owe me a retraction and an apology,' said Crouch.

'No way,' Matt replied. 'Every word I said is true and you know it. If you can't stand the heat, you should resign. You're no longer fit to be the prime minister of this country.'

Matt waited for the inevitable reaction. Crouch was clenching his fists, his face twisted with fury.

'I should never have agreed to this debate – I came here under false pretences. Nobody talks to me like that without paying the consequences. I'll make sure you regret your behaviour tonight.'

Crouch raised his right arm, fist clenched. Hardly able to believe his luck, Matt braced himself for the hit. Instead, as Crouch's right hand came down, he tore the microphone from his lapel and threw it on to the floor. As he stormed off the platform, Matt registered the continuous clicking of what sounded like a hundred cameras.

Was he dreaming, or had the prime minister really just gifted him a full-blown walkout on live television? He saw Rob and Sam in the front row, mouths open, looking equally incredulous.

'Please, Prime Minister, please return to your seat,' Caroline Bruce shouted, pleading with him to stay. 'Come back and defend yourself against these allegations, so you can put your point of view to the thousands of viewers watching us tonight.'

Her appeal was to no avail. Looking straight ahead, Crouch marched down the central aisle, followed by his retinue of advisers and bag-carriers, and out into the street.

CHAPTER EIGHTEEN

'Honestly, Prime Minister, I've got your best interests at heart,' said Penfold, in the back of the Jaguar. 'Don't press charges or have him detained. It'll just create more bad publicity. On the contrary, the least said the better. The incident will soon be forgotten.'

'But he attacked me – the prime minister - and he insulted my mother.'

'Actually, it was the other way round.'

'What do you mean?'

'Technically, you attacked him first. You called him a shady lobbyist and a sleazebag, do you remember?'

Crouch turned his head and stared blankly out of the car-window. How could he have been so stupid? Barker had got one over on him and it hurt. He had never felt so humiliated. His whole image was built around his self-control and unflappability. Away from the prying eyes of the media, he had a sadistic streak and a vicious temper, but nothing had ever been known to rile him in public. Until today. He wondered how he could repair the damage.

'Call off the police car.'

'A wise decision, if I may say so.'

That was one Penfold's standard phrases when Crouch ended up following his advice. They were a strange couple. Crouch valued him more than he would ever admit. Despite often being on the receiving end of Crouch's private rants and tantrums, Giles Penfold had never let him down in the ten years he had worked for him.

Yet Crouch knew that his wheedling subservience was only an act, part of the unspoken bargain between them. Penfold never complained because in the end he always got his way. Wielding power behind the scenes was all he wanted. Thanks or recognition didn't come into it, and would be considered an unwelcome distraction. Penfold could only continue to pull the strings if no one knew he was doing it, and the outside world continued to see James Crouch as all-powerful and impregnable.

The incident with Barker annoyed Crouch because it had exposed a dangerous crack in the façade. Any sign of weakness was dangerous, and would set the vultures circling. Firm and decisive retaliation was called for, out of the glare of the media. No more faffing about. He would see if Penfold agreed. He invariably did, or at least pretended to.

'I really did work my own way up, you know,' said Crouch. 'The suggestion I was helped by my poor father is absolute nonsense.'

'I never doubted it,' Penfold replied.

'Perhaps I underestimated that man Barker, but I won't make the same mistake again. We've got to proceed with the utmost care. No one else must know.'

'Of course, Prime Minister.'

'Naturally, I won't be acting out of any sense of personal pique, but for the good of the country.'

Penfold nodded respectfully.

'Dissent and freedom of expression are fine during periods of peace and stability. When we're faced with global pressures such as now, and the economy's in free fall through no fault of the government, the people look around for someone to blame. Our clear duty at such moments in our history is to promote national unity, by all the means at our disposal. The stronger we appear, the more we can protect the most vulnerable in our society. We can't afford the luxury of allowing rogue elements to roam around the system causing chaos and confusion. In periods of uncertainty, we must encourage our people to rally round the flag. We must all pull in the same direction, otherwise the whole edifice could come crashing down.'

'That would certainly be unfortunate.'

'I've nothing against Matt Barker personally. We've seen today that he can be a smart operator, with a certain talent for public speaking and mobilising the masses. But we can't afford the risk, however slight, of the electoral contest in my own constituency becoming the epicentre of a national earthquake.'

'How would we calm the storm before the earthquake – if you'll excuse the mixed metaphor? Do you have any particular measures in mind?'

'I've got a few ideas about the general situation. We may need to provoke some serious unrest, so we can hit them hard and make an example. We'll probably need a few fatalities. The home secretary won't be happy, but I see no other way.'

'And Mr Barker?'

'In his case, I'm afraid it has to be long and painful. He's left us with no choice. We'll have to get inside his head, and destroy his peace of mind. Bring back the wife from Australia, to muddy the waters. Send him over the edge. Start with the Islamist boy.'

Crouch looked away. This was the most difficult and distasteful part of his job. Few people realised the pressures a prime minister had to face. If he thought too much about the techniques they used, he would never get anything done. He could not allow one individual to stand in the way of the interests of the state. It took courage to take such difficult decisions, and no one ever thanked you for it.

'I'll issue the necessary instructions, Prime Minister. Through the usual channels, so there'll be no trace. Consider it done. He won't bother you again.'

CHAPTER NINETEEN

As they drove at breakneck speed through the suburban streets, one union security car ahead of them and another following, Sam's phone never stopped ringing and bleeping. She eventually turned it off.

'I wonder who'll get to us first – the media or Crouch's mob,' said Matt.

When the convoy entered Matt's street, they saw the photographers and TV crews already waiting outside his flat. Sam asked if they should turn round and drive away.

'No, keep going. I mustn't give the impression I'm trying to avoid the press. They're only doing their job. I'll make a brief statement and take a few questions. I'll do this on my own, and give you a call when I'm back inside.'

The car drove a short distance down the road, and Matt walked the rest of the way. He stood outside the main entrance, with a dozen microphones prodded under his nose.

'Today was a bad day for James Crouch, but a good day for democracy. We reminded the outgoing prime minister that England's still a free country, not a dictatorship or a one-party state. As for his behaviour, we all have days like that, when we say or do things we regret afterwards. On a personal level, I won't hold it against him. Politically, I think he should ask himself whether he's really up to the job. He's been around for too long, and it's starting to show. His attempt to cling on to power looks shameful and undignified. James Crouch should put the country first, and rule himself out for another term in office. The people have had enough of Crouch and the English Nationalists. I believe the Save Our Country Alliance have the policies, the values and the determination that people are calling for. The time has come to end this period of recession and decline, and to start the work of rebuilding England.'

Several questions were shouted out simultaneously: 'Did he apologise? ... Are you saying Crouch should resign? ... Do you have any proof of wrongdoing? ... Are you in with a chance?'

'We'll fight this election with everything we've got, and we'll fight to win. I've nothing further to add,' said Matt. He turned and entered the building.

He ran up the stairs and had a quick but careful look in each room in his flat. This time there was no sign of any unwelcome intruder. Opening the window and looking outside, he saw the cameramen and journalists had left. Reassured, he breathed in lungfuls of the fresh evening air. The street was perfectly quiet again and everything seemed in its place. The two security cars were parked opposite. The cherry trees were in blossom, the birds singing, and clumps of bright spring flowers dotted across every house's front garden. He called Sam and asked her to come round.

'There's more to life than politics,' said Sam. 'I'd love us to go away somewhere, the two of us. To go for walks along the beach, to climb mountains, to lie together in the shade of a tall tree looking down on the sea.'

They lay naked, side-by-side on the bed, Sam's head in the crook of his arm.

'We'll do all that, I promise you, and more,' he replied. 'Just not quite yet. We've other work to do first. I need you here with me. You inspire me - '

'No one's ever said that to me before ...'

'... and give me energy and make me happy. How come you suddenly appeared out of nowhere to change my life?'

'It was all part of my devious plan to seduce you and then kidnap you and hold you to ransom,' said Sam.

'What went wrong?'

'Don't know really ... I suppose you saw my evil intentions ...'

'And then we got sidetracked,' said Matt.

He sounded more serious now.

'That's what invariably happens. Diverted from our original purpose. In the hands of the gods, or whoever decides our fate.'

Sam thought for a moment.

'Do you think it will ever end?' she asked.

'You mean, what we're doing?'

'The politics, the backbiting, the threats and bullying, the sniping, the sheer hypocrisy – '

'Most of that's human nature, so no, it'll never completely go away,' said Matt. 'We'll have to go through all that, you can't avoid it. It's the price you have to pay if you want to try and improve things – or at least to stop them getting worse. The counterpoint is people's essential decency, and the satisfaction of leaving a mark, however small.'

'I realise it's unlikely, but suppose we win, and you become prime minister, then what happens to us? I know we'll be doing a vital job to turn the country round, but won't it just be more of the same, on an even bigger scale? The infernal merry-go-round will keep on turning, faster and faster, never stopping to let you get off. You'll never have a moment of time you can call your own. Where will I fit in? I'm not going to just fade away and let you take all the glory.'

'I'll never allow that, I promise you. Anyway, you're too strong and smart to let that happen. The project can't succeed without your having a major role.'

She stiffened and screwed up her face.

'You should rephrase what you just said. Be very careful. You can stuff your offer of "a major role".'

He closed his eyes, realising his stupidity. He took a deep breath and tried again.

'We'll have to organise our lives differently, in an equal part-nership where we respect each other's strengths, and make sure we don't become prisoners of the system.'

'A bit pompous but that sounds marginally better. Give me one good reason to believe that might happen.'

'Because I want to share the rest of my life with you.'

'Even if we win?'

'Only if we win.'

'Arsehole – it's a deal.'

She consummated the promise and her forgiveness by hungri-ly nibbling his ear. Then they put their arms around each other, made love, and drifted off to sleep. She moved in the next day.

Matt's burgeoning relationship with Sam gave him a huge lift, and there was more good news on the way. Everything was com-ing together at once. The latest batch of opinion polls for West Thameside put Matt in double figures. Crouch was still fifteen points ahead, but the gap was narrowing. Two days later, after a meeting at the campaign HQ in Tufton Street, Matt received the visit of Harish Mukherjee. His usually lugubrious air had vanished, and he was waving an envelope in the air.

'I can hardly believe it,' said Harish. 'We received the news yesterday, confirmed by letter - the Council's climbed down. The threat of court action must have made them think again. We can stay in our homes - I can't thank you enough. You and Ahmed have saved our lives. Nita sends her thanks too.'

Matt gave Harish a hug.

'You deserve this result. It took a lot of courage to stand up to the Council and the developers.'

Matt's next thought was to call the one person who had worked harder than anyone else to obtain this result.

'So you've heard,' said Ahmed, brushing aside Matt's compliments. 'He told me first thing this morning. The real heroes were the families themselves. I just went along every other evening to play football with the kids, and make sure the residents didn't give up. They've obtained justice and I'm pleased for them. They're organising a picnic in the park next Sunday – you should come.'

'I'll be there. You're a rock, Ahmed. You don't like hearing this, but we'd never have recruited so many young people if it weren't for you. Your energy makes all the difference.'

'I'm just doing what I believe in. If I can help other people, it makes it easier to put up with all the shit they throw at us.'

'Who do you mean?'

'I'm probably just imagining things. Let's have a chat on Sunday.'

Matt saw he had another call waiting, so they left it there.

Back on the campaign trail every day, the morose mood of inertia and indifference seemed to have lifted. People in the street began to stop and listen, and more and more volunteers came out canvassing, with many from the local student population.

'I know I shouldn't say this,' Matt said to Rob one day in the office, 'but I can't help wondering if we've turned the corner. Maybe the voters are starting to sense that Crouch is no longer as powerful as he used to be, and we might be in with a chance.'

'Don't get ahead of yourself,' Rob replied. 'The other side will come at you when you least expect it. If you're right and this could

be Crouch's last stand, he's not going to turn round and quietly walk away. It's not just Crouch and the ENP you're taking on
– they're only a front, it's the invisible people behind them that
count. Once they sense they're losing their hold on power, they'll
make you pay a heavy price, even if we win.'

The previous evening, in the White Swan, Rob had briefed Matt
on the situation in the country at large. The overall picture was one
of extreme fragmentation, with wildly fluctuating regional varia-
tions, making predictions hazardous. The ENP enjoyed a clear
lead ahead of the other parties and alliances, but hadn't increased
its share of the vote for several weeks. The polls had the remaining rumps of both the Conservatives and Labour stuck sluggishly
in the mid-teens. SOCA was poised to overtake them both for the
first time and move into second place, benefitting from a growing
war chest financed by several new donors and the concentration of
their resources in key marginal seats. The ENP were cleaning up
most of the votes freed up by the collapse of the traditional parties,
particularly in seats previously held by the Tories in the South East
and East Anglia. Support for the Alliance was steadily growing in
London. In another new development, creating more confusion,
the number of candidates standing as independents or on behalf
of local communities was growing daily.

According to Rob, if these trends continued - and if the polling organisations were not as wildly inaccurate as they had been
in 2015 and 2017 – not only would no single party or electoral alliance have a majority in the House of Commons, but there might
also be no basis for any form of workable coalition. Although a remote possibility, a scenario was even emerging where Independent
MPs could hold the balance of power.

'In other words,' Rob said earnestly, 'the system's imploding.
We're looking at the possibility of a massive vacuum at the centre of English politics. The right-wing press is already screaming
that if the ENP fail to secure a majority, the country will become

ungovernable. The lower-end tabloids are full of talk of alleged conspiracies and planned putsches, union-inspired riots and in-surrections. They're trying to make people believe that only a vote for the ENP can prevent all-out anarchy and civil war. Against all this background noise and frenzy, if we're not careful our message will be drowned out, and the Alliance written off as irrelevant.'

'I'm not worried,' said Matt. 'Chaos, panic and paranoia sound good to me. Look at it this way. We've got five weeks to go, our share of the vote is gradually increasing, the traditional parties are flailing, and the ENP can feel us coming up behind. There's a steady flow of donations coming in, and thousands of new mem-bers are joining every week. It's amazing what we've achieved in such a short time. A lot remains to be done and the most difficult part is still to come, but it's hard not to be optimistic. We're in ex-actly the place I'd like to be at this stage. We're surfing on the tide of history - whatever could stop us now?'

Rob shook his head, clearly not sharing Matt's surge of confi-dence. Matt felt his pessimism was overdone. Of course they had to be careful, and not get ahead of themselves, but events would prove soon enough which of them was right. Leading a revolution and in love with Sam, Matt was the luckiest man in the world, but he wouldn't let it affect his judgement.

CHAPTER TWENTY

As Matt approached the bridge, he saw he was a few minutes ahead of time. Halfway across, he stopped to lean against the stone balustrade, watching the ripples of the water flowing through the arches below and the ducks waddling along the muddy banks. The river helped him clear his mind, and the bridge – especially when he stood in the middle of it - gave him an irrational sense of accomplishment and peace. He liked playing with the feeling that he was moving from one side to the other, of starting in one place and not knowing for certain where he would end up.

Matt had agreed to pass by Ahmed's flat on the way to the park. He had been there several times before.

'Why don't you drop in for a coffee?' Ahmed had said on the phone the previous evening. 'I know everything looks fine on the surface, but there are one or two new members I'm not sure about. I think we may have been infiltrated.'

Ahmed hadn't wanted to say anything more about his concerns over the phone. Matt was unfazed: Ahmed was suspicious by nature and a worrier. Matt knew him well enough to sense when he needed reassurance. As the arduous campaign entered the final stretch, everyone was feeling the strain. Matt would tell Ahmed that, while his fears were probably exaggerated, in the current climate he was right to report anything unusual. Their enemies were undoubtedly growing by the day. They would have the suspects vetted and see if any action was required.

Matt's reverie on the bridge was interrupted by the roar of a plane soaring towards the sky, doubtless after taking off from nearby Heathrow. He could make out the British Airways emblem on the tail. The noise sounded louder than usual, perhaps because there was no cloud cover, or the wind was blowing in a different direction.

He came to the end of the bridge and turned right into a narrow street that led up the hill to Ahmed's flat, which was on the ground floor of what must have once been an imposing Edwardian villa, but that was now crumbling and in need of several coats of paint. He walked slowly up the hill, stopping to look in the windows of the antique and junk shops. Further up the road, on the valley side, pink blossom floated down from a row of cherry trees. Another plane roared overhead, the noise sounding even closer. He guessed he was now directly under the flight path. The sound gradually gave away to a chorus of cawing crows from the upper branches of a tall plane tree.

A little breathless from walking up the hill in the sun, he stood at the foot of the cracked stone steps leading up to Ahmed's front door.

Then he saw the curtains blowing through the open window.

He climbed two steps to see more clearly. As he held back the curtain and peered inside, his stomach tightened.

Leaning forward, he saw the shape of a body hanging from the top of the window-frame, turning slightly from one side to the other with the breeze. Its head was lolling forward, and a belt was fastened round the neck.

The listless body swung round, and he saw the contorted face and expressionless eyes.

Bringing his hands to his head, Matt forced himself to look again.

The swinging body was Ahmed's corpse.

The shock sucked all the breath out of his body and his brain closed down. He was unable to take in what he had just seen. Needing to steady himself, Matt sat down on the bottom step, staring at the ground, his whole body shaking. He couldn't bear to look upwards again.

He hadn't known him long, and they came from different worlds, but Ahmed had become his *protégé*, almost his younger brother. He couldn't think further than the basic, inexplicable, heartrending fact of Ahmed's death. Try as he might, he couldn't get his brain to work or form a single coherent thought. He took one last look at the body, and then sat facing the opposite direction, unable to bear the sight any longer. He resisted the instinct to force his way into the flat and cut Ahmed down, to help bring him to rest. Instead he fumbled for his phone and called the emergency services.

During the twelve minutes that he spent waiting for the ambulance, it felt as though they would never come. To make the time pass more quickly, Matt tried again to work out what might be the cause of the tragedy. In his jumbled thinking, he first asked himself whether he himself was in some way responsible. Should he have seen the signs? He couldn't remember anything strange in Ahmed's recent behaviour. He had certainly never talked about being depressed. What had happened didn't add up.

In a flash of stark clarity, he saw the obvious explanation that had been staring him in the face, but which his stricken state had prevented him from seeing.

Crouch's people had killed Ahmed and made it look like suicide.

Which meant that Matt, who had brought him into politics and taken him under his wing, was partly responsible for his death.

And that, in all probability, someone in Matt's inner circle must have been passing information to Crouch.

After expertly breaking the lock, the crew – two medics and the driver - went straight inside. Left alone in the street, Matt's mind and body slowly began to function again, second by painful second, even though the jarring questions still swirled round his head. He couldn't shake off the image of Ahmed hanging in the window.

'Apparently he'd been dead for a couple of hours,' said the ambulance driver, as he stood in front of the entrance, barring access into the house while his colleagues examined the body inside.

'Do you know the cause of death?' asked Matt.

'We're not supposed to say anything at this stage - we'll have to wait for the post-mortem. You saw the state he was in - didn't seem much doubt to me.'

When the police arrived, they cordoned off the house and went inside. Half an hour later, an officer came out and asked Matt to give his account of what he had found when he arrived at the scene. When he had finished, the policeman stopped recording and put away his device. He thanked Matt for his time.

'That'll be all, sir. We'll be in touch if we need you again.'

Matt didn't want to leave. It would feel like he would be abandoning Ahmed, letting him down.

'He was a good friend. Always so positive. I can't believe he'd take his own life.'

'Looks fairly open and shut to me, sir, but don't worry, we'll do a thorough investigation. Often in these cases you never find out what tipped them over the edge. You'd better be on your way – you've been very helpful.'

Reluctantly, Matt crossed the street and stood there motionless and frozen, leaning against a lamppost. As if in silent vigil, he stared at the house in front of him and the comings and goings of the police and medical staff. Life around him was a blur, the affirmation of normality a blow to the heart, as children skipped along the pavement enjoying their day off school, and people sauntered up and down the hill as if they hadn't a care in the world. Matt had never felt more alone. Anxiety and hopelessness churned away inside him. He felt he was Ahmed's last link with life, before he became a number in a morgue and a name on a death certificate. It was the least he could do: by remaining within sight of the building where Ahmed had spent his last hours, Matt was showing him the respect he deserved.

They finally brought out the body on a stretcher under a white sheet. As the ambulance drove off, Matt waved Ahmed goodbye, his heart in his throat, ripped apart by sadness, fear, and anger.

As he walked back down the hill, he got out his phone. First he phoned Sam and choked out the ineffably sad news. Then he texted Harish to say that unfortunately he and Ahmed wouldn't be able to make it to the picnic. He would explain the reason later.

Back at the flat, Sam made them some tea and toast. Her face was drained of all colour. He sat at the table and she stood next to him, her hand on his shoulder. Matt could feel her looking down at him, worried about him, willing him not to crack up. She knew him so well now. He realised how lucky he was to have her there with him. He hoped he wouldn't disappoint her.

'Even if he was depressed – which I don't believe - he'd have thought of the pain he'd cause others,' said Matt. 'His family first of all, who were so important to him, and he had so many friends. It doesn't make sense. The Ahmed we knew would never have done that.'

'We can't be sure,' said Sam. 'But if you're right ... who did it?'

Matt looked straight ahead.

'Crouch's people did this because of me. If it wasn't for me, he'd still be alive. They killed Ahmed to make me stand down.'

She leaned down and kissed the top of head, her hands gripping his shoulders.

'Listen,' she said. 'It's tough for you on a human level - of course I understand that. But politically you have to put your personal feelings on one side, and show that the fight goes on. Our people will be looking to you for a strong reaction, that gives them hope, despite the tragedy. We can't afford the slightest hesitation or sign of weakness. We're no longer in an old-fashioned political contest about values and policies – from now on this is the ultimate battle for power and survival. There can be only one winner. They'll show no mercy. Ahmed is probably just the first of many victims. We can't let him die in vain.'

Nodding in agreement, he stood up and they embraced.

'Don't let Ahmed's death deflect you from the cause, however heartless that might sound,' said Sam. 'He would want you to stay firm and keep fighting.'

'I'll do my best.'

Half an hour later, Matt emerged from the bathroom, showered and changed. He was wearing a dark suit and tie.

He took out the whisky bottle from the kitchen cupboard and poured himself a generous shot, which he downed in one.

'You're right, I've got no choice,' he said. 'First of all, I'm going to see Ahmed's family. Then I'm going to find Penfold. I'll do whatever it takes to make him tell me the truth. He won't enjoy the experience.'

Although he had known that seeing Ahmed's parents would not be easy, he was not prepared for the blast of utter devastation that hit him as he entered their living room. A single candle burned in the corner, next to the television. The air was heavy with tears. This must be the rawest, hardest kind of grief, to lose a child in such a way.

Ahmed's mother sobbed on the sofa, incapable of speech. His father, who wore a long white robe, tried unsuccessfully to hide his sorrow behind a veneer of excessive outward politeness mixed with cold fury.

'Please come in, take a seat. You are welcome in our house. If it wasn't for Ahmed's younger brother Mohammed, we would have no reason to go on living. Ahmed was our eldest son, we worshipped him. Our world has collapsed, it will never return.'

Matt bowed. He knew in advance how inadequate his words would sound, but he had to say them anyway.

'I can't begin to understand your pain at this terrible time. All I can say is that your son was a wonderful young man, much loved by everyone he met. He had so much to contribute – his death is a tragedy.'

Despite the tears, Matt could see the contempt on the father's face.

'He changed since he started working for you. If he hadn't got involved in all this politics, he'd still be alive today.'

Matt closed his eyes briefly and said nothing. The mother's continuous wailing reached a new pitch.

'Are you proud, Mr Barker?' the father went on. 'Are you pleased with yourself, for recruiting all these young people to your pointless cause? Don't you feel any shame that you're giving them false hopes and poisoning their lives with your fancy ideas of democracy and equality? My son would never take his own life – it's against everything we believe in.'

Matt bit his lip, searching in vain for a form of words that would partially absolve him without contradicting the father.

'I'll do everything possible to find out who was responsible. That's my solemn promise to you.'

'Leave us. Get out of this house,' said the father. 'I don't believe a word you say.'

Matt tracked Giles Penfold down to an address he still had for him in Kennington, within walking distance of the Houses of

Parliament. The flat was on the fourth floor of a nondescript building, next to a massage parlour. He rang the bell and when Penfold opened the door, Matt pushed him aside and forced his way in.

Unflustered, as if he had been expecting him, Penfold walked over to the window, beckoning Matt to follow him. He took out a packet of wipes from his trouser pocket and started cleaning his glasses. He had on the same grey woollen cardigan he had worn at the beach.

'I thought you might try and find me, so we kept you in our sights,' said Penfold. He spoke softly, without looking at Matt, staring out of the window. 'How are the Khans? Come and look at the view.'

Matt stood behind Penfold, arms hanging by his side, fists clenched, waiting for the right moment to throttle him.

'Do you remember Logan?' Penfold went on. 'He's in the kitchen. If you lay a hand on me, you won't come out of here alive. Can you see the top of Big Ben through those trees, and the bend in the river towards Vauxhall Bridge?'

He turned to Matt with a disarmingly boyish smile. For a second, there was something about the gleaming dome of Penfold's bald head and the tortoise-shell glasses made him look quite harmless and unthreatening. The moment passed when Matt caught a glimpse of the icy, unblinking eyes that bore into him from behind the lens.

'Uplifting, isn't it?' said Penfold, gesturing for Matt to come and stand beside him. 'This view of London always moves me, even after all these years. Don't you feel the same?'

Matt clasped Penfold's shoulder and spun him round to face him.

'Careful,' said Penfold, brushing his cardigan where Matt had touched him.

'It was you, wasn't it? You or your people killed Ahmed Khan and made it look like suicide. You can't deny it.'

Penfold inhaled deeply.

'This is going to be hard for you to believe, but it's the truth. I won't deny that we were involved. We never meant Khan to die. He was under interrogation as a security risk – we'd received evidence that he'd been radicalising fellow students.'

'Bollocks. That evidence must have been fabricated.'

'You appreciate that we have take such allegations extremely seriously.

The service wanted to teach him a lesson and extract some information, but tragically things got out of hand. It was a terrible mistake. I can't tell you how sorry I am. That being said, what's done is done. You should take this incident as an opportunity to reconsider your position. Otherwise you might be responsible for other deaths, including people close to you – surely you wouldn't want that?'

His anger mounting, Matt swung a punch at Penfold's nose. With unexpected agility, Penfold ducked, easily avoiding the blow. A clattering noise came from the kitchen, as if someone was emptying the dishwasher or stacking plates.

'You're obviously out of practice. If you want, I can give you the address of a very good gym,' Penfold said, a little breathlessly. 'Don't underestimate me, Matthew. I've been observing you for years, remember. I know better than anyone else what makes you tick. I understand perfectly well why you're doing this and what motivates you. In other circumstances I might have even sympathised with your politics. So don't dismiss me as someone on the other side. When it comes down to it, we're all basically on the same side. Or if you prefer it, we're all on different sides. Whichever you like … it makes no fucking difference, if you'll pardon the expression. It's just a question of choosing the right moment to show our true colours.'

'But you murdered one of my closest friends and supporters … '

'That's nonsense. I deny the charge – and anyway you can never prove it. Another thing, Matthew, I'm surprised you haven't mentioned it.'

'What's that?'

'I haven't told the PM yet about your history of psychological problems and depression. I assume you wouldn't wish this to come out in the election campaign.'

'What are you talking about? You're making this up - I don't have a history of depression.'

'Well you do now. We have the files from the therapist you saw after the tragic death of your sister – '

'Don't you dare mention my sister –'

Matt couldn't bear to hear someone like Penfold talking about Sarah, sullying her name and her memory, dragging her in the dirt.

'I know it's difficult for you, but try and calm down. Logan's watching us on the camera in the kitchen. One false move and you'll regret it. Now hear me out. Quite understandably, you were in a bad way for months after Sarah jumped – '

'Don't call her Sarah ... we don't know if she jumped ... we never found any remains ...'

'That's neither here nor there. Look, I know this is difficult, but you need to face up to reality. Your psychological profile is hardly appropriate for someone who wants the responsibility of pressing the nuclear button. We can easily spread the word that you've only gone into politics because you're clinically deranged and suffer from delusions. Not great qualities for someone aspiring to lead the country in turbulent and dangerous times. Once we release the information, with documents to back up the allegations, you won't last twenty-four hours. You'll have betrayed all your support-ers and your reputation will never recover.'

Matt felt stifled and gasped for air. As Penfold slowly turned the screws, he became desperate to leave the room. He made one last effort to hide his discomfort and save his dignity. As he heard himself speak, his voice sounded tinny and weak.

'So what's the deal? If you're still expecting me to withdraw, it's not going to work.'

'It's too late for that now. Technically, you'll still be in the frame, but in practice we'll expect you to gradually wind down. You can fight on. Just don't fight too hard. No more personal attacks against Mr Crouch. Stop virtually all media activities. Support the prime minister's call for national unity. Express admiration for certain aspects of his record. You can go on bleating occasionally from the sidelines, but no more talk of insurrection please. And finally, we'd like you to manufacture a row with the unions and end your association with them and with Rob Griffiths.'

'And if I refuse?'

'Then when you leave this building, you'll be entirely on your own and they'll destroy you. Very slowly and unpleasantly. Don't expect me to lift a finger this time. I've done all I can, more than you'll ever realise. If I tell them you've rejected this offer, they'll want to dispose of you, and I won't stand in their way. Now get out.'

Logan came out of the kitchen, holding a heavy pistol. He clubbed Matt twice round the head and then dragged him across the floor and out of the flat, before kicking him down the stairs. As Matt struggled to stay conscious, grimacing at the pain ringing in his head and his ribs, the door at the top of the stairs slammed shut. In the darkness at the bottom of the stairwell, gingerly, painfully, Matt managed to stand up and dusted himself down.

As he staggered towards St Thomas's hospital, with every painful step he felt his once indomitable energy and strength seeping out of him. He tried to get a grip of himself, to dig down deep to stiffen his morale, but his mind and body failed to respond. He couldn't take much more of this constant aggravation. He wasn't going to give up completely, and he wouldn't tell Sam, but for the first time he wondered if the objective of wresting power from the nationalists was worth all the trouble. Perhaps, after all, to spare other friends from suffering the same fate as Ahmed, he should seek an acceptable compromise with Penfold. It was the realistic and responsible thing to do.

CHAPTER TWENTY-ONE

He wondered whether Sam had detected his weakening resolve. After dressing his cuts and bruises, she brought out the malt and two glasses. He told her what had happened, without mentioning Penfold's offer of a deal and his own arguments for accepting a compromise.

'Go on, drink yourself into a stupor if you want to,' she said. 'Have a good cry, bang your head against the wall – although in your condition I wouldn't recommend it – and let out all your frustration. Then put it behind you and come out fighting. There's no other way.'

When she told him what they should do, he grimaced and clutched the side of his chest as she managed to raise a smile out of him. The plan was ingenious and he didn't have the strength to resist. He would go on fighting for at least another day, and then review his options. They clinked glasses, downed the last drops, and went to bed, where she kissed and licked away his pain, and slowly, tenderly brought him back to life.

They had chosen Bloomberg's plush and futuristic premises between the Bank of England and St Paul's as the venue for Matt's announcement. In the side room where they waited for the event to begin, blue-tinted fish-tanks full of vividly coloured tropical fish competed for wall space with dozens of TV monitors, which announced minute-by-minute fluctuations in share prices and exchange rates from the four corners of the globe. Matt found this bombardment of unwanted information an irritating distraction. He was keen to get started. Noticing his impatience, Sam made one last check that the microphone was fixed to Matt's lapel.

'All ready?' she asked. 'You remember what we said – no half measures or messing about. Don't hold back.'

'I know what I've got to do,' he replied.

When Matt pushed open the door and walked up to the podium to start the press conference, there was a collective gasp of incredulity from the assembled hacks at his bloodied appearance. Furious jostling and shoving broke out between the photographers and the TV cameramen in the front rows as they competed for the best pictures and camera angles.

It wasn't every day that the man who might be England's next prime minister appeared in public with two black eyes and purple bruises all over his face.

'Good morning. First of all, apologies for my unusual appearance. Please don't take it as a mark of disrespect for the fourth estate.'

The cries came from all around the room, some out of genuine concern, others taking the piss: ' … how did it happen? … who was she? …did you report the incident to the police? … must have had one too many … probably fell over the cat …'

The voices stilled as Matt began to speak.

'Yesterday at around three o'clock in the afternoon, I was assaulted in the street by two men who were unknown to me. I can only presume they were acting on behalf of the English Nationalist

Party, or possibly the security services. They told me that if I didn't withdraw from the election, they would attack me again and – this is a direct quote – 'destroy my family'. I was examined by a doctor at St Thomas's immediately after the attack, and fortunately have nothing worse than mild concussion and a few cuts and bruises. The doctor told me to rest for a few days, but I felt it was my duty to come and give you this information in person.'

Ignoring the barrage of questions, Matt went on.

'This incident is symptomatic of the state of politics in this country. Our public life has reached a new low with the ENP's crude and dishonest campaign in this election. The nationalists are running scared: they're losing all the arguments, so they've resorted to using intimidation and physical violence against their opponents. I've got a message for James Crouch: your scare tactics won't work. I'm not going to stand down. We won't be silenced. Together with our millions of supporters – whose numbers are growing every day – we'll fight back, by peaceful and democratic means, to restore freedom and fairness to the way this country is governed. I'm prepared to put my life on the line, if that's what it takes to win this election in the interests of our people, and make our country free, safe and fair once again. Thank you, that's all for now – as I said, I'm still under doctor's orders.'

Less than two minutes later, their car was speeding through the City. Sam showed Matt the first real-time tweets: they were all overwhelmingly positive, condemning the assault on Matt and praising his courage. 'Serious questions for Crouch to answer' was the title of the Reuters report that came out a couple of minutes later. Sitting together on the back seat, Matt and Sam looked at each other, both poker-faced. As they passed by St Paul's, Sam could hold back no longer and burst out laughing. Matt shook his head, smiling broadly.

'You couldn't make it up,' he said. 'A few well-chosen words at the right moment, and we've regained the initiative.'

Sam continued scrolling through her tweets.

'There's quite a storm out there,' she said. 'Crouch must be seething.'

The prime minister turned off the TV in his office, and threw the remote into the far corner of the sofa. He began pacing up and down in front of the window that looked on to the rose garden. Penfold didn't need to be a clairvoyant to know that an explosion was imminent.

'Barker didn't produce a scrap of evidence for this absurd story, yet they all lapped it up. Why didn't our usual friends in the media go after him and expose this cock-and-bull story as a pack of lies? I thought journalists were supposed to be relentless in their pursuit of truth. Don't they realise there's an election on and they're supposed to do what we say?'

'Perhaps they were caught by surprise. Don't worry, Prime Minister: the media cycle will move on as usual, and in a few hours this ridiculous story will probably be forgotten.'

'"Probably be forgotten" isn't good enough, Penfold. The damage will have been done. I want it killed, immediately.'

'I'll pass the message on to the editors, and to the owners in Paris and Sark. They'll understand perfectly.'

'What about News International?'

Penfold hesitated.

'It's not entirely clear who's in charge at the moment. By the way, Mrs Barker's on a flight back from Sydney tomorrow evening, with the children.'

The prime minister stopped pacing up and down. He suddenly looked more relaxed.

'That could be useful. At first he won't know which way to jump. Keep an eye on her. If necessary, I'll speak to her myself.'

PART 3 – DESCENT INTO DARKNESS

CHAPTER TWENTY-TWO

The following Sunday morning, Sam left the flat early to do some shopping. Matt was still lying in their warm bed, half asleep, when he received the phone call from hell.

'We're back!' said a loud and cheerful woman's voice.

At first the voice's very familiarity disoriented him, and he needed a few seconds before he could place it. Then as the realisation sunk in, his heart plummeted and went into free fall, like a plane with sudden engine failure dropping out of the sky.

Please, not her, Matt said to himself, as he tried to muffle his groan with his fist. Not now, just when everything was going so well again.

While he was excited at the prospect of seeing the children, Jenny was the last person he wanted to meet or talk to. His days were full enough already, with the demands of fighting a general election and the pleasures that came with building a new life with Sam. He didn't need any additional distractions or calls on his time. Matt was certain that Jenny didn't begin to realise the extent to which his life had been turned upside down, and he had become a different person. She would almost certainly try to pull him back to being who he was before. He wished he'd never answered the phone.

'How are you?' he spluttered. 'How are the children? Why the sudden return?'

In their eight years of marriage – and he doubted she had changed, at least not on this point – Jenny had rarely given a direct answer to any question, however simple. Nor did she ever confine herself to a single succinct sentence when she could use several lengthy paragraphs instead. When the mood took her, she was capable of ignoring the question altogether.

'Where shall I start?' she said. Before Matt had a chance to reply, she was off again, treating him to a detailed account of everything that was going on in her life. He guessed this was the official, sanitised version, and wondered how long it would take her to come round to explaining why, if everything had been so marvellous, she had decided to leave it all behind and suddenly come back to England.

'In case you were wondering, I haven't come back because I was missing you.'

He supposed that was some kind of consolation.

'We all had a wonderful time,' she said. 'The children absolutely loved it.'

He waited for her to get to the point.

'It's funny how sometimes things all come together at once. I was beginning to feel a little homesick for the music school and my old pupils – nothing serious, just the odd pang of regret. Then out of the blue the school sent me an email offering me a pay rise in my old job if I came back, and the chance of promotion. A day or two later, quite separately, I met a man and we started seeing each other. His name's Ross. He's in minerals.'

Jenny stopped talking for a moment. Knowing she was waiting for his reaction to her news, Matt remained silent, and she continued.

'Ross had to go to England for a few months to work on a project, and he asked me to go with him. So here we are. You two should meet.'

Now there was no holding her back. Matt sat up in bed, rearranged the pillows behind his head and let her gush away, mostly over his head. She reeled off a long list of places and people he had never known, nor ever wanted to. Perhaps she had taken too much Australian sun - she sounded very upbeat. Matt thought he heard a slight twang in her voice: it would be typical of Jenny to drop a screaming hint to make sure that everyone knew that she had just come back from somewhere far away, necessarily a place where the sun shone, the surfers adored her and the living was easy.

Only half-listening as she droned on, he pulled up the covers and played around with his iPad. Skimming through the political pages of the online edition of the Sunday papers, he managed in time to suppress a chuckle when he saw The Observer had named him "Winner of the Week" after his altercation with Crouch.

Matt considered for a moment whether or not he cared about Ross's arrival on the scene, and quickly decided that, if Ross was hitting on Jenny, he should be given every encouragement.

She gave him a blast about the nice man who had complimented her on how well behaved the children were in the departure lounge at Sydney airport. His name was Bill and they were on the same flight. It turned out that he had a niece and nephew in England who were the same age as Sophie and Jack. She accepted his offer to buy her a coffee, and as boarding commenced, they exchanged phone numbers.

'You shouldn't do that,' Matt said.

'What do you mean?'

'Things have changed a lot since you left. From now on, you have to be careful about giving information about yourself and the children to people you don't know.'

'Don't be ridiculous – this man was just being friendly and passing the time. Has going into politics made you even more paranoid than you were before?'

'I'm not joking, Jenny. We shouldn't be discussing this over the phone.'

'It sounds to me that you need someone to bring you back to earth. That was always my role before we broke up.'

Matt punched the pillow, but let it pass.

'Come round to the house and you can tell me whatever's on your mind. The children are dying to see you. How about tomorrow some time? I'll cook something nice and we can have a proper conversation. We haven't spoken for ages – we've got a lot to catch up on. Are you with anyone these days? Bring them along – they'd be very welcome.'

He hesitated about whether he should tell her about Sam and decided against it, on the grounds that he couldn't face the fake enthusiasm and stream of questions that would inevitably follow. He had nothing to hide, but equally it was none of her business. Rather than being bounced, he would be the one to choose when it was the right moment.

'I'd love to come round, but the timing's difficult. I've got election meetings all day.'

He heard Jenny snort.

'Surely you're not so busy that you haven't got time to see your own children for the first time in almost a year – '

'Six and a half months – '

'Whatever – you know if you wanted to, you could find the time. Sophie and Jack talk about you non-stop. They wouldn't understand if you didn't come and see them as soon as you can. What's this obsession about politics anyway? I hope you're not getting things out of proportion.'

Matt counted to ten, and then breathed out, making a low whistling sound.

'You never really understood did you? You never even tried to understand. I'll come round this evening around six, before the children go to bed. Later on, I'm making a speech to several thousand people at a football stadium and doing two TV interviews. So I can't stay for supper.'

'Please yourself. Thank you for giving us some of your valuable time. I hope you'll forgive me for reminding you that you've got two wonderful children who love you to bits.'

The choice before him was between swallowing his pride and going round to strangle her.

'You must be tired after the flight,' he said. 'Recriminations are a waste of everyone's time. See you later. Just one thing – why did you come back?'

The line went dead. Matt shrugged and went off to take a long cold shower, trying to wash any Jenny-related worries out of his mind. Now that she was back, he had to deal with the situation. She didn't mean anything to him any more. He wasn't going to let her unsettle him or spoil his life.

As he was drying himself in the bathroom, he heard the key in the lock.

'Have you only just got up?' Sam shouted out. 'Some people have all the luck, spending the entire Sunday morning in bed, leaving the rest of us to do the work.'

'I'm sorry,' he said. 'I had some unexpected news.'

After he had dressed quickly and helped Sam put away the shopping, he made some coffee and they sat at the kitchen table, in their usual places, facing each other.

'You can't imagine how pleased I am to see you,' he said.

She looked surprised.

'What's the matter?' Sam replied. 'I've only been away for a couple of hours. You look as though you've seen a ghost.'

'I have, in a way. Heard, not seen. Let me explain.'

'That's wonderful,' said Sam, after Matt had told her about Jenny's return, sounding as if she really meant it. 'Seeing the children again will do you the world of good. You hardly ever talk about them, but I'm not stupid – I know how much they mean to you. I can't wait to meet them.'

'I'm sure you'll get on well together. I wish they hadn't come back at the start of the most hectic period in the whole campaign. Their being back in the country opens up another flank of weakness and vulnerability. I'll be scared stiff for their safety.'

'We can handle it,' said Sam. 'I'll block off some time in the diary for you to see Sophie and Jack every other day, and speak to Rob about getting them some discreet protection. I'm ready to stand in for you whenever that's feasible.'

Sam seemed to have thought of everything. Her smooth efficiency reassured him. Yet he knew that the problem he faced went way beyond matters of internal organisation and time management. Simultaneously protecting his children, preserving his sanity, and overthrowing the government would be a testing set of challenges at the best of times. He felt encircled and hemmed in. Everywhere he looked, he saw nothing but obstacles. How was he going to cut his way through the thorns and thickets that barred the path to victory? He thought of what might lie ahead for Sophie and Jack, Sam and him, Rob and the others and the hundreds of thousands of Alliance supporters all over England, and for the country: he knew he couldn't let them down, and hoped they would all survive.

CHAPTER TWENTY-THREE

As soon as he entered the old house, Matt succumbed to the warm welcome. The children – Sophie in a fuchsia nightie and Jack in light-blue pyjamas with a kangaroo motif – were waiting for him in the hallway, beside themselves with happiness and excitement.

'Come on you two, race you upstairs!'

He made a point of huffing and puffing and arriving last on the landing.

'Have you come home?' asked Jack, jumping up and down in his bare feet on the pile carpet.

'I'm here now,' said Matt. 'Even when we're not together, I'm always thinking of you. The whole time.'

'Daddy,' said Sophie, grabbing his hand, 'I want to see you more often, so I can tell you about my friends at school.'

'Of course, sweetie. I want to hear about everything you do. We can have nice chats on the phone.'

'It's better when I can touch you. Sometimes I try to call you but you don't answer.'

He rubbed his eyes and forced a smile.

'It'll be easier now you've come home. Come on, let's sit down together.'

They went into the children's bedroom, and the three of them snuggled up in the creaky rocking chair. He read them several bedtime stories, as they listened with serious concentration. By the time he had finished, Jack's eyes were firmly shut and Sophie was yawning. He lifted them up and dropped them gently on their beds. Before turning out the light, he tucked them in and gave each of them one last kiss. As he left the room, he stopped in the doorway to listen to their soft and even breathing. He could have stood there forever.

When he went back downstairs, despite the layers of dust and piles of unopened boxes, the house felt friendly. He smelled what he guessed was Jenny's walnut bread baking in the kitchen, and the sweet scent from a tall vase of peach-coloured roses which stood on the grand piano – Jenny's only true love, he used to call it - in the living room. Jenny must have worked hard to make everything look nice.

She came out of the kitchen, wearing a colourful print blouse over her jeans, and a pair of coral earrings that he had given her during their year in Italy. He was even cheered by the familiar sound, which always used to get on his nerves, of Hamish the hamster relentlessly spinning on his squeaky wheel in his cage next to the microwave. The children must have retrieved Hamish from the neighbour who had looked after him while they had been in Australia.

After telling Matt to sit outside on the deck, Jenny brought a bottle of sparkling white wine which she asked him to open, and produced some tasty snacks with tiny pieces of smoked salmon and cream cheese on oatmeal biscuits.

'However did you find the time to prepare all this?' he asked.

'Luckily the shops were still open,' she replied. 'You and I haven't seen each other for ages, and I wanted everything to be just right.'

'I suppose tomorrow you'll tackle the garden. That's always the worst part of coming back when you've been away. The garden takes on a life of its own.'

'Actually, I've been thinking about redesigning it. Making it easier to maintain. But I won't bore you with that now. Cheers.'

Matt raised his glass a little warily.

'Here goes,' he said. 'Welcome home.'

They sat there in the gathering dusk, swatting away the midges, separately staring at the sky.

Jenny suddenly jumped up and came to perch on the arm of his chair. Putting her arm round his shoulders, she kissed him affectionately on the cheek, as old friends might do, in all innocence. Despite himself and without taking a conscious decision, he felt a barely discernible tremor around his ribcage, and instinctively recoiled from her by no more than a millimetre. Jenny must have felt it, for she immediately took her arm away and went back to her chair.

'Please stay for supper,' she said, a little too giddily. 'Please, Matt, just this once. Surely it's not too much to ask.'

He really didn't want to appear as if he was rejecting her invitation, but he couldn't see any other way out.

'It's very kind of you, but I told you I can't. In twenty minutes from now, I'm supposed to be at a meeting. Thanks for asking me round - it's been great to see Sophie and Jack again. Let's stay in touch.'

He felt Jenny's eyes boring into him. Her expression had hardened.

'In that case, there's something I want to tell you. Come inside for a moment – this won't take long.'

They sat down in the living room, Matt on the sofa and Jenny two yards in front of him in an armchair, legs crossed and arms folded.

She observed him, looking him over, apparently not liking what she saw. Her earlier reasonableness had vanished. He wondered where the first poisoned dart would land.

'You've got to decide, Matt. Either you give up politics or I'll make sure you never see Sophie and Jack again.'

She's lost it, he thought.

'You've no right to do that.'

'You're blind, Matt, you can't see how your life looks to people on the outside. As long as you remain in politics - with all the violence, the threats, the name-calling - you can't offer the children the stability they need. Quite the contrary – you're a danger to their emotional development. Any family court judge would agree with me. Face up to it.'

She must have prepared this cheap trick in advance.

'That's utter nonsense – '

'I know you prefer speaking to listening, but for once, hear me out. Stop grandstanding: you're not addressing an adoring crowd at a political rally, you're in the living room in the house where you used to live, with the mother of your children. I asked you round this evening so we could make a fresh start, but you've made it obvious you're not interested. I'm trying to save you from yourself, but you won't let me come anywhere near you. It's time you stopped drifting along in your private fantasy world, and came down to earth. This crazy political adventure is never going to work. You should get real before it's too late – for the sake of the children, if you don't want to do it for me.'

He hadn't expected her to turn on him so soon. How quickly she could change from kindness to small-mindedness. He knew he mustn't rise to the bait.

'I realise it must be hard for you to understand,' he replied. 'So much has changed while you've been away. After the election, I'll decide what to do with my life, but I can't stop now. There's too much at stake.'

Jenny tossed back her hair.

'Do you know what I think? That you're doing this entirely for yourself. You're on some giant ego-trip, and to justify what you're doing, you pretend your motives are noble and worthy. In fact you're doing it out of selfishness. You're only happy when the whole world's looking at you. Thank God I had the courage to leave you.'

'Let's have this conversation some other time,' said Matt, standing up to leave. 'You've never had any interest in politics or respect for politicians, and I don't expect I can change your mind over the next five minutes. I've got better things to do with my time this evening.'

As soon as he said it, he wished he hadn't.

'I'll remember that, and I'll tell the children,' she said. 'Since you've got better things to do, I suggest you leave this minute. I don't want to hold you back. As you can't be bothered to explain why you've embarked on your one-man crusade, I think I'll give my vote to someone who's more honest and straightforward. James Crouch strikes me as definitely the right person to lead the country.'

'Very funny. Sarcasm doesn't suit you. You always did lack a sense of humour.'

'I mean it. I'll campaign publicly against you. Crouch's office phoned me yesterday to ask for my support –'

'- That's ridiculous. They'd never do that.'

'You'll see soon enough. I told them I wasn't interested, but I've changed my mind. I'll tell the whole country what a complete shit you are under that smug exterior. You can tell your girlfriend that I'll come after her too. I'm surprised you haven't mentioned her, if she's so important to you. I've been asking around, and I know everything about her past, probably more than you do.'

'You're making this up - anyway my relationship with Sam has got nothing to do with you.'

He began walking out of the room.

'If you think I'm inventing things, ask your little friend why she never told you about her affair with Rob Griffiths.'

How pathetic – it couldn't possibly be true, thought Matt, slamming the front door behind him and breathing in the fresh night air. Sam was the one person in the world he completely trusted.

CHAPTER TWENTY-FOUR

In the days and weeks following his difficult reunion with Jenny, everything started to go wrong, so much so that Matt almost forgot her snide insinuation about Sam's alleged affair. He had no doubt that the story was fabricated, putting it down to Jenny's malicious intent – anyway, with everything else that was going on, it was the least of his worries. He still trusted Sam. He stored the question at the back of his mind and forgot about it. Nor did he take seriously the idea that Jenny might take revenge by allying with Crouch. She was trying to wind him up.

What weighed most on his mind was Jenny's threat to deny him access to the children. He rang her to ask forgiveness for his behaviour that evening at the house. He was prepared to prostrate and humiliate himself, and unilaterally accept all possible blame for every cross word that had ever passed between them, if only he could get her to change her mind.

'I'm terribly sorry if I hurt you in any way. It's no excuse, but life is a bit stressful these days. Let's forget what we said to each other that evening.'

'Is this an apology?'

'I said I was sorry and I mean it – what more can you want? All I'm asking is we simply apply our agreement that I'll look after Sophie and Jack one afternoon a week and every other weekend. I promise they'll have my full attention and they won't come to any harm. I'll make sure they're happy and we'll have fun together. It'll do them good. That way, you'll have some free time for yourself. Please. You know it means everything to me.'

'I'll think about it,' Jenny replied. One week later, she relented.

His momentary relief was not enough to slow down or ultimately prevent the opening of other hostile fronts in his increasingly flaky and fragile psyche. The whole world seemed to have it in for him, and he couldn't understand why. He had only ever tried to act for the common good, as he saw it, yet his name was being continuously dragged through the mud on the Twitter. '*Serial paedophile*', '*mental dickhead*' and '*fatcat lobbyist*' were among the least offensive descriptions of him on that were trolled all over social media.

Rebutting every accusation soon became too time-consuming, and he tried to ignore all but the most serious. As soon as he had dealt with one ridiculous, unfounded allegation, another would emerge, in a deliberate strategy of relentless bombardment. If it wasn't sexual misconduct, it was financial impropriety. One day, fake evidence would be produced to show his links with human trafficking in Romania; the next day, he would be accused of tax evasion and the alleged possession of several bank accounts in the Cayman Islands; at regular intervals, he would have to rebut suggestions that he had a long history of harassment and sexual assaults against teenage girls.

Of course, he knew the accusations were grotesque and calculated to distract him, and he shouldn't pay them any attention, but their sheer volume and creepiness started to make him feel weak and unclean, as if the poison had entered his bloodstream and was attacking his vital organs. He had never felt so drained and diminished.

'Aren't you rather overdoing it?' Sam had said one evening, as she picked up the bottle of whisky that he had bought two days earlier and saw that it was already half-empty.

'I've always been able to take my drink. It helps me to sleep. We all have our little weaknesses.'

Without saying anything, and with a sad and prissy expression that irritated him, she put the bottle back in the cupboard.

'No moralising,' said Matt. 'I'll decide how to live my own life, thank you very much.'

Sam turned and went into the bedroom without a word. He could sense her disappointment, and knew that he should apologise, but something held him back. He went to the cupboard and poured himself one last shot, but didn't feel any the better for it.

Early one morning he received a call from his credit card company saying that his card had been used for purchases of luxury items – mainly jewellery, high-end designer clothes and electronic equipment – in Moscow and Hong Kong. The goods purchased amounted to over twenty thousand pounds. Had Matt bought these goods? Horrified, he replied that he had never visited either of those places and that his credit card must have been hacked into. The card company was very understanding, and promised him a complete refund and a new card, but the procedure would take several weeks.

At the same time his bank statements showed that four transfers of five hundred pounds each had been made to an account in Panama. A copy of one of the fake payment orders was retweeted twenty thousand times in less than twenty-four hours. The nationalist tabloids were salivating. Again, the bank promised a full investigation, which unfortunately would take at least two months. They offered to raise Matt's overdraft limit, and waive any charges, but the damage had been done. His reputation was being gradually destroyed, he had to ask Alan for a loan, and above all he felt he had lost all control over his life. He couldn't shake off the image of complete strangers poring over his personal details, with the aim of causing him maximum embarrassment and distress. Nothing was sacred or secret any more. He didn't know who to trust or where to hide.

'The plan's working,' said Penfold. 'Barker's losing his grip. In my view he won't last the course until polling day – he'll soon be in meltdown. To remove any doubt, we'll slip something in his drink to bring on hallucinations – the frightening variety. Once he starts getting violent, we'll make sure he's captured on camera. We'll have him sectioned under the Mental Health Act and placed in a secure environment.'

'At which point I will express my deepest sympathy,' said James Crouch. 'I can see the press release already: *"We may have had our differences, but that is part and parcel of the democratic process. Matt Barker was a formidable opponent, and I send him my warmest wishes for a full recovery and a speedy return to public life"*.

'Very neatly put, Prime Minister. We're not there yet, however. With respect, we shouldn't get complacent.'

'You're probably right – I was getting slightly carried away. Before you administer the *coup de grace*, I thought I might pay him a little visit.'

It was late afternoon on Wednesday, which was Matt's day to look after the children. Because his flat was too small, he had agreed that he should come over to Jenny's house while she went out for a few hours. She had recently resumed her old job as music teacher at the local secondary school, and had a full programme of piano lessons that afternoon.

The children were playing in the garden and Matt was alone in the kitchen, clearing away the mugs and plates after tea. They had shared a carrot cake and some chocolate hobnobs which Matt had brought with him. The children had eaten with relish, especially Jack whose voracious appetite, Matt proudly noted, increasingly resembled his father's. Being with them lifted his spirits. Watching them laugh and giggle, and tell silly stories about the teachers at school, and smear themselves with chocolate, and spray each other's faces with lemonade through straws, reduced him to tears of joy. Their cheerful innocence and total lack of malice rubbed off on him. This was a better world than the one he usually inhabited. For a few hours, the daily trials and tribulations of the election campaign, and Matt's insecurities, were pushed out of his mind.

As Matt finished tidying up in the kitchen, he ran through the programme for the rest of the afternoon. For once there was no pressure or deadline to meet – they could take their time and do whatever they felt like. First of all, he would play with the two of them for a while in the garden. They might kick a ball about – quite aimlessly, back and forth, or in a triangle, not all competitively – and Sophie might want to show him her cartwheels. Or they could catch the bus to the high street and go to the toyshop, taking care not to buy anything that would annoy Jenny – in other words, no guns or swords for Jack, and nothing pink for Sophie.

He had just switched on the dishwasher when he heard the scrunch of gravel as a car drove on to the driveway, followed by doors slamming and then two muffled thuds. He wasn't expecting anyone. The steps of several people marching up the garden path grew louder. Then came two insistent rings on the doorbell. He wondered why his security detail hadn't prevented whoever it was from intruding on the property. Not expecting visitors, and feeling a tingle of apprehension mixed with resentment at the disturbance, he carefully hung up the dishcloth he was holding. He took a large kitchen knife in a sheath out of the drawer, stuck it in his back pocket and went to answer the door. They were probably Jehovah's Witnesses or people collecting money for a local charity.

There on Matt's doorstep, looking indecently pleased with himself and flanked by two beefy, sullen men, stood the prime minister. A smile lit up James Crouch's unnaturally white teeth, as his pushed his way past Matt and took up position in the hallway, standing with his arms crossed next to the grandfather clock. The two men with him had also come inside and now stood in front of the door, which they had closed behind them.

'Aren't you going to ask me in?' said Crouch. 'I won't keep you long. We need to have a little conversation.'

Matt had no time for Crouch's silly games – he had only one concern drumming in his head.

'Where are they? You've got a bloody nerve,' he shouted, as he rushed forward, trying to push past the two men and reach the door. They roughly pushed him back, but he managed to reach the window in the hallway. He opened it wide and stuck his head out, and searched in every direction, but couldn't see any trace of them.

'Sophie! Jack!' he called their names repeatedly, but there was no reply.

'Don't worry, we've got everything under control,' said Crouch, standing behind him. 'We saw your two lovely children when we came in. I had a little chat with them, just to say hello. There's plenty to keep them busy outside. We're keeping an eye on them, and you've got absolutely nothing to worry about. In case you were wondering, we've tasered your security men – they'll wake up in a few minutes with a headache, but in the meantime we won't be disturbed. Now if you don't mind, could we sit down somewhere?'

Without waiting for Matt to reply, Crouch went in to the living room and sat down on the sofa. Matt stood over him, shaking and glowering. He saw that he was still in the sightline of the other two men, who remained in position by the front door.

'What've you done with my children? Who do you think you are?'

Crouch languidly crossed his legs. His left shoe dangled in the air, exposing the heel of his silk burgundy sock.

'Who do I think I am? That's an interesting question, but probably not uppermost in my mind at this precise moment. You want to know that your children are alive and well, and I want you to face reality. It should be perfectly easy to come to some arrangement.'

Crouch plumped up the cushion next to him, but Matt refused to sit down. Matt heard the sound of children's laughter outside, but before he could run to the window, the two men moved quickly over and pinned his arms to his side. Matt felt one of them pull the knife out of his back pocket. Crouch burst into laughter.

'Expecting trouble, were you? How charmingly old fashioned. Relax. I've come to help, not to harm you. All this is getting a bit too much for you, isn't it? I completely understand – believe it or not, I've been there myself many times. Politics can be such a bitch. She worms her way inside your head and feeds off your brain cells until you don't know which way to turn. On top of everything else, you've been unlucky with the timing – three weeks before an election is not a great time to have a breakdown.'

Crouch nodded at the two men, who let go of Matt's arms.

'I'm fine, thanks.'

'You don't have to pretend,' Crouch went on. 'I'm not one of those people who make cheap jibes about mental health issues. Quite the contrary, I know psychosis is a disease like any other and is nothing to be ashamed of – those who suffer from it simply need treatment and rest. You've got some very able colleagues who can pick up the torch when you drop out. I'm sure they'll achieve a perfectly reasonable result. Then in five years time, you'll have completely recovered. I'll have retired and you'll sweep the board.'

'You're wasting your time. I'll never accept your offer. It's not going to happen.'

'You've misunderstood. I'm not making you an offer. I'm telling you what you have to do. Anyway, you're probably not the best judge of your condition. What you need is to take some time off and see a therapist. Unless you do what I say, not to put too fine a point on it, you're fucked. Now let's see what the little ones are up to.'

Crouch stood up and walked to the front door, accompanied by his two heavies. The three men stepped outside, and started walking down the path, with Matt following close behind, his heart heaving and his eyes straining to find Sophie and Jack.

Suddenly there they were, unperturbed, playing behind the apple tree on the far side of the front lawn. Crouch had seen them first. Instead of proceeding down the path towards the car, Crouch strolled on to the lawn and, taking his time, kicked an old football across to Jack, who smiled and kicked it back. Matt shouted at Crouch to leave his son alone. Paying no attention, Crouch sauntered over to Jack and, putting a hand on his shoulder, ruffled his hair.

Two metres away, Sophie sat on the swing that was fixed to an upper branch of the apple tree, absorbed in twirling a pigtail. She didn't notice Crouch approaching her from behind, and almost fell off the swing when he pushed her hard from behind. Her initial grin of excitement was soon replaced by fear and growing panic, as Crouch kept pushing the swing higher and higher. The more she shouted for him to stop, the higher he pushed it. Matt, maddened with worry but helpless, was vainly trying to wrestle his way out of the grip of the two bodyguards. At last, Crouch stopped pushing the swing and let it slow down slightly, and then aimed a sharp kick with his shiny black shoe at the small of Sophie's back. Propelled forward off the seat, she banged her head hard against the jagged-edged bark of the tree trunk.

Matt, freed at last, ran at full tilt across the lawn towards his screaming children and scooped them up in his arms. As Crouch climbed back into his sleek black car with tinted windows, he waved at Matt. The car drove off at speed, scuffing up the gravel.

As he dressed Sophie's cut and consoled his children with a glass of milk and some more biscuits, Matt wondered where Crouch would strike next. After Sophie and Jack had washed their hands and had begun quietly watching the cartoon channel in the living room, he went upstairs to the bathroom.

Sitting on the edge of the bath, he held his head in his hands and wept. He hoped Jenny would arrive soon, and he would be free to disappear. He had put his political ambitions before his children's safety, and he would never be able to forgive himself. For their sake, he wished they had never come back.

CHAPTER TWENTY-FIVE

Crouch and Penfold sat opposite each other in the prime minister's study, Crouch in his favourite high-backed chair glowering down on Penfold, who was squashed into a corner of the low sofa.

'You won't want to hear this, Prime Minister, but it's my duty to give you the facts, however unpalatable. For whatever reason – I can't see any rational explanation – support for Barker's movement continues to grow.'

'I thought you told me he's suffering from delusions and serious depression and he's about to withdraw.'

'That's a slight exaggeration. The problem's not Barker and his mental state, it's about the shift in public opinion. The mood is volatile, but all the polls tell the same story: SOCA is gradually moving ahead. People are fed up with the traditional parties and the same old faces and they're desperate for something new.'

'But don't they realise I've always been in favour of change – it's my brand, it's what I'm known for. I never stop reinventing myself.

We've reformed our party structures, we're proposing a series of radical new policies, we've slashed taxes - what more do they want?'

'They probably don't know themselves, Prime Minister, except they feel let down by the system, and some of them are blaming the ENP. Barker and SOCA are offering change, and much of the electorate seem prepared to take them on trust. However unlikely the prospect, if the trend continues, they could even win the election. We need to do something dramatic to regain the initiative. Our options are limited and we haven't got much time.'

Crouch walked over to his desk and, one by one, picked up the three silver-framed photographs and looked long and hard at each one – portraits of Winston Churchill and Margaret Thatcher, and a photo of Crouch himself being blessed by Pope Francis. He had recently removed the one of him shaking hands with Donald Trump in the Oval Office and placed it in in his bottom drawer. It was a pity, they had got on so well, but *sic transit gloria mundi*. Even presidents come and go and outlive their usefulness.

He held up the photo of the Pope and made the sign of the cross. Crouch had always been good in a crisis. With God's mercy on his side, he was confident he would find the right way forward.

Martha Hunt stirred half a spoonful of sugar in her tea and smiled across at the prime minister in anticipation. From her relaxed demeanour, she probably assumed that this sudden summons to an unplanned meeting heralded a change of heart on Crouch's part, or that he wanted to ask her a favour for which she would be suitably rewarded.

'We've got one week to defeat our enemies,' said James Crouch to the home secretary, 'and this is how you're going to do it.'

Hunt's face blanched and she carefully placed the teaspoon on the side of her saucer.

'You'll provoke a situation of general unrest, so we can then crack down with maximum force. Anyone suspected of supporting SOCA will be a legitimate target. You should expect fatalities.'

Horrified, Hunt opened her eyes wide.

'Would that be within the law?' she asked. 'Quite apart from the political risk?'

'I'll take care of the legal niceties,' Crouch replied. 'You get on with doing your job. As for the political implications, we'll present the electorate with a clear choice, between a strong government defending the national interest, and a bunch of anarchists attacking the foundations of the state. I admit it's a risk and a heavy responsibility, but we can't afford to be sentimental. Believe me, it's the right thing to do for the country.'

Hunt shook her head, apparently not wholly convinced. Crouch made another effort.

'Listen to me, Martha. This'll be your chance to go down in history as a woman of great courage, who put the defence of public order before her own personal safety, by standing up to the rabble. First thing tomorrow morning, we'll declare a national emergency in Cobra, and you'll be granted special powers to take all necessary action. I'll make sure the tabloid coverage is overwhelmingly positive.'

Her hint of a smile encouraged him to continue.

'Any previous suggestions that you're weak and indecisive – which I never subscribed to myself – will be immediately forgotten. Your reputation will be transformed overnight, and you'll become the undisputed favourite to succeed me, when I step down in a couple of years' time. His Majesty the King will thank you personally.'

She looked as if she was going to be sick. Crouch wondered if he had miscalculated. He didn't want her bottling it – that would seriously jeopardise the plan. She was supposed to be his buffer, and the person both to take the flak and to carry the can if events got out of hand.

'I know this won't be easy for you. If you feel at all worried, let me put your mind at rest. I'll make absolutely sure nothing untoward or unpleasant happens to you. I give you my solemn promise.'

Her eyes gave a brief flicker of hope.

'One more thing: I'll be right behind you every step of the way. You can count on my unswerving loyalty and support.'

From the way her face suddenly went blank, Crouch wasn't sure if his stirring words had had the desired effect.

'You can contact me any time, Martha,' he called after her, as she shuffled out of his office, head bowed. 'I'll always be there for you.'

She didn't look back. At least she hadn't resigned. Over the next few days, she would have a vital role to perform as a political shield. After that, she would have served her purpose and he could send her to the House of Lords. She would probably be begging for mercy by that stage.

Crouch reached for the phone and had his private secretary set up a secure conference call with the Chief of the Defence Staff and the Commissioner of the Met.

'Start moving into position,' said the prime minister, when they came on the line. 'Operation Bonecrusher starts at midnight tonight.'

James Crouch settled down for a long evening. He sat on the sofa in the small living room of the flat above Number 10, sharing a bottle of prosecco with the lustrous Valentina. He had never expected he would become so dependent on her. From the first moment they met – she had been designated as his official interpreter during a trade mission in Donetsk – something had clicked between them and she had shown unfailing loyalty ever since. It annoyed him that the excessively polite and up-themselves Downing Street staff had never accepted her. Penfold had once explained that they had nothing against Valentina personally or her Russian nationality, it was the principle of the prime minister having a live-in mistress above the shop. It was felt that this might set an unfortunate precedent. Crouch resolved to start his next term of office by terminating the service of some of the stuffier retainers among the staff. Their social attitudes were so outdated.

As the first reports of street violence and the uncompromising military riposte began to come in, Crouch snuggled up to Valentina and refilled their glasses. This was going to be a night to remember. Even by his own high standards of self-congratulation, the first phase was turning out exactly as planned. It had only taken a few simultaneous sparks to light the tinderbox – firebombs thrown by anonymous demonstrators at half-a-dozen SOCA offices located in different regions - and the flames soon fanned out all over the country.

When Sir Christopher Jenks sent up a detailed report of the numbers of killed and wounded, Crouch asked Valentina to bring him a black tie. When she came back, without saying a word she brushed some fluff off his jacket collar, as he stood in front of the mirror and shaved with an electric razor. If the situation deteriorated during the night and he had to address the nation on TV, he would be ready. After giving Valentina a friendly pat on the bum as he dispatched her to bed, Crouch waited, alone and statesman-like, to learn the country's fate. How little people understood the loneliness of power.

He sat down and made himself comfortable, stretching out his legs in readiness for further reports on the mounting violence. Regrettably but inevitably, by midnight the death toll was approaching a hundred. Over twenty people had been killed in one incident in London alone, when the army had shown commendable decisiveness by coldly machine-gunning a group of protesters that had occupied the National Bank of China in Threadneedle Street.

Crouch noted down the place-names and the numbers of fatalities. Fires were raging, alongside widespread looting, in the centres of all England's main cities – including Birmingham, Manchester, Newcastle, and Bristol. Waves of racist attacks and hate crimes had been perpetrated in different parts of the country. The police presence was so minimal that, in some areas, the anti-migrant movement had the streets to itself. Scores of halal butchers and Polish food stores had their windows smashed and their produce destroyed. "The government appears powerless in the face of such widespread violence, and the country is sliding into anarchy," chirruped the BBC's slightly excitable political editor, Emily Marshall. The operation had been perfectly executed and its objectives secured.

At five o'clock in the morning, Crouch decided he wouldn't need the black tie after all, and put it back in a drawer. After congratulating the army and police commanders on the success of their exemplary action, which he asked them to continue, Crouch informed Penfold and Jenks that he would be taking a step back. He would refuse all media appearances until further notice. He instructed them to impose a total news blackout. The more the panic and mayhem spread over the next two days, the stronger his position would become.

He went upstairs, undressed and slipped under the silky sheets alongside his lover. Her gentle snores gave way to a sharp intake of breath and then a susurration of low groans, as the prime minister, taking her from behind, claimed his recompense for a hard night's work. As he lay back, panting and flicking off pearls of sweat after reaching his clammy climax, he promised that Valentina would receive her due in the next birthday honours.

Over the next two days, while the repression continued unabated, Crouch disappeared from view. The Downing Street switchboard was instructed to divert all calls for the prime minister to the cabinet secretary. When the questions raised were legally complex but politically innocuous, Jenks was to pass them on to the home secretary. Apart from issuing a brief statement to say that *'The prime minister is devoting all his energies to defeating this grave threat to our democracy,'* no contact was made with the increasingly irate and hysterical media.

As Number Ten came under siege, Crouch observed that Sir Christopher Jenks, usually so unflappable, appeared to be losing his grip. After several hours of enforced inactivity behind a wall of silence, in an unprecedented breach of protocol, Jenks burst into the prime minister's office without knocking.

'You've got to address the nation – the people need your reassurance,' he said. 'And the White House is unhappy. They're not used to being kept in the dark by their closest ally.'

The prime minister was unmoved.

'We've just got to keep our nerve for another twenty-four hours,' he replied.

At five o'clock on the second day, when the number of fatalities had reached two hundred, he sent in the Special Forces and the anti-riot police. First they distributed water, food parcels and fuel to those taking the government's side. Once the ENP's supporters had received enough essential supplies to keep them quiet for a few more days, the work of repression began in earnest.

One by one, every SOCA office was broken into, ransacked and razed to the ground, while its occupants were arrested and imprisoned under the revised Prevention of Terrorism Act. Under the unprecedentedly harsh legislation that Martha Hunt had rushed through, under orders, at the end of the outgoing parliament, the police had the power to detain suspects without charge for forty days. The liberal outcry to these draconian measures had barely lasted a few days – Crouch knew that, in the new England, *habeas corpus* was a dead letter. Nobody in power cared any more. In parallel the ETP – the emergency torture programme that had been approved by the Privy Council but kept out of the public domain - was activated to obtain all relevant intelligence.

It was time to claim victory. James Crouch had the crested lectern installed in the street outside, facing the massed ranks of the waiting press. He knew better than to betray any signs of self-satisfaction or complacency. As he put on a crisp white shirt and took the black tie out of the drawer, he softly hummed the chorus from "Danny Boy". In front of the mirror, he practised speaking with the right balance of gravity, authority and humility in his voice and expression. Dabbing on some gel and combing back his hair, he rattled off his statement. *"Today our thoughts and prayers are with the victims of these heinous crimes and their loved ones, friends and colleagues. No words of mine can begin to express the pain they feel, but we will always remember the sacrifice of those who gave their lives. Thanks to the bravery of our armed forces and the police, I am able to tell you that the rebellion has been crushed. Our country is safe again."*

Pitch perfect. In his imagination he heard the spontaneous applause from the assembled journalists. Looking suitably grim, he bowed to himself in the mirror and went downstairs, to deliver his historic statement to the waiting world.

On the other side of London, at a hastily arranged press conference in a church hall before a much smaller audience, Matt struggled to find the words to condemn both the violence and the cynical attitude of the prime minister. His message was not getting through.

'These acts are unspeakable,' he said. 'While we share the grief of the families of the victims, one person alone is responsible for this tragedy: James Crouch. I accuse the prime minister of deliberately provoking the violence that led to their deaths, and call for an independent inquiry to establish the full facts. He has brought anarchy upon this country for base political reasons, because he knew he was losing the election. We can't let him get away with this despicable crime.'

The questions thrown at him were all hostile.

'Won't you admit any responsibility yourself? Will you withdraw from the election out of respect for the dead? Rather than blaming Crouch, didn't SOCA start the violence? Have you any proof that the prime minister acted illegally? What's your message to the families of those that have died?'

Why didn't they understand? Were they all Crouch's stooges? As he shouted above the uproar, he was surprised to hear the mounting anger and bitterness in his own voice.

'We'll make sure they haven't died in vain. We'll take revenge by fighting the nationalists in the streets and through the ballot box. We'll hunt them down and make them pay for what they've done - '

Sam pulled him off the platform and led him away from the baying pack.

'SOCA calls for revenge and armed insurrection' was the headline of the first agency reports shown to the prime minister.

'Mission accomplished,' said Crouch to Penfold. 'Why did this idiot ever go into politics?'

CHAPTER TWENTY-SIX

In his recurrent nightmares through the nights that followed, Matt heard the screams of his friends and supporters as they refused to reveal his identity or whereabouts, while having their faces slashed or their bones broken. Even if he only saw these scenes in a dream, their pain was his fault. He knew he had to help them but didn't know how. If he sent in the trade-union militias, they would be slaughtered. If he did nothing, the Alliance would lose all hope of winning the election.

Late in the evening, Matt was sitting alone in his flat, at his lowest ebb, when Sam came home with her shirt ripped and her face covered in blood. Leaning against the door, gasping for breath, she told him what had happened.

'They beat me up on my way home from the office … I did my best to resist but never stood a chance. Four of them dragged me down a side street opposite the bus station … they went on hitting me and kicking me until I lost consciousness. Two neighbours who I vaguely recognised eventually came by and helped me home. They said I ought to go to hospital, but I preferred to come back here. I didn't want to have to explain to anyone what they'd done to me.'

'The bastards,' Matt said. 'My poor love.'

'They called me "Barker's little slut".

He put his arms round her and led her to the armchair in front of the fireplace. He brought her dressing gown from the bedroom. As he placed it over her shoulders, he could feel her trembling. A rivulet of blood was dripping down her face. As Matt started wiping her cheek, Sam snatched the cloth away from him.

'I don't need your sympathy,' she said. 'I want to know when you're going to get off your arse and start fighting back.'

He flinched and gave a little shake of his head, but said nothing. She was in shock, understandably. It wasn't the right time to try and explain his thoughts, in all their complexity and contradictions. Doubtless she was expecting him to leap into action and join battle at once, for her and for their common cause. If only things were that simple.

He stood motionless with his back to the window. The world was collapsing around him and now this latest disaster. None of this was supposed to happen.

'Our people have suffered terribly and want to see action – of course I understand all that,' said Matt. 'But we've got to choose the right moment to fight back - there's no point in launching an attack if we're going to be massacred. I'm not interested in glory for its own sake. You know we can't take on the army – we haven't got the means. We can only win by convincing people to support our ideas and our values, not through more bloodshed.'

She was looking at him fixedly with a contempt he had never seen before, as though she was seeing him differently, taking her distance, judging him.

'Betrayal. That's the only word to describe your behaviour – complete betrayal. You marched us up to the top of the hill, and when it didn't work out as you had expected, you ran for safety. Tell me it isn't true.'

His face was burning. He had expected a little more understanding for the dilemma they faced.

'Answer me!' she shouted. 'Show me I'm wrong.'

Before the words were out of his mouth, he regretted them.

'Why don't you get some rest. Then we can talk about this rationally.'

The silence was excruciating. A shutter came down on Sam's face.

Grimacing with pain, grasping the arms of her chair, she slowly got to her feet. She stood unsteadily in front of him in her torn and bloody shirt. As she began to speak, he could hear the self-righteous venom in her voice.

'Let me spell it out for you once more - this is the situation we face. Two hundred people have died, many more of our closest supporters are being tortured as we speak. You set up our movement - you're our leader. Our people would follow you anywhere. One word from you, and they'd come out in the streets and risk their lives to overturn this mean-spirited, godforsaken government that's destroying everything this country stands for. Yet you've abandoned them. I'll ask you one last time: when are you finally going to do something about it?'

'It's not that easy, Sam –'

'- I thought you had courage, and that you'd stand by your principles and fight to the end – how wrong I was! All you can do is talk – you're in love with an idea and with your own voice. When the call comes for action, to risk physical injury and even your life - as thousands of others have done in your name over the past few days - you just run the other way and disappear. Thank God I've finally realised what a sham you really are, a fake hero, a coward …'

She paused for breath. He couldn't let this pass. Perhaps she was still in shock, but he wasn't going to take any more. He had to make her see sense. As he moved towards her and tried to put his hands on her shoulders, with both arms she pushed him away.

'This isn't a simple choice between right and wrong,' he said. 'The future of our country and millions of people's lives depend on what we decide to do. I wouldn't be human if I didn't find that decision daunting. I admit it, I'm lost, I'm flawed, as we all are. At this moment, I can't see straight. I need some time to get my head round all this, and work out what we need to do. And find the strength. I'm sure I'll recover – hopefully in a couple of days - and take the right decision, with or without your support.'

Sam's face went blank. If anything, she looked bored, in a hurry to end the conversation. If that was what she wanted, he would let her go. If she felt they needed a few days apart, so be it.

'We don't have time, Matt, don't you understand that? Can't you just be honest for once about your intentions. If you don't start organising the resistance now, this minute, I'm leaving.'

'Leaving what?'

'I'll take my things and never come back here. If you haven't the balls to fight, I'll go to someone that has.'

He felt the kick in his stomach. He tried to work out what she meant. A dim light flickered in the back of his mind. And then he got it.

'You mean Rob?'

'Of course, who else?'

He knew he shouldn't dig himself into this particular hole, but ploughed on anyway.

'Stands to reason, I suppose. When was it exactly, your affair with him? You're the one who's always going on about honesty. Looks more like hypocrisy to me.'

She stood up and moved towards him. The scorn that showed in her battered face had sucked out all her usual tenderness.

'Don't be so fucking trivial!' she said. 'People are being murdered and all of a sudden you're behaving like a jealous idiot.'

Hating himself, he continued in the same vein.

'I couldn't give a shit about what you got up to with Rob - I'm only asking you to tell the truth. Instead of pretending you occupy the moral high ground ...'

She was no longer listening.

He watched her as she went into the bathroom. She quickly stuffed a random selection of cosmetics and a hairbrush into a washbag, and then grabbed some clothes from the cupboard and threw them into a suitcase. Matt wanted to tell her to stop, but the words wouldn't come out. He stood rooted to his spot in front of the window, paralysed by the speed of what was happening, powerless to stop the giant boulder that was rolling down the mountain in slow motion, getting closer and closer, about to crack open his head.

'I'm sorry,' he said. 'Don't go. Please stay.'

Without another word, Sam, his lover, his saviour, his rock, walked out of his life.

At least now he could get some peace. Shaking and sweating, Matt opened the cupboard and took out the malt, already half-finished. Two more bottles were hidden in his wellington boots behind the washing machine. He poured himself a large glass and switched off. Feeling disconnected was his only remaining pleasure. Something had snapped and he was no longer in control of his life, and most of the time he didn't care. He had done his best, but there were too many problems. He couldn't be expected to solve them all on his own. That would be unreasonable.

None of the blurred thoughts that crossed his mind seemed worth pursuing. He had to conserve his strength to deal with the shadowy enemies that surrounded him. They knew exactly where his weaknesses lay and could pounce out at any moment.

He no longer had anyone to turn to. He had lost all the women he had ever loved – Sarah, Jenny, and now Sam. The two people to whom he had been closest – Rob and Sam – had both betrayed him. All the usual reference points of his life – his work, his belief in the cause, his reputation, his self-respect – had vanished or been snatched away from him. It was like having his wallet stolen, only a thousand times worse: money, credit cards, the photos of his children and his very identity had been pilfered and turned over to some anonymous backstreet dealer in human suffering, who at that very moment was cutting up his last remaining means of survival and most cherished possessions into scraps and shreds. His component parts were being recycled in some other, unknown location. He would soon be nothing at all. The person he used to be no longer existed.

Every so often, the vague memory floated across his brain that, not all that long ago, he had been on course to become prime minister. Well, that time in his life was all over now. Looking back, how laughable and totally pointless it all seemed.

For three interminable, hazy days he drifted, knowing he ought to be thinking of how to face up to his demons and win Sam back, but unable to find the courage – the mere thought of the word felt like a kick in the teeth. He spent most of his waking hours watching daytime television. He didn't change his clothes or shave, and hardly ate. Every evening he would drink half a dozen cans of lager and several tumblers of whisky, before turning up the music: any kind would do – drum and bass, Irish jigs, hard rock – the louder the better. An hour or so later he would pass out, dead drunk.

Throughout these days, Sam took up permanent residence at the back of his mind, lurking and reminding him of his weaknesses every time he started to sober up. He kept hearing that unmistakeable catch in her voice, that unbearable huskiness, which made him shiver and weep. She always said the same thing.

'I believed in you, but I was wrong. You ran away at the first sign of trouble. I never want to see you again.'

Whenever he tried to answer and explain, she disappeared.

On the third night, waking up full of drink, he decided to stagger down to the river. Collapsing on a bench, he amused himself by trying to count the stars, until he lost track somewhere in the middle of the Milky Way and fell fast asleep.

When he woke up, he found himself lying on the grass verge, surrounded by pigeons scavenging for crumbs. The sun was shining brightly, drilling into his eyeballs. His head felt as tight as a drum and his tongue tasted like sandpaper.

A blur of yellow stood over him, and then he heard a woman's voice.

'Are you all right, sir?'

Matt sat up, shielding his eyes and feeling the warmth of the sun on his face.

'We know who you are, sir, but you'll understand we have to ask you to move on,' said a second woman's voice.

The shapes around Matt slowly came into focus, and he realised that he was being spoken to by two policewomen in high-vis jackets. A small crowd was forming in front of the boathouse, some twenty yards away, waiting to see if the comic scene with the drunk and the policewomen might turn into a full-scale incident or at least provide further entertainment.

Matt tried to think of something he could say or do that would give him back a semblance of dignity. He failed to come up with anything. Hearing someone shouting, followed by a peel of laughter, he glanced in the direction of the crowd. Like a bucket of cold water being poured over his head, he suddenly saw in blinding clarity that the mother of all fuckups was racing towards him. Scrambling his fuddled brain into unfamiliar action – he had to kickstart the engine several times by slapping his head before it finally spluttered into action - he estimated he had approximately thirty seconds to save his life. He needed to escape from the gawping onlookers before someone recognised him.

'I must have dropped off,' said Matt to the two policewomen. 'I'd better be going home.'

He managed to get to his feet, and brushed the crumbs and blades of grass from the front of his shirt. Swaying slightly, digging deep to draw on what little strength he still possessed, he set off at a brisk shuffle. If only he could make it to the high street on the other side of the bridge, he might be able to merge into the crowd of early-morning office-workers, commuters and schoolchildren without being identified.

In the dank darkness under the arches of the bridge, gulping for breath, Matt tucked his shirt into his trousers, patted down his hair and emerged into the sunlight. His face pointing resolutely downwards as he walked, imagining that he was protected from knowing looks by an invisible protective shield, he willed himself to appear unnoticed. He fired himself up by promising that if he made it back to the flat unscathed, he would do whatever it took to make amends for his moment of weakness. He would set off for the battlefield immediately. Naturally, he would never touch another drop. There was still time to inflict a crushing defeat on Crouch and the ENP.

Twenty minutes later, sweat pouring down his face and the back of his neck, suspended halfway between exhaustion and delirium, he was home. Apparently no one had spotted him on the way. Coming up in the lift, panting hard, he almost buckled under the wave of sheer relief that swept over him. He had behaved like a fool, and it had been the narrowest of escapes, but he could now put the episode behind him.

Matt had just turned the key in the lock, when two figures emerged from the shadow of the stairwell. They pushed him through the door and slammed it shut behind them. They had been waiting for him.

CHAPTER TWENTY-SEVEN

In the late afternoon, sitting together in the prime minister's study, Penfold was showing Crouch the video of Matt Barker's nocturnal escapade by the river. He had just suggested it be sent from an anonymous source to one or two selected news outlets.

'Good idea - I think we've hit the jackpot with this one,' said Crouch. 'Barker's campaign will never recover. I always knew he was a loser.'

And then the emergency phone rang, wiping the glee off his face. The home secretary's voice was trembling, and she was struggling to sound coherent, as the words came tumbling out. Crouch put her on loudspeaker.

'It's just horrific ...pandemonium ... pools of blood and children's screams coming from all directions,' said Martha Hunt. 'A van drove into the east stand of the O2 Arena and then came an enormous explosion, just as people were leaving the concert ... the carnage was horrendous ... people of all ages, families out for the evening together, including teenagers and young children. Over thirty dead already, including three members of the band, and the numbers are bound to increase.'

Crouch sank on to the nearest armchair, his face taut and impassive, simultaneously trying to follow what she was saying and deciding how he should react. This was truly a cruel and tragic blow, just when he thought he had successfully re-established law and order.

'We've reason to believe that another attack is imminent, so we've moved the threat level to critical,' Martha Hunt continued. 'I have to ask for your authorisation to bring in the military.'

'Of course, Martha. You must have all the resources you need. We're still in a state of national emergency, after the crackdown on the opposition, so that makes things easier in a way.'

Seeing the frown on Penfold's face, Crouch realised he hadn't quite hit the right tone.

'I'll put out a statement immediately,' he went on, lowering his voice to make it sound more grave, 'condemning the atrocity and expressing our deepest sympathy with the victims and their families. Killing and maiming innocent children at a pop concert is an attack on our whole way of life, and we'll never let the terrorists win.'

Penfold, who was listening carefully and taking notes, caught Crouch's eye and mouthed something at him. Crouch nodded back his agreement.

'Perhaps I'll add a few words about our brave emergency services,' he went on. 'We'll convene Cobra within the hour. Any idea who was behind the attack – presumably the Islamists again?'

Martha Hunt hesitated before replying.

'That's always a possibility, prime minister, but the police seem to think that this time it was the English Patriotic Front. It may be just a coincidence, but all the bands at the concert were black or Asian or both, and most of the audience too.'

'Holy shit!' said the prime minister, despite himself. 'The police must have got it wrong.'

Crouch frowned and then closed his eyes, weighing up the situation. This latest information was potentially embarrassing. Although it had never been publicly proved, as one of its founders Crouch knew that in practice the Patriotic Front had close links with the English Nationalist Party. Some even called it the ENP's military wing. He had to prevent these alleged connections from surfacing during the election campaign and losing him valuable votes. The moral dilemma in these painful situations was always the same: how soon after the tragedy could you decently bring the political calculations into play? Life had to go on, after all.

'We'd better keep quiet about that for the moment. We don't want to create a new climate of fear without having all the facts at our disposal. Just say the identity and motives of the attackers remain unknown.'

Penfold was making a circular gesture with the fingers of his right hand. Crouch took the cue.

'And that at this stage the police are not ruling out that the perpetrators of this heinous crime are linked to a network of Islamist terrorists.'

'Very well, Prime Minister. I'll call you as soon as we have any further information.'

After the line went dead, Crouch stared silently at the ceiling. Turning his head in the hope that Penfold wouldn't see him, he took a monogrammed handkerchief out of his jacket pocket and dabbed the corner of his eye. Although he rarely got any credit for it, he was as human as the next person. This lack of recognition was deeply unfair but – as so many times in the past –he wouldn't let it deflect him from his purpose.

Penfold was rubbing his hands together in the far corner of the sofa. This generally indicated that he was about to say something Crouch didn't want to hear.

'You'd better schedule a visit to the victims in hospital,' said Penfold.

'You're right – though we don't want any media scrum. Keep it discreet and tasteful. Just one camera crew from the pool will do – make sure we get there in time for the ten o'clock news.'

Pursing his lips, Penfold scratched his right ear lobe.

'This rather puts the kibosh on the Matt Barker story, wouldn't you say, prime minister?'

'What on earth do you mean?'

'According to precedent, after a terrorist act on this scale, you'll be expected to suspend all election activities for at least forty-eight hours and make a solemn appeal for cross-party unity – "what we have in common is more important than what divides us" etcetera. You can't afford to give the impression that you're involved in a personal attack on your main opponent at a time of national crisis.'

Crouch knew that Penfold was right – he just wished he wasn't so sanctimonious about it. Penfold was a trusted adviser and good on detail, but he had no feel for the big picture of raw politics. The man had no balls. When he found himself in the heat of battle, his instinct was to run for cover. Whereas Crouch knew that exceptional situations required exceptional measures, and strong leadership. If he had a chance to destroy Barker once and for all, he would grasp it. He couldn't allow the power of his office to slip out of his hands, merely on account of some half-baked precedent or prissy principle.

'I would never dream of trying to make political capital out of the mental health problems of a political opponent. What sort of politician do you think I am?'

Penfold left the prime minister's question unanswered, as they both turned to look at the breaking news on the wide TV screen. Ten more fatalities had been announced, eight of them young girls in their teens.

As Matt was propelled into the hallway of his flat, for the first few seconds he feared for his life. How naive he had been to think he could get away from his enemies so easily.

Then he recognised the familiar voices, and smelled the grapefruit tang of her shampoo, and his heart missed several beats as a wave of relief swept over him.

'We missed you. We thought you might need some company,' said Rob, playfully punching him on the shoulder.

'I'm sorry,' said Sam, before throwing her arms around him and kissing him.

'I'll put the kettle on,' said Rob, disappearing into the kitchen.

'Those bruises suit you,' said Matt, gently running his finger over the scar above her left eye. 'Gives you a kind of battle-hardened look.'

'Idiot,' she whispered, her head gently nuzzling against his neck.

Time stopped, and all his fears fell away. Standing alone with her and feeling her embrace was like receiving an electric charge. Matt wanted to shed his outward skin of drink and grime there and then, and pick up his life anew as if the nightmare of the past few days had never happened. He was desperate to show her that, despite appearances and everything they had gone through, he was his old self. He could still lead the crusade.

Sam pulled away from him, wrinkling her nose. They stood facing each other.

'Where have you been?' she asked. 'I'm sorry I was so hard on you – I wasn't feeling too well myself. We called you several times a day and left messages but you never replied. I was worried stiff. We had to change the entire campaign schedule - Rob did most of the filling in for you, and told the press you were rewriting the manifesto. They didn't believe a word of it. Then this morning we got an anonymous call saying you were heading this way from the river, looking as if you needed help, and we came straight over. What were you doing all this time?'

If he told her, would she understand? He had to take the risk. There was no point in making up an excuse, or pretending he felt contrite. Nor should he put some of the blame on her for walking out on him. It wasn't that simple, far from it. Tentatively, he started to explain, while looking her in the eye, daring her to express her disapproval, even disgust, at what he was about to say.

'I couldn't call you because I wouldn't have made any sense. I was ill, so I had to lie low for a few days. However hard you try to resist, sometimes the demons win. Now I'm back, the same as ever, ready to fight again, you have to believe me ...'

Sam laid a finger on his lips.

'You don't have to say anything. Whatever caused you to do this, you're forgiven. I'm on your side.'

She took a step back and crossed her arms.

'Although there's still one more thing we've got to clear up, where you haven't been entirely straight with me.'

'What do you mean, I've been completely open –'

'– Depression is one thing, and there you have my sympathy, but there's something else you need to do. For both our sakes, and for what we both want to achieve. You know what I mean. No more drinking.'

Squirming, Matt closed his eyes. This was unfair. Didn't she realise that he could never survive the darkness without the bottle?

'I'll support you, and we can get you some help, but it's up to you. What you need now is to get back to doing what you do best. I know you don't like flattery ...'

That was before. A few compliments right now would go down quite nicely. Try me ...

'... But your strengths far outweigh any occasional moments of weakness. It may sound strange, even trite, but you can't get away from the simple fact that the people need you, Matt. They admire you. You've got the gift – you inspire them. And you know it works both ways: when you sense you're lifting them, you feel energised. You could call it a positive form of egotism. But the precondition is you stay sober. Let's talk later, if you feel like it. Now have a wash and get some rest. We need you back on the campaign trail first thing tomorrow morning.'

Although he knew that she was right, he was desperately reluctant to move away from her. She must have been reading his mind.

'We've got the whole night ahead of us. In the meantime, I'll be waiting for you, right there,' said Sam, pointing at the sofa. 'I won't move. I'll never leave you again, I promise, unless you throw me out – and provided you do what I say.'

He saw the mischief back in her eyes, as the old complicity started to flow again between them, binding them together.

'Now you'd better be telling the truth …' he said, putting on a solemn face. 'Desertion in the face of the enemy is a treasonable offence.'

Awash with gratitude, but not wanting to show it, Matt showered and went straight to bed. His last thought before losing consciousness was that he had better hide the bottles behind the washing machine before she found them. He might even pour the contents down the sink as a secret gauge of his good intentions and conversion to sobriety. He hated being lectured – particularly when he was in the wrong – but he would do anything to keep her. Well, almost anything. And then he was lost to the world.

After sleeping straight through until the late afternoon, and shaving off his week-old stubble, he put on some clean clothes. He felt positively buzzing and glowing from the unaccustomed cocktail of rest, cleanliness and the chance of redemption. Before going into the living room, he sat on the bed and thought about his next move.

His mind seemed so clear that he almost felt apprehensive, as if he was still under the effects of some euphoria-inducing substance. Whatever the source of his inspiration, he knew what he had to do. The key to his survival would surely be to destroy the person who was most responsible for trying to push him over the edge.

It wasn't exactly about taking revenge, more like redressing the balance in favour of decency and dignity. He would never stoop to Crouch's methods. Eliminating those old ways was the point of their battle.

Sam was waiting for him, as she had promised, sitting on the sofa and staring into mid-air. When she saw him, she wiped the worried look off her face, and went to make them a pot of tea. The living room and kitchen were spotlessly clean and a delicious smell came from the oven. There was no sign of Rob.

They sat at the kitchen table at their usual places, facing each other. He saw that Sam was watching him tenderly but warily. They each began by profusely apologising, talking over each other, and then agreeing to draw a line. It was nobody's fault, and anyway they had more important things to discuss.

When she said with mock seriousness that, from now on, under no circumstances would she ever let him out of her sight again or do another runner, he trusted her totally and felt exhilarated.

'I've put a chicken and some potatoes in the oven,' she said. 'In the meantime – where shall we start?'

'Nothing less than total victory will do. We've lost a couple of days but we can still make it happen.'

'Of course we can.'

Her eyes shone as she looked at him, but her expression had switched to solemn and serious.

'There's something you need to know. While you were asleep, there's been some more bad news.'

What could she mean? He couldn't bear the thought of another setback, just as he was starting to leave the darkness behind and embrace reality again.

After reaching across to him and placing her hand over his, Sam tentatively began to tell him about the O2 bombing, describing the attack and its deadly consequences for the victims, many of whom were young people barely in their teens. As she spoke and he took in the scale of the atrocity and the suffering, Matt flinched under the weight of his shame. Threatening clouds of doubt fluffed around his thinking, and his head felt fuzzy. He forced himself to push aside all the preying distractions and concentrate on what Sam was telling him.

'Your silence has been noticed, of course, and already condemned by our opponents. We presume Crouch knows about your disappearance, but so far he's not gone public because he knows it wouldn't look good in the current circumstances. Tomorrow you've got to be back in the front line. If you're not, we'll lose everything.'

'Give me a moment,' he said, plunging his head in his hands.

Yet another tragic blow. At first he wasn't sure he could take any more. The thought that during his disappearance so many young and innocent people had suffered such pain was unbearable. The attack wasn't his fault, but his failure to react immediately and show sympathy was unforgivable. He owed it to the families of the victims to show he was on their side.

He was right to feel the shame, yet feeling guilty would be of no practical help to anyone. He began composing in his mind the statement he would send to the press and on social media. If he didn't find the right words to react to the tragedy, his reputation would never recover. More importantly, he had to stop the country from sinking further into the mire of violence and hatred.

As Sam waited for Matt to reply, she gave him one of her long, stern looks, with no visible hint of sentiment or affection. If she was still unsure that he was capable of showing leadership, he would prove her wrong. He drank the last dregs of his tea, before pushing the cup and saucer away from him.

'So what will you say?' Sam asked.

He spoke hesitantly at first, as much to himself as to Sam, before quickening the pace, and imbuing his words with purpose and rhythm.

'I'll tell them this must be the last attack. The violence has to end. People are tired of hearing politicians produce the same old platitudes, while the attacks keep on happening. This time it's got to be different. The whole country has to make sure nothing like this ever happens again. It's not the moment to play the blame game or point the finger at minorities, it's a time for national solidarity, for everyone to stand together. This isn't about me, or Crouch. The only people that count this evening are the victims in the O2 Arena and their families. Everything else is secondary, mere background crackle and interference. The stakes couldn't be higher – we've crossed a line tonight, with what looks like the first mass attack by English white supremacists on the Muslim community in London. The government's only answer to violence and hate is more of the same. They've imposed a news blackout again, which the mainstream media are slavishly applying. They're bringing in the army, yet they're losing control – England's tearing itself apart. We've got to stop the bloodshed, and heal the wounds.'

He knew he had her with him now. The clouds of doubt had lifted from Matt's mind. Neither needed to spell it out - this was the moment he had to decide for himself. He hardly had to think – the pieces were falling into place in his mind of their own accord.

He sat up very straight in his chair, and told her what he would do.

'Call Hassan at The People's TV in Shoreditch. Tell him I want to make a statement at midnight tonight. In the meantime, you can trail a few lines on social media. It's my duty to stand up for what we believe and do what I can to prevent another massacre. My message will be brief, down-to-earth and unsentimental. No ''hand of history on our shoulder" stuff. The only way we can stop Crouch's guns is to win the people's hearts.'

After devouring the chicken and potatoes – his first proper meal in days - and refusing Sam's offer of a glass of wine after a second's hesitation, he set to work. She cleared the table and brought him a cup of strong coffee. He had two hours to find a way of staving off a national tragedy of immeasurable proportions. Fear and rationality were beside the point. Precisely because the challenge was so impossible, he knew that if he found the right words, he was in with a chance.

CHAPTER TWENTY-EIGHT

'I'm sorry to interrupt,' said Sam as she and Matt sat on the back seat of the speeding car on the way to the studio in Shoreditch. 'There's something I think you should see.'

Matt looked up from correcting, for the umpteenth time, the text of his statement, and glanced at Sam's iPad. The headlines couldn't be clearer: in a long interview with the BBC's political editor, Crouch had declared Matt unfit for public office, alleging that he had a history of mental illness and depression. Matt gave Sam back the tablet.

'He can say what he wants – it won't make any difference. Personal attacks are not what people want to hear right now. It makes him look cheap.'

Matt didn't know how to change a plug or fix a leaking tap. Didn't know or couldn't be bothered. Instead his mission was to save the country. Communicating effectively with hundreds of thousands of people - for example, by making a crucial speech that could change the course of history - was what he was capable of doing well. Soaring above the day-to-day, the mediocre. Finding the words, the tone, the flow and the lyricism that move to tears or give hope, that was what he tried to do. Experience had shown that it usually worked.

This time he had to inspire an entire people to rise up against the political system. Logically he had little chance - England was a conservative country, after all. But approximately once every two centuries - as exemplified by the Peasants' Revolt, Oliver Cromwell and the Tolpuddle Martyrs – the people had broken with tradition and shown their innate streak of radicalism, by opposing the ruling class. Was this the time for them to do so again?

Things could always go horribly wrong, and doubtless one day they would, but tonight disaster was unthinkable. He thought of those who had lost their lives, and knew he had no choice but to succeed. The possibility of failure was not so much feared, as a recognised part of the process. Like stage fright. He had to feel nervous, in order to stay calm.

As they drove through the darkened streets, Matt put aside his script and looked blankly out of the window. Preparing for the ordeal, the hardest test he had ever faced. Alone, untouchable, cut off from the world around him, even from Sam. That was how he liked it and how it had to be. She knew him well enough by now. He would only come down and return to his normal self when the last word had been spoken and the last microphone switched off. Until then he would stay locked away in his separate state, calmly prepared to risk everything.

To the recorded sound of Big Ben striking midnight, Matt appeared on the screen, seated behind a desk of stripped pine. He spoke into the camera, firmly, calmly, with authority and a hint of steel. His eyes never flickered.

Friends, fellow Englishmen and women: my appeal to you tonight is quite simple. We must act together to save our country and pull it back from the brink of disaster. For years we hoped it would never come to this, but now the moment of reckoning has finally arrived. We no longer have any other choice, but to stand up for what we believe in, to stand and fight, whatever the risks.'

Matt had the impression that, unusually, every single cameraman, sound engineer and technician in the studio, as well as focussing on their jobs, was waiting to hear what he would say next.

'Our opponents will tell you that those who support the Save Our Country Alliance are enemies of the state, filled with hatred and bent on revolution, and that only the English Nationalists can protect and guarantee order and prosperity. Don't listen to them. These are the arguments that have been used by fascists down the ages. They will tell you that I'm a manic depressive and unfit for public office. Don't listen to them. In all humility, I would point out that their mean-spirited equivalents at the time said exactly the same about Winston Churchill and Abraham Lincoln. Moreover, it was probably true. But their mental condition didn't stop either of those great men from saving their country from destruction and oblivion. Some medical experts say it even helped them.'

He hoped Sam appreciated that last reference. He had included it with her in mind.

'The time for action and resistance has come. If we look around our country, we see state-sponsored killings, racist attacks and government corruption on an unprecedented scale. If we don't act, the unthinkable will become reality: the evil of fascism will have taken root in the country of Shakespeare and Churchill.'

'James Crouch and the leaders of the English Nationalist Party already have blood on their hands, but they're still not satisfied. They will cling on to power whatever the cost. Although they sense they're losing this election, they want to drag the country down with them. We shouldn't underestimate the seriousness of the situation we face.'

Matt leaned forward, speaking directly to the viewers at home, the tone of his voice softer than before.

'Many of you watching may be saying to yourselves, and to your family and friends, "Who's this man who's suddenly appeared from nowhere, who

no one had ever heard of only a few months ago? What's this movement he's set up? Why should we trust him?" You're right to put these questions – here's my answer. What this new movement has achieved over the past six months, week after week, month after month, has no precedent. When we started out, they told us it was impossible, but they didn't understand the spirit and the strength of the people of England.'

The rhythm of the words began to flow as he stepped up the pace and intensity.

'The old ways are finished. Our opponents know the tide has turned against them. Day after day, we've proved the doubters and the naysayers wrong. They threw everything at us, and we went on fighting. When they knocked us down, we picked ourselves up and continued the battle. We never gave up, because we knew that England had to change.'

'In ten days' time, if you give SOCA a majority in Parliament, that process of profound transformation will begin. SOCA is the only political movement with the courage to confront reality, and to answer the people's call for fairness, justice and change. The old divisions between left and right, young and old, London and the rest, must be healed. We'll offer you a new vision for a new era, where individuals count and local communities are empowered. Where business can be a driving force of prosperity for all, instead of a vehicle for tax evasion and short-term profits for the wealthy few. Justice not corruption. Equality not elitism. A tax system that supports job opportunities for the young, and public services that serve the public. A root-and-branch reform of all our national institutions, to ensure they are no longer shackled to the past, but provide a solid foundation for renewal and reform.'

He paused and took a deep breath. He had to put everything in to the final message of his statement. His voice took on a new level of gravity.

'Tonight we're within sight of victory. Over the next ten days, the world will be looking at England. We must show them the best of the English char-acter, and the strength of our moral purpose, by comprehensively rejecting this corrupt, self-serving government, which has become a laughing stock

in the eyes of our friends in Europe and around the world. We must show that England can rediscover its true self, its true identity. England's coming home.'

'Victory in this election will belong to those who fight the hardest and want it most. You've shown, by your full-hearted energy and commitment, that there's nothing we can't achieve together. Let me end by asking you two favours: to make sure that the election that takes place a week on Thursday is free and fair, by resisting all attempts at intimidation and obstruction. And above all, to give your vote to the candidate in your constituency who represents the Save Our Country Alliance. Listen to your heart and soul, think what the future can hold for those you love, and do what you know is right. Good night and good luck.'

There had been so much to say and so much at stake that the distilling into plain, resonant language and striking the right balance was never going to be easy. As they removed his makeup, Matt thought the statement had come across fairly well. Not quite as brilliantly as he had secretly hoped for, but he felt reasonably satisfied. As always in the first few minutes after these occasions, while pretending to look cool, he craved reassurance and compliments.

'How did I do?' he asked Sam.

'An unmitigated disaster,' she replied.

His face fell.

'That's surprising. I didn't think it was that bad.'

'Idiot – you hit them out of the park. You're on your way to Number Ten. Now let's go home before you start feeling too pleased with yourself.'

A small press pack was waiting at the exit from the studio, on the corner of Shoreditch High Street and Bethnal Green Road. Matt greeted them good-naturedly as he walked to his parked car and told them he wouldn't be taking any questions – he'd said quite enough already that evening. There was a rumble of disappointment among the hacks, as they realised their hour-long wait in the cold had been for nothing.

'So when's the class war then? When are you going to man the barricades?' shouted Harry Walker from the Daily Standard into Matt's face. 'You're pretending to be a proper little working class hero, but you're not fooling us. Coming from a former lobbyist, you've got a nerve. You're just playing with people's lives to further your own career.'

It was late and Matt was tired. He knew Harry was trying to wind him up, and he shouldn't reply, but he wasn't in the mood to let it go.

'This is serious, Harry. Can't you act responsibly for once? You've been playing games all your life, spewing out hatred and prejudice and whipping up people's fears. You could say what you wanted because you were always protected. Now your cosy life is coming to an end – you'd better get used to it.'

Harry Walker stood in front of him on the pavement, barring Matt's way forward, recording every word on his smartphone.

'Ever heard of the freedom of the press? Or won't that count for anything when you Trots take over?'

'Let me go through, Harry. It's been a long day for both of us.'

'I want an apology first. You questioned my professional integrity. Or are you feeling too depressed – '

Matt knew he shouldn't, but this had been building inside him for months, even years. The tabloids had had everything their own way for too long.

He gripped Walker's shoulder with one hand and kneed him in the stomach. While Walker was bent over and gasping for breath, Matt then punched him squarely in the face with a straight uppercut, which landed on the side of his nose. To Matt's surprise, as he turned away and wiped his hands on his trousers, above the clicking of the cameras he heard the rest of the press pack give a loud cheer.

Sam bundled him into the waiting car.

'People like you shouldn't be allowed out in public,' she said. 'That wasn't exactly the ideal image for a future statesman. We'd better get you home before you decide to clobber someone else.'

She slipped her hand in his as they sat together on the back seat. He settled down to watch the fleeting images of the sleeping city through the car window – the tacky neon lights above the all-night shops, the forbidding façade of the Bank of England, solid and indomitable St Paul's, the refuse collectors and the huddled homeless, unsteady late-night revellers, fading imperial buildings, and the lights still on in Whitehall offices for civil servants working into the small hours, juggling to stave off the multiple crises. Matt had no regrets. The clock was ticking and the world was closing in on him. He wondered what he had unleashed and where it would all end.

PART 4 – CLIMBING BACK

CHAPTER TWENTY-NINE

With just over a week to go, there was no doubt that Matt's message had got through. The touch-paper had been lit. In the days that followed his dramatic midnight appeal, a new mood – wild and euphoric, but brittle too, swept through most of England. At rally after rally, on the airwaves and on social media, around the kitchen table and in the pub, people made clear their determination to defend the country and defeat the nationalists.

Moved beyond words, Matt had never experienced anything remotely like it. He had touched a nerve and released a burst of energy and hope on a scale that caught everyone by surprise. He marvelled at the sight of the massive crowds wherever he went. He had always known that the English people possessed a deep reserve of courage and decency that had been stifled for too long by those in power. Yet he had never imagined such an outpouring of passion and anger.

With each day that passed, SOCA inched up in the polls. The Alliance welcomed a hundred thousand new members in two days. The Tufton Street phones were permanently jammed and the

SOCA website temporarily crashed. It seemed they could do nothing wrong.

'There's a Justin Fishbourne on the line,' said Sam one morning. 'He's tried to reach you several times. He wants to make a large donation. Shall I say we accept?'

'Tell him to pay back what he owes his company pension fund first. Then if he crawls naked down Whitehall, I might consider his offer.'

The three of them met for a lunchtime strategy session in Sam's favourite Indian restaurant across the road.

'Don't let it go to your head,' said Rob. 'It could all change from one day to another. And you know what they say comes after pride ...'

'I understand how fragile it all is,' said Matt. 'We've got to keep up this momentum until election day. If we show any sign of weakness or complacency, or our support starts to drop, they'll attack us even more brutally than before. We mustn't let up for a second.'

Looking affectionately at his two comrades, he banged his fist on the table.

'Stay strong,' he said. 'Enjoy the week ahead, and drink in the enormity of what's happening around us. We'll never live another moment like it. This is our time – although the prize is so much more important than you and me, or Crouch, or any bunch of politicians. History's on the march, and we happen to find ourselves caught right in the middle, at the precise moment of truth. We can't afford to screw up.'

They each had the same niggling concern at the back of their minds.

'What's happened to Crouch?' asked Sam. 'We haven't heard a word from him or his camp since Matt went on TV. Apparently he's been spotted a few times on the streets in West Thameside, campaigning, but they've cancelled his daily press conferences. He hasn't been seen outside the constituency for several days. He must be biding his time, but for what?'

'He's a puffed-up dictator, but he's not stupid,' said Rob. 'He must realise the country's turning against him. Perhaps he's trying to organise a dignified departure.'

'Bollocks,' said Sam. 'He's up to something. Anyway, he doesn't deserve to be treated with dignity after all he's done. I know we're supposed to be magnanimous in victory and all that, but we can't let Crouch escape without making him pay for his crimes. Our people would never forgive us if we just let him quietly retire without punishment. He and his supporters deserve no pity, no mercy. What they did – first ruining the country for their personal gain, and then causing the deaths of hundreds of innocent people - can never be forgiven. They've never shown any flicker of concern for their fellow-citizens. Crouch should be treated like a war criminal.'

'Hang on,' said Rob. 'It's not the French revolution – we're not going around chopping off people's heads. Let's focus on what we've got to do now, rather than taking revenge later.'

'Why do you always defend Crouch?' Sam threw back at him.

This was getting out of hand. Matt felt he had to shut them up before the argument escalated.

'Stop quarrelling like an old couple,' he said.

They both looked at him dumbfounded, and then the three of them burst into laughter.

'Perhaps not the ideal choice of words in the circumstances,' said Matt.

The brief moment of tension had been defused, even if accidentally. Matt wasn't unduly worried. Anger and revenge were rarely good counsellors, but they were playing for high stakes, and a degree of nervousness before the last big offensive was understandable. He knew that many of their supporters shared Sam's opinion about Crouch, and her directness was an essential part of the mix between the two of them. If it were confession time, he would even say that Sam's strong views neatly balanced out his own tendency to overcomplicate life and endlessly sit on the fence. He needed her beside him. She was right that they would have to decide what to do with Crouch. It was just that first, they had to win the election, and then they had to take power and form a government. Once in office, he would do whatever needed to be done, within the law.

His thoughts were moving elsewhere, and his vision of where his duty lay was changing. In talking to the press, and even with Sam and Rob, he was careful never to sound complacent. In his own heart of hearts, he felt that surely nothing could stop them now. Even as someone who prided himself in being rational and measured, it was hard not to feel buoyed up by the adulation, and further exhilarated by the sweet smell of revenge.

It was time to start preparing for his first days in power and forming his team in Downing Street. He blinked at the thought of walking through that door. It wouldn't be easy to transform SOCA, which up to now had essentially been a loose alliance of disparate voices of protest, into a cohesive force for governing the country. He would have to strike the right balance in his choice of cabinet ministers, and insist on discipline and total loyalty from the outset. The full implications of what it meant to wield power, and the crushing burden of responsibility, were beginning to sink in.

The outline of a new and harder mindset started to take shape in his head. There would undoubtedly be difficult decisions ahead, which no one else could take but him, and him alone. One of his principal missions would be to restore justice. If that meant making the guilty pay a heavy price, he would do his duty in the national interest without any hesitation. Truth and reconciliation, if necessary, could come later.

CHAPTER THIRTY

S everal hours later, towards the end of the afternoon, Rob brought him back down to earth.

His interviews over for the day, Matt was sitting at his desk in the Tufton Street office, flicking through the sports pages in the evening paper. Despite it being the middle of the cricket season, the main story claimed that even football was now being affected by the national crisis, and the sense that an era was coming to an end. 'The glory days of easy money and lax tax regimes for sheikhs and oligarchs will soon be over', the article read. SOCA had promised new legislation to change the structure of club ownership, place a cap on transfer fees and 'return the clubs to the fans'. The richer Premier League clubs, usually so careful not to express political preferences, were distancing themselves from the ENP. Invitations had been cancelled, favours denied, requests for photo calls with players refused. Ripping off fans in Newcastle and Manchester while floating the club on the New York stock exchange was about to get a whole lot harder, if the polls were right.

About time too, thought Matt. Football was yet another area of national life in desperate need of reform and an injection of fairness and common sense rather than dirty money. The piece in the paper was further confirmation that the policies in SOCA's manifesto accurately reflected public concern.

As Matt folded the paper, he saw Rob bearing down on him, looking miserable as usual.

'I'm afraid we've discovered one exception to the national trend,' said Rob, drawing up a chair.

'Where's that?'

'West Thameside.'

'You're joking.'

'We should have seen it coming. It's like Custer's last stand – they're throwing everything at it. We were level pegging last week, but today Crouch has moved three points ahead of you. Now we know why he's been keeping quiet – he's been focussing on his re-election.'

'Don't let's get too excited,' said Matt. 'There's often a wobble in the polls over the last couple of weeks.'

Rob looked exasperated.

'And elections are often lost because the candidate gets complacent,' he replied. 'You need to stop swanning around the TV studios and spend more time in the constituency. Get out on the doorstep, connect with people. Ramp up the campaign and take a few risks. Otherwise SOCA might win a historic victory, but you'll be on the outside looking in. We can't allow that to happen. I haven't given up six months of my life to end up on the losing side.'

So that was Rob's problem – nothing to do with loyalty to the cause, more the idea that the result might prove he had made the wrong choice. He was as hard to pin down as ever. Matt reluctantly decided he had better humour him, to bring him back in the fold and make him feel loved.

'I'll make some space in the diary tomorrow and the next day to spend more time in the constituency. I don't share your pessimism - you're getting things out of proportion. Crouch's credibility is draining away. We've got an excellent set of policies and moreover they're all costed. The people see us as responsible and on their side. We've got to keep our nerve.'

Rob drew his chair closer to Matt's desk.

'You still don't get it, do you? Let me give you a quick lesson on the facts of life.'

Matt wondered what was behind all this agitation – it wasn't in Rob's character.

'We've got one week to go. One week. It's now or never. If we don't get you elected, all the work we've put in over the past year will mean nothing. I know what you're going to say – it's not just about you, it's about transforming the whole country, your usual spiel. For you to become prime minister, you have to be elected in West Thameside. At the moment, your chances don't look good. To be safe, we need to find another three thousand votes. That means we'll have to start taking a few risks. We might even have to get our hands a little bit dirty from time to time.'

'That's fine,' said Matt, 'as long as we don't compromise our principles and our policies.'

Rob blow out noisily through his lips and shook his head.

'Sometimes I wonder why I bother - we should have had this conversation months ago. You have to get it in your head that politics isn't all about la-di-da speeches and fine-sounding principles – if you want to get elected, you have to cover the grubby side too. You don't win elections just by receiving the highest number of votes – it's also about organisation behind the scenes. That's the way it's always worked.'

'That may be the way you do things in the unions, but I believe in a different kind of politics -'

'And let your opponent clear up those extra votes that are going begging? When people go into the ballot box, most of them don't give a toss about policies and principles. They vote for what they think's in it for them.'

This sounded a bit cynical, but Matt had to admit that Rob probably had a point.

'What do you have in mind? What are our options for making up the difference – apart from my spending more time next week on the doorstep?'

'Let's start with postal votes. Nearly twenty per cent of voters vote by postal ballot nowadays, and the system's completely out of control. Across the country, thousands of households are registered for multiple votes and so-called ghost voters – which means that people who've been dead for years or may have never existed go on receiving ballot papers. The result is that someone else fills them in and sends them back. That's just one example - you wouldn't believe what goes on. An official enquiry said recently that there were at least fourteen different ways in which postal ballots can be misused.'

'But surely that couldn't happen in West Thameside?'

'I wouldn't bet on it,' said Rob. 'But don't you worry. We've made sure James Crouch won't be able to take advantage of the failings in the system. More to the point, we ought to do quite well ourselves.'

Matt bristled - this was completely unacceptable. How could Rob have imagined that Matt would stand by and let him break the law?

'There's no way I'm going to let you deliberately commit fraud on my behalf,' said Matt. 'I thoroughly disapprove of these methods.'

'Of course you do,' said Rob. 'But you want to get elected, don't you? So you can change the country for the better?'

Matt couldn't deny it.

'Politics is a rough old business. For every good deed done, there's always a price to be paid.'

'I'm not prepared –'

'Hear me out. All sorts of things go on behind the scenes – trade-offs and paybacks, blackmail and bribery - that nobody ever hears about. We cling on to the fallacy that democracy still works, while under the surface, money is constantly changing hands to buy votes and people are forever knifing each other in the back. It's a mug's game really – the only thing that's certain is you can't trust anybody. There's no point in getting steamed up. The deadline for postal votes has already passed – the votes are in and there's nothing you can do about it.'

Matt had never heard such blatant cynicism. He understood better now why Rob was often accused of playing both sides against the middle – because he was completely devoid of any principles of his own.

'Are you saying you went behind my back and acted illegally in my name?'

'I wouldn't put it quite like that myself. It's more about using the system to maximise your vote, so you can carry out all those wonderful promises you made.'

Matt felt cornered, powerless. Whether or not this was the reality of the way things worked, he hadn't entered politics to win by rigging the vote. Even if he understood the point that they had to be realistic.

Rob hadn't quite finished.

'And I haven't told you yet how we can squeeze a few extra votes out of the count. We've neutralised a couple of tellers.'

'I don't want to know. Just get on with it. I'm late for the train.'

Matt picked up his briefcase and headed for the exit.

Rob shouted after Matt, 'I'll be the first to congratulate you on the night. Even if you don't thank me.'

Matt didn't look back, pretending he hadn't heard. As he walked to his waiting car, he told himself the clear priority was to focus on the future and the transition of power. He couldn't let himself be distracted by shadowy shenanigans carried out by others, about which he had never been consulted and knew nothing.

CHAPTER THIRTY-ONE

S OCA's rise in the polls had been noticed abroad. From the numbers of calls and requests for appointments, Matt could see that the general excitement about the fast-changing national mood had even taken hold among London's usually staid diplomatic corps. The message went back to national capitals that England might be at last coming in from the cold. To the sound of crashing gears and screeching brakes, one after the other, governments who had shamelessly worshipped at Crouch's feet during his heyday made clear their support for Matt and his movement. His diary was in danger of clogging up with all the requests for meetings from ambassadors scrambling to join the winning side.

Matt observed these developments with mild amusement and detachment. This new layer of adulation was like the icing on a cake that he had neither the time nor the inclination to eat. The posturing and warm words passed him by. He kept the diplomats waiting.

He hadn't realised it at the time, but understood later, that Sam had taken a different view on the usefulness of diplomacy.

The new departure that events were soon to take started quite innocently, one morning when they were together in the car, going into London.

'How should we deal with Europe?' she had asked. 'You're always saying we live in an interconnected world. Shouldn't you go over to Paris and Berlin, and even Brussels, to build alliances, show you're a natural-born statesman – which is true by the way.'

'They're not very keen on the English after what we did to them,' Matt replied.

'That was in the bad old days, when the nationalists were in charge. Make sure they understand that things have changed. A SOCA Government will do things differently, make a fresh start, repair relations.'

'You might have a point. I'll think about it.'

Which meant, as Sam knew only too well, that as far as Matt was concerned, the idea wouldn't go any further. He had enough on his plate domestically without taking valuable time off from the election to court foreign dignitaries. Matt had noticed Sam's irritation at his disinterest and the glint in her eye. So when the call came through one week later, after getting over his initial surprise, he had a fair idea of where the initiative had originated.

By pure coincidence, or so he thought, Bernadette and Sam just happened to be in his office, going through the diary for the following week.

When he felt his phone vibrate, he passed it to Bernadette.

'Can you deal with that please,' he said, absent-mindedly.

He noticed Sam and Bernadette exchange glances.

For some reason, as she took the phone, Bernadette sat up very straight in her chair. Only after she had crossed her legs, pulled down her skirt and tossed back her hair did she speak into the phone. Matt heard her talking loudly and rapidly in French.

'*Oui, il est ici. C'est un grand honneur. Je vous le passe …*'

Bernadette nonchalantly passed the phone back to Matt, dead-pan, with just the faintest hint of Gallic smugness.

'The President of the French Republic would like to have a word.'

Matt was aware of President Jules Masson's reputation as a rogue and a charmer. Modesty however was not one of his strongest suits. True to his image of a man who always seemed in a hurry and fizz-ing with energy, he came straight to the point.

'Congratulations Mr Barker – your campaign has been stu-pendous. The crowds at your rallies, your speeches - so emotional, straight from the heart – that dramatic statement on TV in the middle of the night – you were brilliant. So un-English, if I may say so. Your style is straight out of my playbook. You will win, I can feel it, and I'm never wrong about these things.'

Flattery usually made Matt suspicious, but he had to admit a certain warm satisfaction at hearing the flow of compliments from the President of France, even if the superlatives were a little overdone.

'Thank you, Mr President, you're too kind –'

'Call me Jules. Matt, I want you and I to become friends after you've won the election -'

'The election's not over yet, Mr President. The current Prime Minister, Mr Crouch, is a strong opponent. He could still win.'

'Nonsense! He's a racist, a nationalist *poseur,* and an enemy of France. You must defeat him. What can we do to help assure your victory? We can provide money, arms, and files on your opponents' crimes and infidelities. What would be most useful?'

Although the conversation had been going on for less than a minute, Matt felt that he was already losing control.

'Mr President, Jules if you prefer... I don't think that would be appropriate –'

'Say no more, Matt, we understand each other. You don't want to be personally involved or 'fingered' – isn't that your English expression? Don't worry, this is a completely secure line. Just tell Bernadette – she's my cousin, by the way – who you want to delegate as your intermediary, and our intelligence people can do the rest. *"Discretion is the better part of valour"*, as Hamlet said –'

'Falstaff.'

'What did you say?'

'The quotation is from Falstaff, not Hamlet.'

'Are you questioning my knowledge of Shakespeare and English culture?'

Interesting, thought Matt, Monsieur le President has a sensitive side. Or perhaps it was just French pride.

'Of course not, Jules, I wouldn't dream of it. Your English is impeccable. Much better than mine.'

In the stony silence that followed, Matt remembered too late that the French didn't do irony.

'There's something you need to understand, Barker.'

'Yes, Mr President,' said Matt, a little too eagerly, although pleased at the reintroduction of a degree of formality.

'We all know the London and the City are finished. You Anglo-Saxons have been living on borrowed time – the party's over. Paris will return to her historical vocation as Europe's cultural and financial centre. That is the modest price of my support for your campaign and likely victory. I will help you in other ways too. Is that clear?'

Far from it, thought Matt, but he'd better keep up appearances.

'I understand what you're saying, even if I don't -, '

'- One more thing. You should go to Brussels. We have to pretend that's where all the decisions are taken nowadays. I've arranged everything for your visit - the President of the Commission has a proposal that might interest you. Our two countries have a great future together. I look forward to seeing you in Paris after the election. Come and have lunch – you may have heard that we have an excellent cellar at the Elysee. I understand that you like the occasional drink? Please bring your lovely companion, she looks delightful. *Au revoir, cher ami.*'

The call was over. Matt looked across at Bernadette and Sam, eyes rolling.

'I thought that went very well,' he forced himself to say. 'What a remarkable man. Now let's have a look at the diary. I suppose it wouldn't do any harm to raise my international profile and squeeze in a trip to Brussels. We need to tell the Eurocrats a few home truths.'

On their arrival in Brussels three days later at the Gare du Midi, two official cars took Matt and Bernadette to the Commission's sprawling headquarters in the Berlaymont building. They were accompanied directly up to the 12th floor in a noiseless lift and ushered into the President's office, which was the size of a small football pitch. Jean-Michel Schmidt greeted Matt with an unexpectedly exuberant bear hug. His welcome was so warm that Matt forgave him the unmistakeable smell on his breath. After all, Matt was not best qualified to throw stones …

The four of them – Matt and Bernadette, Schmidt and Pierre Fanti, the President's tall and bald-headed *chef de cabinet* - sank into plush leather armchairs. Matt declined the tempting offer of a glass of Chateau Petrus 2005. At four-thirty in the afternoon this was surely a joke or, more likely, an eccentric gesture of self-parody on Schmidt's part.

'A wonderful year, but sadly the wrong time of day,' said Matt, trying a little Euro-schmoozing, much to the amusement of his host.

Matt accepted coffee and two spicy *speculoos* biscuits instead.

'Thank you for coming to see us at such short notice,' said Schmidt. 'May I express my admiration for your remarkable achievements so far. You've given us all hope. We're on your side - the whole of Europe supports your movement for change and looks forward to your victory in the election. The EU and SOCA share the same values – fairness and prosperity for all in an open, inclusive society. A win for SOCA is a win for Europe. We look forward to welcoming England back to the continent.'

Schmidt sounded as if he was reading out a pre-prepared script. Such sugary effusiveness was perhaps the usual way of starting a conversation in Brussels, but it wasn't Matt's style.

'As far as I'm concerned,' he replied, 'England never left Europe. At heart the English people have always wanted to have good, constructive relations with our neighbours. We got into this mess because the people were lied to and betrayed by a small clique of nationalists, whose only concern was to further their own interests. Their refusal to recognise the disastrous consequences of leaving the EU, which were inevitable from the start, was the biggest con-trick ever played by a government on its people in England's history.'

Schmidt was beaming all over his face.

'At last an English politician who understands the real world,' he said. 'We've been waiting a long time to hear those words.'

'We're only now seeing the full extent of the damage,' Matt went on. 'Once they realised the true facts of the situation, the vast majority of English people – or British as they were then known – had no desire for their country to leave the European Union. If we're elected next week, on my first day in power I'll propose the renewal of our membership, so that England can reclaim its natural place in Europe.'

Schmidt grinned at him, his look of self-satisfaction tinged with mischief.

'We'll be delighted to welcome you back. You can count on the Commission to assist you every step of the way.'

President Schmidt noisily crunched another *speculoos*.

'Of course, as I'm sure you realise, there will be a price. Since you left, the cost of subscription to the club has gone up. But you mustn't worry – I can offer you a special discount.'

The room fell quiet. This didn't sound too promising. Matt hadn't come to Brussels to be patronised.

'I thought it better that we should be straight with each other,' Schmidt went on. 'It seems to me we have a mutual interest. The European Union is attacked on all sides, and I myself am not in the best of health. I'm not sure which of us will expire first.'

Schmidt stared fixedly at Matt, as if trying to gauge his reaction. Matt wondered whether this linking of geostrategic considerations with the state of his health was another of Schmidt's elaborate jokes, or perhaps some kind of test? Matt decided to say nothing, and wait for Schmidt's next move.

'To be honest, I've never been particularly keen on you Brits. I never trusted you, and given what's happened, history has probably proved me right.'

This was a bit rich.

'I haven't come here to be – '

' – don't get flustered. Listen carefully to what I have to say.'

The man had a nerve. Reluctantly, Matt let Schmidt continue.

'This is hard for me. You're probably too young to understand. As one gets closer to the end, there are moments of unusual clarity and lucidity. They tend not to last very long, but it's important to grasp their meaning.'

Matt found it hard to follow Schmidt's train of thought. How much longer would he go on rambling?

'I've recently come to realise – and as a devoted European this is one of the great ironies of my life – that a rejuvenated England represents Europe's best hope for the future. England's return, under your leadership, will bring new stability to our continent. It will show that the nationalists are on the run. In time, I even see you as a possible future successor. We will give you all the help you need.'

Matt was not going to let himself be smothered in warm words.

'I'm grateful for your support. I'm not looking for a job, and England isn't asking for charity – we can look after ourselves.'

Schmidt oozed out an extra drop of condescension.

'You may be on course to win the election. But do you think your opponents are just going to stand aside and let you take over without a murmur of protest? I've got to know James Crouch well over the years. He's not a man to give up without a fight. He still has powerful friends. That's where I believe we can help you. Without Europe you cannot survive.'

'What kind of help do you mean?'

'Financial support to rebuild your cities. Generous grants to your young people under the EU's Erasmus Plus programme. Plus a fast-track procedure for England to rejoin the Union. We can even send in the European Defence Force if you wish, to help keep the peace. Give me a call the morning after your election, and we can discuss your requirements.'

Matt looked at Schmidt in horror. If ever word got out that Matt was negotiating the use of EU troops on English streets, he would be political toast. It was time for Matt to reassert himself and play the old man at his own game.

'We'll decide the terms of our return, not you,' said Matt. 'Europe needs fundamental change and reform.'

Schmidt gave a little Gallic shrug, as if he had heard it all a thousand times before. Words alone meant nothing, he seemed to be saying. Ignoring the gesture, Matt delivered his *coup de grace*.

'I mean what I say. I shall tell the press that, as a condition for our return, I'll call for your resignation.'

Instead of looking mortified, Schmidt's eyes twinkled, even reassured.

'Perfidious Albion again – some things never change. I'm impressed by your political skills, Mr Barker, but I have to disappoint you. Many have tried to threaten me over the years. It's never worked – as you see, I'm still here. If it wasn't for my health, sometimes I think I'll stay in this job for the rest of my life. Don't get too full of yourself – it didn't work for your country in the past, and it won't work now. Europe is bigger than all of us. Pierre will see you out.'

Schmidt held out his hand, which was slightly shaking.

'I stand by every word I said. Good luck on Thursday.'

By the time they reached St Pancras, the news was out. A large scrum of jostling journalists and camera crews waited at Arrivals. As soon as they spotted Matt, they began shouting out their questions.

'Are you taking us back to Europe? … Did Schmidt agree to resign? …How much did you agree to pay? …'

Bernadette had had a word with Emily Marshall on the phone from the train, giving her some exclusive background about the meeting with Schmidt and promising her preferential treatment. She discreetly steered Matt in her direction, making it look spontaneous. The security detail cleared a narrow space as Matt spoke into the BBC microphone.

'England's destiny is to play a leading part in Europe. The failure of the outgoing government to engage with Europe was a betrayal of the national interest. I told President Schmidt that the EU has to change and finally become accountable, and he has to consider his position. If the terms are right, I'll propose that England should rejoin the European Union. Our return is long overdue – and it's what the people want.'

'Have you had any reaction from other European leaders?' asked Emily Marshall.

'President Masson of France fully supports my position. As does, naturally, the Irish Taoiseach. I'll be speaking to the German Chancellor later this evening.'

'Do they consider you a government-in-waiting?'

'They won't have to wait much longer, Emily. Thank you everybody and good night.'

CHAPTER THIRTY-TWO

Four days before polling day, James Crouch walked behind his security detail along the long underground passage that led from Downing Street to the War Room – a nuclear bunker deep under Admiralty Arch. He was having an animated conversation with Giles Penfold. The meeting was due to start in five minutes, and they still hadn't decided on the best strategy for achieving Crouch's objective. Penfold wasn't being much help.

'These decisions are eminently political, Prime Minister,' he said. 'It really wouldn't be appropriate for me …'

Without finishing his sentence, Penfold cleared his throat.

What was the matter with the slippery bastard today? Penfold wasn't usually so shy about giving his views on all manner of eminently political subjects. Typical civil servant, always covering his arse and afraid of his own shadow.

The likely reactions to Crouch's announcement were hard to predict. Would the others fall into line of their own accord, or would he have to resort to threats, or even force? The meeting they were about to attend, in the utmost secrecy, would make or break his political career and determine his legacy. His throat was dry, and the dim lighting occasionally made him stumble and grasp Penfold's elbow to keep his balance. He hoped that, under the bright strip lights of the War Room, his nervousness wouldn't show. He felt no qualms or trace of guilt, or so he told himself. Once the decision was announced, he was confident that eventually – after some initial hesitation that would be largely for show to cover their backs, so that if things went wrong later they could point to the minutes - the others would follow. If they didn't, he would have to use force. He hoped that wouldn't be necessary.

The two protection officers that walked in front of Crouch and Penfold paid no attention as the prime minister occasionally raised his voice, his words reverberating off the walls of the tunnel. As they approached the end of the passage, Crouch glanced over his shoulder. He was reassured to see that the third man he had asked to join them, who wore a baggy dark suit, was still there, several discreet paces behind. Crouch counted on his ally to add an element of surprise to the meeting and act as his secret weapon. He beckoned the man to come forward and join him.

They had known each other since Crouch's earliest days in business. They rarely met but had kept in touch. Each was under no illusions about the trustworthiness of the other. Crouch had seen him as his sleeper, to be paid off and kept sweet for as long as necessary, waiting for the big day - the moment when England's decrepit institutions would be consigned to history and the old liberal order torn down. That was when Crouch would make his move and bring his associate out of the darkness. He would use him against his unsuspecting enemies, to dispose of anyone who got in his way.

That day had come. The man Crouch had summoned out of the shadows to stand by his side was Rob Griffiths.

When Crouch had first told him about his plan to put an end to Matt Barker's pretentions, it only took Rob a few seconds to get over his initial shock and see that the idea provided him with an opportunity. Crouch could almost see inside Rob's head as his brain whirred, making his calculations of where the advantage might lie. For the right reward – not only financially, but also in terms of political influence - he would end up doing as Crouch asked. That was what Crouch had always liked about Rob's style. He was a man of action and a tenacious negotiator. But the reward was important.

Rob had arrived at Number Ten shortly before midnight. Crouch instructed the doorman to let him in through the back entrance off Horseguards Parade. When Rob was shown into the upstairs flat, Crouch hugged him warmly and brought two cans of beer from the fridge. Crouch ripped them open, handing one to Rob. They didn't need to bother about glasses.

As they each took a first swig, Rob was eyeing him, sizing him up.

They sat down in two facing armchairs.

'Good to see you, PM. How's Valentina? Still in London?'

'She's safely tucked up in bed - you just missed her. Needs her beauty sleep. She's a great support to me.'

'I bet. Give her my warm regards. You made a good choice there - you're lucky to have her. '

Rob sounded rather wistful. Perhaps he was being sincere for once. He had always claimed he liked living alone, and plotting and conspiracies were his meat and drink. Hard on the outside and soft on the inside, Crouch reckoned, with twin streaks of stubbornness and heartless cruelty. You wouldn't want Rob Griffiths as your enemy. If he decided he was on your side, he would do anything for you, unquestioningly. At least that had been Crouch's experience on the previous occasions they had worked together. What Crouch was about to ask would be the most difficult test of all.

'You've spent a lot of time with Matt Barker recently. What state's he in these days? Does he wander around in deep depression, or does he still think he's going to conquer the world?'

'He's an idealist – completely out of touch with reality. He's still standing though, despite everything you lot have thrown at him. The more he's attacked, the tougher he gets.'

'Hasn't he ever suspected anything?'

'The only time I thought he might see through me was when he got all steamed up about my ancient affair with the girl. But I put on a great show of loyalty and devotion, and we soon became best mates again.'

'You've played him well,' said Crouch, 'but the game's over. His movement's become a serious danger to national security. The deep state's finally lost patience, and the generals are demanding that SOCA should be declared an illegal organisation and disbanded.'

Rob face hardened. He took another swig of beer and sat back in his chair, his eyes never leaving Crouch's face.

'That sounds a bit dramatic, PM. Do you really believe that's the right course for the country? It might backfire. You look rather jumpy. Are you sure about this?'

Crouch put his can of beer on a side-table and loosened his tie.

'The thought that I might lose the election fills me with despair. I can't accept to be forced out, after all these years. After everything I've done for the people.'

Rob showed no sympathy. Nor did he appear too concerned by the prospect of Crouch being defeated.

'You'll get over it - that's democracy. You can't always be on the winning side.'

'As a general rule, that's true. Except this time it's different. The people that count in this country – those that have always had its interests at heart - have made it clear that they won't accept Matt Barker as prime minister. They've no desire to give up power, and neither have I.'

'If he wins the election, you won't have much choice.'

'We'll see about that. There's a growing consensus that we need a different system. Liberal democracy's no longer up to the job, history's moved on. We can't have an idealistic clown with no experience running the country in cahoots with a ragbag of disaffected Greens, Trotskyites and communitarians. We'd be the laughing-stock of the world.'

Rob crossed his arms, his face still impassive.

'From the moment the polls close,' Crouch went on, 'there'll be a gun pointing at Barker's head. England deserves better than that. Within days the pound will be worthless, the economy will collapse. Barker might even try to get rid of the royal family – I'm told he's a closet republican. SOCA's only got a chance of being elected because of the perversity of the system. We need new, stronger institutions run from the top down, and a government formed of people with direct experience of running a business or defending the country from our enemies. Of course, if the ENP wins the election, nothing will happen.'

'Naturally,' said Rob.

Crouch wondered if he was taking the piss.

'And if they lose, and the military take over, what will you do?'

'If asked, I'll be ready to serve, wherever I can be useful.'

Rob looked at him in wide-eyed disbelief.

'Let me see if I've got this right. You, the current prime minister - who if I remember correctly was democratically elected - are saying that if your party doesn't win the election, you're ready to support a military *coup d'état* and become the generals' puppet – is that your position?'

'That's a gross misrepresentation of the facts, but broadly correct. Sadly, we'd have no other choice. We mustn't allow the saboteurs to take power – they'd destroy everything we believe in. Barker must be killed and the insurrection crushed. That's where you come in. This is what I want you to do.'

When Crouch entered the War Room, with Penfold and Rob Griffiths standing next to him, he immediately sensed that something was not right.

'Come in, Prime Minister,' said General Sir Nicholas McIntyre, Chief of the Defence Staff. 'We've been waiting for you. Take a seat.'

The four-star general was dressed in full military regalia, and wearing an impressive array of combat and service medals.

He was sitting at the head of the long rectangular table, in the place usually reserved for the prime minister.

'Find yourself a chair,' barked the general. 'It's time we made a start.'

There was no point in making a fuss. Crouch spotted an empty chair halfway along the far side of the table and sat down between two naval officers. Before Penfold could hand him his file, General McIntyre started speaking.

'At different periods in our history, many decisions that were vital for our country have been taken in this room,' said the general, looking round the table. 'Whichever branch of the armed forces or society we represent, I'm sure we're all aware of our responsibilities.'

Crouch raised his hand and asked for the floor. The general gave him a dismissive look.

'If you insist,' said the general, and began speaking to the aide sitting next to him.

'With respect, General, the convention is that it's usually the prime minister who opens these meetings –'

Turning to look at Crouch with an expression of amazement, McIntyre let out a loud, booming guffaw, triggering ripples of laughter all round the table.

'Could I point out, Crouch, that this meeting is secret. It isn't actually happening.'

More titters of laughter. Trying to hide his irritation, Crouch knew his face was burning from the slight. He looked around the table for potential allies who could speak in his favour, but saw no one. Over half those present were in uniform, from all three services, their peaked caps, embellished with copious quantities of scrambled egg, lying in front of them on the table. Two of the three air force representatives were women, smartly dressed in sky-blue serge. Wedged in between the khaki, the navy blue and the gold braid, Crouch counted half-a-dozen owners of newspapers and TV channels, several CEOs of FTSE 100 companies, and two bespectacled note-takers whose over-serious, constipated expression gave them away as courtiers from the Palace. Penfold and Griffiths were leaning against the far wall, both studiously avoiding his gaze.

'*Ergo*,' the general went on, managing to look both serious and indecently pleased with himself, 'if the meeting isn't taking place, the usual rules can't apply. Which doesn't mean that we're not keen to hear what you have to say. I'm sure we'll all be on the edge of our seats. All in good time. Do you mind if I continue?'

Gritting his teeth, with a wave of his hand Crouch graciously allowed General McIntyre to go on.

'Before I was interrupted … I was reminding everyone here of the historical significance of this room. Winston Churchill's greatest victories – his finest hour – were meticulously planned and prepared within these four walls.'

An air of solemnity descended on the meeting room. Crouch found the air thick and dank, and felt the perspiration seeping on to his shirt underneath his armpits. This was not turning out as he had expected.

'In our different ways, we've all been involved in the fight to defend democracy and freedom, both in this country and around the world. We're here tonight to prepare for the worst-case scenario in tomorrow's general election. If by mischance the subversive alliance wins a majority, we shall act swiftly and ruthlessly to bar their route to power. I take it we're all agreed that we should do our duty to stand up for England?'

The room erupted with cheers and the noise of the generals and admirals thumping the table with clenched fists. The civilians present merely clapped loudly.

'That's settled then. Everything's in place to uphold the values we and our forebears have fought for since time immemorial, across the globe in the days of Empire and, when duty called, against the barbarians on the other side of the Channel. Prime Minister, are you with us or against us?'

The pompous git. In the perfect silence that followed the scratching of chairs on the floor as their occupants shifted position, Crouch felt all eyes upon him.

'You can count on me to remain in Number Ten for as long as I have your agreement and support.'

He smiled and looked around the table, expecting praise and gratitude, but none came.

'Good man,' said General McIntyre. 'We'll be in touch. Now who's volunteering to command a battalion in Parliament Square?'

Crouch knew his fate was sealed. He could remain in office, but not in power. In a way he was not surprised – the military had been itching to wrest power away from the politicians ever since the successive years of draconian defence cuts in order to finance austerity. The abandonment of Trident - and the accompanying humiliation in the eyes of the Americans - had been the last straw. No more freebies to Washington or late-summer training exercises in the Med. He knew how much they resented the loss in hard-earned status and privilege.

In all their bluff and bluster, they had underestimated him. Crouch would go along with them for now, to ensure his own survival, but once the election and its aftermath were over, he would find a way of sending the square-headed squaddies back to barracks. Despite their invariable professions of loyalty to the country and the government, they were not always very quick on the up-take. He would eventually outmanoeuvre them and exact revenge. In the meantime, he might even confound them by winning the election. Democracy was such a blunt instrument.

PART 5 – ON THE BRINK OF VICTORY

CHAPTER THIRTY-THREE

'I need a quiet moment, and I'd like you to come with me,' said Matt to Sam, the afternoon before polling day.

Neither spoke as the driver took them to the Muslim Cemetery in Waltham Forest, known as the Gardens of Peace. They took off their shoes before walking between the graves to the place where Ahmed was buried. The grass was dry and freshly cut.

The past few weeks had seen a gradual improvement in Matt's relations with Ahmed's parents. Matt had spent many hours in their home explaining the background to Ahmed's death, and eventually his father Mustafa had almost forgiven him. At least he accepted the sincerity of Matt's admiration and affection for his son.

Before going to the cemetery, Matt had told Mustafa of his intention, and he had voiced no objection. He said he and his wife Nasreen prayed for Ahmed's soul every day. The youngest son Mo sat on Ahmed's old bed for hours, when he came back from school, as if willing Ahmed to return from his long journey and start playing football with him again and helping him with his homework. Mo didn't show much emotion, but his parents knew his bottled-up grief for his big brother hurt him as much as ever. They were worried about the boy, and two weeks earlier had taken him to see a doctor, who had given them a prescription for some anti-depressants, to use in moderation. Mustafa still hadn't been to the chemist's to get the pills. He wanted to help Mo, but drugs didn't seem right somehow.

Matt didn't pray or hope that Ahmed would reappear, but he too thought of him almost every day. Not when he was out on the streets or in the TV studios or in the middle of something, but at certain moments late at night, or when he was alone, or at those times when he became introspective and wondered about the meaning of what he was doing and what would be the final outcome.

The stooges of the country's rulers who had no heart had cut short Ahmed's life, brutally and deliberately. Like the little boy Mo, Matt would never completely get over his feelings of sadness and guilt. He knew too that at any time they could do to him what they had done to Ahmed.

When they arrived at the simple white headstone showing Ahmed's name, Sam squeezed Matt's arm and took a step back. He said nothing and made no gesture, but was grateful to her.

He shuffled half a step forward and bowed his head, his hands clasped behind his back, speaking softly to the grave.

'Sorry, my friend,' he whispered. 'You were the best of us. We'll drink to you tomorrow – orange juice, of course - if all goes well, or even if it doesn't. You're still on the team, we won't forget you. You did more than most to help make all this happen. Have a good rest.'

The tears rolled slowly down his cheeks until he wiped them away with the back of his hand. Matt turned to Sam, shaking his head.

'It wasn't worth it, was it?' he said.

'That's the wrong question. If Ahmed were with us now, he'd be furious to hear you say that. You remember how he used to get so worked up when he believed he was right about something and the rest of us didn't understand.'

The memory made Matt cry a little more as he forced a smile.

'Ahmed would want us to go all the way. Whatever the result tomorrow, whatever the cost and the pain – and who knows, there may be more to come - it's been the right thing to do. You know that's true.'

This time Sam put her arm through his, as they walked back between the graves.

'I suppose, paradoxically, I should tell myself I'm lucky,' said Matt. 'Lucky to be here at this time, and to have this chance.'

They reached the car. Before getting in, Matt rested his elbows on top of the car, leaning forward, scanning the high-rise flats towards the horizon, before glancing back towards the cemetery. He suddenly banged the flat of his right hand on the roof, and turned to face Sam, his eyes blazing.

'The countdown begins tonight. No more soul-searching. Nothing can stop us now.'

When they got home, Matt told Sam that he had one more visit to make before meeting all the campaign workers for a thank-you drink at the White Swan.

He had to see the children one last time before everything blew up. Taking his time, Matt walked through the park to the old house. As he crossed the driveway, he saw Jenny waving at him from the kitchen window. Almost immediately, the front door opened and Sophie and Jack came running down the path towards him.

The children chattered and giggled, each holding one of his hands and pulling him from one side to the other. The big news was that, three days earlier, they'd bought a dog, a chocolate Labrador puppy, which they'd called Betsy.

'Where is she?' asked Matt.

'Fast asleep,' said Jack. 'She never stops sleeping.'

'Who looks after her?'

'We all do,' said Sophie. 'She belongs to all three of us.'

Matt closed his eyes and swallowed hard.

'Mummy and I do most of the work. We have to clear up all the mess. Jack just plays with her.'

Matt patted them both on the head, and then gave Jenny a perfunctory peck on the cheek. She didn't seem to mind that he wasn't more affectionate. Since that first disastrous encounter after her return, they had both stopped pretending. The children began to chase each other round the old chestnut tree, while Jenny and Matt stood together on the front porch. He noticed they both had their arms crossed, and quickly put his hands in his pockets.

'I can't stay, I'm afraid. But I wanted to see you all before my world gets turned upside down.'

'The children probably won't even notice that anything's changed. They don't see much of you any more as it is.'

'I'm not emigrating, you know –'

'You might as well be. I hope you'll invite us to your new planet from time to time.'

They both knew they were going through another parting. Each time it was both the same yet worse, as they had less and less to say to each other. He wouldn't admit it to her, but Jenny was right that he was about to partly disappear from the children's lives. He could make promises, block off whole hours of his time in the diary, but the truth was that from now on he would no longer be in control. He would probably see them less than before.

'Say goodbye to them for me.'

'You can't just sneak off - give them a big hug before you go.'

She clapped her hands and like magic the two children appeared from behind the tree. Matt leaned down and they ran into his open arms.

'Now what did I tell you to say to Daddy,' said Jenny.

Sophie and Jack looked at each other and each burst out laughing. Sophie whispered something in Jack's ear before saying loudly, 'One, two, three!'

'Good luck, Daddy', they both shouted at the top of their voice. He pulled them close.

'Look after Betsy,' he said. 'I want to see her next time I come. And Mummy.'

He hugged them once more and let them go. He began walking backwards away from them, first blowing kisses, then waving goodbye as his heart sank like a stone, before he turned into the road and was gone.

CHAPTER THIRTY-FOUR

As Matt entered the Oak Room of the White Swan, he was assailed by a blast of background music and cheerful chatter that almost knocked him back through the door. Fifty familiar faces radiated warmth and easy friendship. When they spotted him, a loud cheer broke out, as they continued partying. Waves of laughter rose and fell. Matt guessed that, under the surface, the nervousness levels were at an all-time high.

As he surveyed the scene, he thought of all they'd been through together - the frequent disagreements and arguments, often no sooner expressed than regretted and quickly patched up, the breakups and reconciliations, the temporary wobbles in people's normally unswerving loyalty. Yet there they all were – Sam and Rob, naturally, but also Bernadette, Karim, Malik, Marta, Jack, Bogdan, the Hancock Grove crowd, and so many others - still passionately true to the cause and, for the most part, enjoying each other's company and pulling in the same direction. If elections were decided by the devotion and enthusiasm of the candidates' supporters, Matt and SOCA would already be clear winners. In a little more than twenty-four hours, they would know if that had been enough.

Tonight he would be saying goodbye, from the edge of a precipice. Whatever happened, he would miss the comfort of their company more than they would ever realise. Tomorrow, as polling day unfolded and gradually gathered pace, he would be suspended, alone in no man's land, during the long wait before the announcement of the result. And then… who knew where he would be transported? He repeated to himself that he had no regrets.

As he moved into the midst of his friends and supporters, at first he feared that some might reproach him for not having spent more time in the constituency while they were doing all the work on his behalf, and for the days when he had gone missing. He needn't have worried: with much backslapping, kisses and handshakes, he was welcomed back into the fold like a long-lost comrade returning to his home village after fighting bloody battles in a distant land. They were his people, and it felt good to be with them again.

Karim, Ahmed's successor as the leader of the student volunteers, was among the first to come up and shake his hand. He spoke loudly into Matt's ear.

'We've missed you on the doorstep. I can't believe it's nearly over. Trudging the streets has become what we do. It's going to be hard to fill the day.'

'Don't worry, there'll still be enough to keep you busy,' said Matt. 'The world doesn't change overnight because there's been an election. That's when the real work begins.'

Karim wagged a finger at him.

'Don't let us down. There's two thousand young people giving you their vote tomorrow, and they've all got their eye on you. Keep listening to what we have to say. I've taken a risk in backing you – don't dump us when you become somebody important.'

Matt replied without a moment's hesitation.

'You've every right to keep an eye on me and hold me to account. But it's a two-way process. If I'm elected, I'm going to need your support more than ever, to get the results we all want. I can't walk into Downing Street and wave a magic wand. If we're in government, we'll have to go on fighting for what we believe in. I'll never abandon you and your friends, and I'll expect the same support from you in return. Agreed?'

They sealed the deal with a high-five and Matt pushed forward to join Sam, who was sitting on a table on the far side of the room. As he slowly moved through the crowd, someone turned off the music. By the time he reached Sam, the general hubbub had subsided. Rob clapped his hands and called the meeting to order, and silence descended on the room. The party atmosphere had vanished.

Rob took them through the items of practical business that needed to be sorted for the following day – confirming the names of volunteers who would variously act as tellers, give voters a lift to the polls, and be officially present at the count. He kept hammering home the message that no effort should be spared – 'no shirkers, no going off to the pub' – and that every single vote mattered. By now, after months of practice, the machine was so finely tuned that the discussion only took a few minutes. Matt was struck by the contrast between everything that hung on the result of the election and the banality of the necessary practicalities to make it happen. After Rob had finished giving people their instructions, there was a brief silence and one or two nervous giggles. A few heads turned to look at Matt.

It wasn't just that no one knew what to say; Matt understood it was more than that. The feeling hit them all at the same time, if perhaps to differing degrees. He understood what was going through their minds. Even though they had carried the date of the election in their heads for months, the fact that it was tomorrow, in only a few hours' time, had caught up on them without their having seen it coming. One moment they had been laughing and joking in their usual slightly forced and ostensibly carefree way, and then suddenly they came to a collective standstill.

Enveloped in the silence, Matt suspected that everyone shared the same sense that not only was a chapter coming to an end, but also that they were drained and shattered. Suddenly, out of nowhere, the earlier cheerfulness had given way to the weight of fatigue from all those nights of lack of sleep, and the relentless efforts of cajoling and persuasion deployed over thousands of doorstep conversations and confrontations. The nervous tension that had produced the adrenalin and kept them going for so long, beyond the usual limits of endurance, had started to seep away.

Standing next to the table, trying not to show that he too was close to cracking up, Matt dug deep one last time to find the right words.

'I think you all know how much I appreciate you, as individuals and as a team. You know I'm not usually one for dramatic words or grandiose statements, and tonight I'll just say this: love's not too strong a word. I'll never forget what we've achieved together.'

Looking around the room, drawing everyone in, Matt nodded and gave a little, tight-lipped smile, as if to say that he knew exactly how they were feeling, because he was feeling it too.

'This isn't the time for speeches – that'll be tomorrow.'

Matt paused for a second, looking down, momentarily lost in thought. As the silence round the room returned, he felt its force. People were expecting more from him. He caught Sam's eye and saw the mock-reproachful look on her face: she had understood where he was heading. They both knew what invariably followed whenever a politician said that it wasn't time for speeches. And so it proved. He moved across to take up a central position in front of the table, and the rest of them shifted and shuffled in their places to get a clearer view.

'I can see a few tired faces round the room this evening, mine included,' he began. 'We've come a long way over the past year. It wasn't always easy, far from it, but we never gave up. Our movement has grown way beyond our expectations, but so has the mindless violence and brutality perpetrated by the nationalists. We lost one of our dearest friends, to whom we owe more than words can say … Let's take a minute to remember Ahmed.'

Head bowed, Matt stared at the floor, unflinchingly.

Not a single sound came from inside the room. In his mind Matt thanked Ahmed and promised him that he would fight to the last, and give his life if he had to, to defeat their enemies. That was how important tomorrow and the next few days would be.

'Thank you.'

He allowed a few seconds for people to switch back to present time and the task in hand.

'What we've achieved together, in creating this movement, is remarkable, and I thank you from the bottom of my heart. I'm so proud of you all.'

Matt switched on what Sam called his ethereal smile and looked around the room. He had experienced on one or two previous occasions the almost mystical moment that followed. Concentrating hard, he felt a direct line of connection with each person in the room. Several nodded back at him. Some muffled intakes of breath could be heard. Already one or two people were swallowing or biting their lips. Others stared resolutely at the ceiling.

'The day after tomorrow you can take a well-earned rest,' he continued. 'But as we all know, before we can start to relax, we've got to get through one more day. I'd ask you all to do me one last favour.'

Everyone looked up, wondering what was coming next, but ready to do whatever Matt asked.

'Don't worry, it's quite simple – I want you to enjoy tomorrow. Make the most of it, savour it, drink it all in. Write it down in your diaries when you get home, tell all your friends and family. It'll be an unforgettable day, I promise you. I hardly dare say we'll be making history, but it won't be far off. Thank you, everyone.'

Not waiting for the applause, Matt headed straight for the exit. He turned round one last time and waved goodbye, before disappearing into the street, leaving the pub door behind him, swinging on its hinges.

A distant police siren blared from the other side of town, followed by the clattering of a train crossing the railway bridge over the river. The sky was clear and the silver moon almost full, its serene and steady glow standing out against the pinpricks of lights from the planes holding and circling before coming in to land.

CHAPTER THIRTY-FIVE

He was on home territory this time and would leave nothing to chance. General Sir Nicholas McIntyre was the last appointment in Crouch's diary on the evening before polling day. The prime minister had decided to receive him after dinner, in the Cabinet Room at 10 pm. The Chief of the Defence Staff had been told to come alone.

On entering the room, McIntyre came to attention and saluted. Crouch bowed his head in approval. He appreciated the show of respect, even if the way the military used excessive politeness to cover up their smugness irritated him profoundly. Crouch gestured for the general to take the seat opposite him at the Cabinet table, directly under the crystal chandelier. Giles Penfold sat on Crouch's left, fiddling with his files.

'Let me start by reminding you what this is about,' said Crouch. 'Not a word of this conversation must ever leave this room.'

'Of course, Prime Minister.'

'I've every confidence that I'll win the election and remain in office. I need hardly remind you that as long as I'm prime minister, you take your orders from me.'

The general opened his eyes wide.

'That goes without saying, sir.'

Crouch stared him down, before resuming his instructions.

'The objective is to put in place precautionary measures to guarantee public order and safety, in the unlikely event of any major disorder. Most probably, they won't be necessary. The police will be our first line of defence and hopefully they'll be able to deal with any trouble – your troops will be waiting in reserve. Not a move will be made nor a shot fired without my express authorisation.'

A muscle twitched in the general's cheek. He frowned and flashed a disapproving glance at Penfold, who showed no reaction.

'Now tell me, General, what do you propose?'

General McIntyre opened his briefcase and unfolded a map of central London, covered in different-coloured dots.

'From the moment the polls close, our troops will be ready to take up position. The 3rd Battalion of the Parachute Regiment will be billeted in the barracks on Birdcage Walk, and the Royal Tank Regiment will come up from Salisbury Plain during the night. Their mission, once the order is given, will be to secure all government buildings, starting with Parliament and Downing Street. At the same time, if required, our IT engineers - with a little help from the boys and girls in GCHQ - will be available to close down all major media and print outlets.'

Penfold passed Crouch a note, which he quickly skimmed before reading out the contents.

'I must remind you that should military action prove necessary, loss of life must be kept to a strict minimum. But at the same time, you and your troops must do your duty.'

'That's absolutely clear, Prime Minister.'

'If the saboteurs are stupid enough to let events get out of control, you must react with appropriate force. You should target the leaders of any insurrection, not the crowd.'

'Understood. Snipers from Special Forces will be placed at strategic points along the route of any demonstration or mass protest.

If we reach the stage where we need to use them, their orders will be unequivocal – shoot to kill. I take it you're onside?'

Suddenly, Crouch's neck felt rather stiff. He twisted it from side to side. Then he saw that McIntyre was still looking at him. He returned his gaze with what he hoped was an expression of iron determination.

'Let's hope that won't be necessary, but you have my support. You seem to have thought of everything – I'm most grateful. I expect to confound the doomsayers and win by a comfortable majority, but one can't be too careful when our country's future is at stake.'

The general pursed his lips and nodded in agreement.

'With your permission, Prime Minister …'

'Go ahead.'

'May I say how grateful I am for the confidence you've placed in my soldiers and myself. Together I believe that, if called upon to act, we can do the country a great service. Make a clean break at last. In taking these decisions, we're reflecting the will of the great majority of our fellow citizens. I salute your leadership, Prime Minister - my troops will be with you every inch of the way.'

Crouch blinked twice: such deference was unusual from General McIntyre. He was seized by a sudden urge to confide in him. Crouch leaned forward, softening his voice as he spoke.

'You and I are on the same wavelength, General – we've both got the country's interests at heart. Off the record, if a few lefties get their bums blown off, I couldn't give a shit. They've had it all their own way for far too long.'

Crouch smiled and sat back, waiting for the general to agree with him, but instead McIntyre looked alarmed. He and Penfold exchanged knowing looks again.

'Let's all try and get some sleep,' said the general, before giving another stiff salute. 'Perhaps Mr Penfold could kindly escort me out of the building through the back entrance.'

Left alone in the Cabinet Room, Crouch stretched his arms and let out a long, self-satisfied yawn. Everything was proceeding as planned. Perhaps a little rest and recreation might be in order, before going over the top.

As he stood in front of the mirror, adjusting his tie and patting down his gelled hair, Crouch saw Valentina looking at him from the back of the room, a smile on her face. After dimming the lights, he scratched his crotch and took her in his arms. She nestled up to him, pressing against his groin, and they were ready to dance.

They began with an energetic quickstep to the Glenn Miller Orchestra playing "In The Mood", with Crouch expertly guiding Valentina around the small space in front of the fireplace. Ballroom dancing had always been his secret passion, the one pursuit where he felt peerless and instinctively in control. He was light on his feet and a natural dancer - he didn't have to work at it, it just came to him. When the music stopped, he kissed her on the side of the neck. She closed her eyes as the tip of his tongue darted in and out to lick the pale white skin.

With a touch on the button of the remote, he fast-forwarded to "Stardust" and they morphed into a slow waltz, his left arm theatrically outstretched, tango-like, and his right hand clasping her left buttock. She wriggled in pleasure and they swayed in time to the music, in perfect harmony. In a few minutes he would carry her through and throw her on to the bed, but for the moment he was lost in her bergamot scent, her gentle gyrations and the compulsive rhythm of the song. He wanted the moment to last forever. They fitted together perfectly and she danced like a dream. When the breathy, velvety tenor sax solo came on, he grabbed her tight and could hardly hold back any longer. He was in heaven.

When the music stopped, he took her into the bedroom and fucked her like there was no tomorrow. When he turned her round, she howled and hollered like a prairie bitch. As he approached his climax, he felt the whole of Number Ten rocking on its very foundations, the ship of state loosening its moorings, buffeted by the raging sea of his passion. Free at last and on top forever.

They lay breathless, side-by-side, for a few minutes, and then Valentina went into the bathroom. He heard the sound of the shower and then the hair-dryer, before she came back with two towels and a bottle of nail varnish. After throwing a towel at Crouch and placing the other on her lap, she began doing her nails, sitting on the side of the bed.

'Are we staying or moving?' she asked. 'I need to know.'

Crouch stopped rubbing himself down. He was surprised at the question, and found it cheeky.

'I'm going to win. Even if I don't, we're staying here. Trust me.'

She looked hard at the nail on her left forefinger under the light, apparently not satisfied.

'From what they say on TV, it's not that simple,' said Valentina, dabbing another drop of varnish on the little brush. 'We Russians are a strong people. We don't back losers. Suppose you're defeated – what then?'

'It won't happen. I'll always be there for you.'

'That's what you say now. Who can see into the future?'

She put the top back on the bottle of nail varnish, and stood up to her full height, raising her head, looking down on him, flaunting her naked body.

'Come here,' he said, pulling back the sheet so she could slide in next to him. She shook her head impatiently.

'I've got to let my nails dry. Anyway, we've had our fun. It's been interesting to see how you screw people at the heart of government. I've learned a lot. Now it's time for me to get dressed and go to the airport. My flight leaves in two hours.'

Couch sat up in bed, trying to grab her hand.

'Why? You can't go anywhere – I need you here. Where are you going?'

'Didn't I tell you – my mother's sick. I'm going back to Moscow.'
'I thought you came from Donetsk?'

Without replying, she leaned over and kissed him on the forehead, before taking some clothes out of the cupboard and going back into the bathroom, locking the door behind her. He soon heard the sound of the radio, which was playing a selection of loud and melancholic Russian love-songs. She knew full well he couldn't stand them. He shouted at her to turn down the volume, but she pretended not to hear him through the closed door. Over half-an-hour later, she reappeared in all her splendour, dressed in a matching black jacket and skirt, and five-inch heels. As Crouch feasted proudly on her beauty, she put her hands on her hips and spat out her goodbye message.

'If you want to see me again, you'll have to treat me with more respect. Less rough sex, more nights in the box at Covent Garden. A proper job with a nice title. By the way, I've been reporting back every week. Moscow told me I'm worth my weight in diamonds. Let me know one day what you really intend.'

What had come over her? She had never complained before. He heard her stop as she walked across the living room. Then came a clicking sound, and the crackly music started playing. He knew the words well – they often danced to the song in the early days of their romance. The lyrics had always made Valentina laugh – "It reminds me of how stupid and naive the Americans are," she used to say.

Crouch heard the front door closing as the syncopated words drifted into the bedroom: *"Don't sit under the apple tree, with anyone else but me, anyone else but me …Till I come marching home.'*

He couldn't believe it. After everything he had done for her and all the good times they had enjoyed together, the bitch had dumped him at the moment he needed her most.

Draping the towel around his waist, he went over to the window and pulled back the curtain, to catch a last glimpse of his sulphurous lover that was. To his amazement, he saw Valentina elegantly stepping into a dark blue Jaguar, one of the official Downing Street fleet. Her skirt rode up her thighs as she sat down inside the car, and the person holding the door for her was Giles Penfold.

CHAPTER THIRTY-SIX

M att wondered if the waiting would ever end. It was now close to five o'clock in the morning, and the first rays of midsummer sun shone through the line of windows on each side of the school hall, giving an unreal, dystopian glow to the proceedings. The light appeared too bright both for the time of day and for the solemn announcement that was now imminent. He counted that around five hundred people were still present in the hall, nervously awaiting the final verdict. As the low chatter around the room gradually subsided, he could hear birdsong outside. Its cheerful, chirruping normality sounded out of place, and grated on his nerves.

As the candidates waited for Mrs Fortescue, the returning officer, to take up position centre-stage and finally give the result, Matt scrolled through the hundreds of missed calls and good luck messages he had received on his iPhone. The Archbishop of Canterbury and the director-general of the CBI were among those requesting an early meeting. He'd never had any contact with either of them before. Most of the other messages were from people who were completely unknown to him. He shook his head and looked up at the rafters in disbelief, as if appealing either for confirmation from on high that this was indeed his destiny, or for a sign that none of this was really happening.

Strangely, he didn't feel remotely tired, despite having been up since dawn the previous day. The news he had received just before coming on to the podium had given him an intense early-morning rush. He couldn't remember feeling so wide-awake after a sleepless night since his late teens. Only in those days, he had survived on generous doses of drink, mischief and sex. Tonight he had got through on a less heady cocktail of hope, ambition and milky tea. Presumably, the energy would quickly drain out of him once the ordeal was over. He steeled himself to keep on going for just a few more minutes.

It would be a relief to leave the cavernous school hall. There was something oppressive and disturbingly institutional about it. Despite the calm efficiency of the tellers, and the guarded politeness of the other officials he had spoken to, Matt couldn't quite shake off the feeling that he was taking part in a mysterious experiment inside a giant laboratory. Soon he would have to return to the real world outside, and deal with his many enemies.

At the start of the evening, Matt had found it vaguely interesting to observe democracy in action as the counting began. As the hours passed, one pile of ballot papers began to look very much like another. He was less interested in the process of the count than in the result.

All through the night, Matt had refused to contemplate the possibility of victory and its inevitable consequences. He could see from the piles of papers laid out on the long trestle tables, ward by ward, polling station by polling station, that he and Crouch were a long way ahead of the rest. The Green candidate was some way behind in third place, neck and neck with Labour. Crouch had presumably received most of the votes from the few remaining Conservatives, whose candidate was trailing badly. The smaller parties – including the Liberal Democrats and UKIP, both fast-disappearing relics from a bygone age – had received negligible support. In some areas, Matt's piles were much higher than Crouch's; in others, Crouch seemed to have the advantage: it looked extremely tight and too close to call.

Crouch had insisted on the recount. After the first count had been completed, Mrs Fortescue summoned all eight candidates and their agents into the makeshift office behind a dark blue curtain to tell them the result, before the official announcement. They nervously shuffled their feet and formed a loosely grouped semi-circle, with Matt and Crouch at opposite ends, ignoring each other. Matt was surprised that he felt so calm. They all listened intently as the returning officer read out the number of votes obtained by each candidate. When she had finished, for a moment no one spoke. Everyone except Crouch looked at Matt. He had won by just over three hundred votes.

Matt had put on his magnanimous-in-victory face, when Crouch lashed out.

'That's not possible. There must be a mistake - I was ahead in over half the wards. This is blatant fraud.'

So gracious, thought Matt. Typical of the man.

Mrs Fortescue bent her head and looked over her glasses at Crouch with a smile so withering as to reduce most grown men to jelly. Crouch curled his upper lip and said nothing.

'No personal attacks, please,' said the returning officer. 'If you're unhappy, there's a procedure to deal with that, as you well know.'

Matt could see that Crouch was still trying to keep a lid on his anger, for fear of upsetting Mrs Fortescue. What the hell, if he wanted a recount, Matt wouldn't oppose it. The end result would be the same. And so it was decided, officially by amicable agreement but in reality through gritted teeth, to proceed to a recount. His demand satisfied, Crouch stomped out of Mrs Fortescue's office, followed by his agent. Matt braced himself for another two-hour wait at least before the final result was confirmed.

Throughout the evening, Matt had followed on his smartphone and on TV the news coming in from across the country. Rob and Sam updated him continuously on SOCA's performance as the exit polls were followed by the first results. At last the picture was becoming clear and, from what he could tell, looking increasingly positive for SOCA. After doing the rounds of his friends and supporters in the hall, thanking them and telling them he was cautiously optimistic, Matt sat down with Rob and Sam in a secluded corner to analyse the situation. With one eye on the TV screen fixed to the wall in front of them, Matt asked Rob for a summary of the latest overall position.

'Hold on to your chair, and make sure you're sitting comfortably,' Rob began. 'You won't believe this, but SOCA candidates are performing better than expected in every region across the country, except the Home Counties and East Anglia. The ENP are also doing well, but not enough to win a majority. With three-quarters of the results confirmed, the pundits on all TV channels are predicting a narrow overall majority of ten to fifteen seats for SOCA. The way things are going, you'll be asked to form the next government.'

Matt barely had time register the news, when Sam prodded him in the stomach. 'It looks like it's going to get even better,' she said, pointing at the TV screen.

'We have some dramatic breaking news from West Thameside, where unofficial reports claim that the Prime Minister James Crouch has lost his seat after a recount ...'

Loud cheers erupted all over the hall - news travelled fast.

'We repeat that the official result of the count has not yet been announced – indeed we understand that formally the count is not yet finished – and this news should be treated with the utmost precaution. If true however, it would be a devastating blow to the English Nationalist Party and to James Crouch personally. And of course a defeat for Crouch on his home turf would open the way to Number Ten for Matt Barker, as leader of SOCA and potentially the next prime minister. But let's wait and see if this crucial result is confirmed before we start drawing any conclusions.'

The other two looked at him, wide-eyed. Matt straightened his tie.

'One step at a time. Let's wait for the final figures. Anyone feel like another cup of tea?'

Half an hour later, the returning officer walked on to the platform carrying a sheaf of papers. Matt quickly put away his phone. From his place at the end of the line of candidates, he noticed her sturdy brown lace-up shoes. At that precise moment, for him Mrs Fortescue represented everything that was best about England – dependable, unflappable, no sufferer of fools, ever mindful of the general interest but never making a fuss about it. He wanted to kiss her on both cheeks. Not a sound could be heard in the hall, as Mrs Fortescue raised the microphone an inch or two on its stand and tapped it a couple of times. Reassured that everything was in working order, she began to read out the final result of the election of the Member of Parliament for the West Thameside constituency.

Matt looked down the line of candidates at James Crouch. His face was white and his mouth was quivering. He caught Matt's eye and gave a stiff little bow, which Matt reciprocated, his eyes narrowed, with a barely perceptible move of the head. This wasn't a cricket match or the moment to invoke the Olympic spirit. Crouch deserved every ounce of the crushing public humiliation that would be heaped upon him. Matt had no time for him any more.

Crouch had killed and maimed and shown no mercy. Let him suffer and rot.

Matt wondered if Mrs Fortescue realised that her announcement would fire the first shot in a national revolution. On balance, it was likely that she understood perfectly well. She was Middle England, coming together, doing its duty.

He felt the moment of culmination rushing towards him, scattering all other thoughts and impediments in its wake. In a few seconds, the phalanx of cameras would swivel in his direction, and in a trice the image of Crouch's defeat and Matt's victory would be immortalised and digitalised around the world. The preternatural calm required at such times enveloped his body and very being. He instinctively composed himself to look serene, humble and strong.

When the returning officer began reading out the number of votes received by each candidate, Matt barely listened to what was being said. Then he heard Crouch's name and result...'James Maxwell Crouch, English Nationalist Party, twenty-seven thousand, nine hundred and seventy-three ...' followed by the thunderous cheers of his supporters. They were convinced their man had won. Then came Matt's turn.

Was it his imagination, or was Mrs Fortescue hesitating? Perhaps they had somehow got to her at the last minute. She took out a handkerchief from her sleeve and wiped her brow. Her arms stiffened, tightening her grip on the document she was holding with both hands, as if frightened that someone might snatch it from her. She let out a deep breath, which was audibly amplified by the microphone, and began to read the number of votes obtained by the next candidate on the list.

'Matthew Frederick Barker, Save Our Country Alliance, twenty-eight thousand –'

Pandemonium broke out before Mrs Fortescue could finish. The majority of those present stamped and whistled, screaming and cheering to the rafters. A minority – Crouch's irate supporters

– booed and jeered. A few scuffles broke out at the back of the hall. Mrs Fortescue appealed for silence and then repeated Matt's tally. Above the din, straining his ears, Matt just managed to hear her final words.

'I therefore declare Matthew Frederick Barker to be the duly elected Member of Parliament for this constituency.'

The deafening applause rang out again. Matt could hardly make himself heard as he thanked the returning officer, and was rewarded with a wink and the hint of a smile from Mrs Fortescue. He moved centre-stage to begin his acceptance speech and thank his supporters for this historic result.

'Tonight the people of West Thameside have turned back the tide. We have defeated the forces of repression, and given our country a fresh chance. All we ever asked for was fairness and justice for all – '

There was no point in continuing. As the SOCA chant 'Justice Now, Justice Now' was quickly picked up all across the hall, Crouch was bundled off the podium by his protection officers. Waving aside his own security detail, preceded by a dozen TV cameras and twice as many photographers, Matt stepped down from the platform and weaved a triumphant procession through the frenzied crowd, shaking outstretched hands, accepting congratulations and kisses, thanking everyone over and over again for all the hard work that had brought about this truly historic result.

'Tonight this is your victory, and a victory for the people of England,' he shouted at his supporters above the din. 'The nationalists are finished. Our time has come.'

Outside, a light rain was falling. As Matt crossed the car park, breathing in the fresh air, he saw the silhouette of a familiar face behind the window on the driver's side of a beaten-up blue Volvo. The man was wearing earplugs and seemed to be talking to himself. Matt tapped on the window; it opened to reveal a rotund, bald, bespectacled man whom he knew only too well. On any other day he would have smashed his face. The man removed his earplugs.

'Good morning, Mr Penfold,' said Matt. 'What brings you here? Are you going to join your lord and master – or are you jumping ship?'

Penfold stroked the top of his pate, playing for time.

'I'll sit tight for a few days, watch which way the wind's blowing. We civil servants are supposed to keep our heads down until the next government's been formed.'

'It must be difficult for you, to be on the losing side for once. Aren't you going to congratulate me?'

'Personally, I'm delighted. But you should be careful. The real battle's just about to begin – the generals are getting restless.'

'Haven't you understood – you can't frighten me any more, Penfold. Things have changed.'

'Good luck, Matthew.'

The car-window closed and Penfold drove off towards the blue lights flashing at the exit to the car park. As the prime minister's convoy moved away, Matt could see Penfold's old Volvo following at a discreet distance behind.

Matt told his driver to wait five minutes, to make sure Crouch's caravan was well ahead of them. He needed to cut himself off from everything that had gone before. Time stood still as Matt first sat in silence, taking it all in, and then told the driver they could leave. The rain stopped and the sky cleared as Matt began his dreamy, unforgettable journey, first speeding through the outer suburbs, past the sun-kissed semis shyly preening themselves in the early-morning light, before picking up speed between the high-rise office buildings along the Great West Road, across from the gleaming temple of Westfield shopping centre. He heard the faint growl of a helicopter flying directly overhead. After a nod to the wisteria-clad townhouses on Cheyne Walk, and to the bustling stretch of river opposite, they turned into Horseferry Road and right into Tufton Street. At they entered the road, the driver slammed on the brakes: the street was already packed with a rapturous crowd waiting for Matt's arrival.

Soon the car could advance no further and Matt decided to walk the last hundred yards. After the police had made a narrow channel, Matt began his procession through the cheering throng, shaking hands, kissing babies and old ladies, thanking everyone, calmly taking in the extraordinary fact that his chance – their chance – to turn the country round and heal the wounds had finally come.

'Justice Now,' the crowd chanted, over and over again, alternating with 'Crouch Out, Crouch Out'.

'Kick them where it hurts,' an elderly man shouted in his ear. 'Never forgive, never forget. They're traitors and we want revenge. Make the bastards scream with pain before we kill them.'

'That's not the way we do things,' replied Matt, but the man had turned away.

CHAPTER THIRTY-SEVEN

Matt would never forget the tears of joy on the faces of his closest supporters when he entered the SOCA headquarters that morning, with dawn breaking over London, and the office lit up by the sun streaming in through the windows and the central skylight. Swept up by an immense wave of relief and sense of accomplishment, they deserved their moment of glory. Messages of congratulations and support poured in from all over the country and around the world. Previously sworn enemies shamelessly declared undying friendship and unqualified support. As SOCA won seat after seat, and the nationalists' defeat became clear, Matt's people looked on open-mouthed, almost frightened by the scale of their victory that exceeded all predictions. In the course of a few hours during the night, the old politics had been swept away and the face of the country changed beyond recognition.

The Whitehall machine was not to be outdone in the business of pirouetting and operating three hundred and sixty-degree turns. Shortly after five o'clock in the morning, Matt was standing on a table, celebrating with a glass of water, when an immense cheer lifted the rafters: the Alliance had passed the magic threshold of 326 seats and had won an overall majority in the House of Commons. Barely thirty seconds later, the call came through from the cabinet secretary.

In his rare dealings with Sir Christopher Jenks, Matt had always found him distant and unresponsive. A major league hand-wringer and arse-licker – which to give him his due were probably both necessary qualifications for the job – Matt had always found him too obviously and unctuously close to Crouch. Today the tone of his voice sounded warm, almost purring with pleasure. Matt jumped off the table and shut himself in his office to take the call.

'Congratulations, Mr Barker,' said Jenks. 'We're all delighted at the result. Personally, I was expecting it – it's great news for the country.'

Do these people have any feelings of their own behind the smooth-talking facade? Matt wondered.

'We're here to make sure the transition is as smooth and orderly as possible, and to deal with any bumps in the road that might crop up.'

'Bumps?' asked Matt. 'What do you mean? The result's perfectly clear. Surely there's a procedure Mr Crouch is obliged to follow? He's presumably packing his suitcase as we speak. '

Matt heard Jenks clear his throat.

'Of course, you want to get started right away, that's perfectly natural. The entire civil service is looking forward to giving you their full support, and helping you to achieve your objectives, just as soon as you've crossed the threshold.'

'What threshold? I've just won the election – what else do I have to do?'

'Just show a little compassion to your opponent, Mr Barker, that's all I'm suggesting. This result was a shock to the outgoing prime minister – '

'- Everyone knew he was likely to lose. Where's he been the past few weeks – '

'- and he may need a few hours to come to terms with his defeat. Nothing to be worried about, I've already been in touch with the Palace. You'll get the call this afternoon from Timothy Fitzjohn, His Majesty's private secretary, and the King will ask you to form a government. In the meantime, if there's anything I can do to help, anything at all, don't hesitate.'

Still as smarmy as ever, but at least he's trying to be helpful, or pretending to be.

'Thanks for the offer,' Matt replied. 'I'm glad to hear you're respecting the constitution and applying the usual procedures – I'd expect nothing less. Mr Crouch lost the election, so he has to leave Number Ten as soon as possible. I suggest you send round the removal vans.'

Matt heard another half-stifled cough at the other end of the line.

'Of course, I completely agree. I'll try to get him out by lunchtime,' said Jenks. 'There's a car waiting for you in the street below, if you'd like to go home and get a couple of hours' rest. You'll find a file on the back seat with a list of the more pressing issues facing the new government, and some modest suggestions from my side on how you might wish to deal with them. Feel free to call me any time.'

'Give me an hour or two and I'll get back to you.'

The call over, Matt looked out of the window, and saw a silver grey Jaguar parked on double yellow lines on the opposite side of the road. Two dark-suited men stood next to it on the pavement. The transition was already under way and the system seemed well oiled. The same state that for months had tried to destroy him was now offering its protection. The sole difference was that, in a few hours, he would be holding the reins of power.

Sam came to stand next to him.

'So those are the two men that are going to whisk you away from me,' she said, resting her head on his shoulder.

He tried to smile but couldn't deny it. That was the choice he had made.

'Do you trust them and what they represent?'

'Of course. We don't have any choice. We're the leaders now– we mustn't make the same mistake as our opponents and govern the country in an atmosphere of permanent mistrust. Despite everything that's happened, our institutions are stronger than ever, and the majority of the people are behind us. Thank God England's still a democracy.'

CHAPTER THIRTY-EIGHT

Crouch was back in the War Room, surrounded by assorted generals, admirals and air marshals, each looking supremely self-important and none of them so much as even pretending to show him the slightest respect. He had been ordered to sit at the bottom end of the table, and left there to languish, ignored while the military brass chatted noisily among themselves. He hadn't been allowed to bring anyone with him, and when he asked the way to the washroom, he was told that no one was allowed to leave the room, for security reasons. From time to time someone would look in his direction, mutter something inaudible behind their hands to the people sitting next to them, and burst into laughter.

This wasn't the outcome Crouch had anticipated. The lights were too bright and the room lacked air. He could feel the nausea rising, and looked around for a suitable receptacle in case he had to be sick. He couldn't find one, not even a paper bag or a waste-paper basket. In desperation, he tried some deep breathing exercises that Valentina had taught him when they had gone together on a yoga retreat in the Swiss Alps. How the world had changed.

At last General McIntyre called the meeting to order and everyone immediately stopped talking and sat up straight. McIntyre looked straight at Crouch, staring him down.

'I'm not sure you understand. You're no longer in power.'

Crouch heard the odd titter of laughter from the more senior officers around the table. From their amused expressions, he could see that they enjoyed nothing more than the drubbing and dressing-down of an uppity civilian. When the man in the stocks was a politician, their happiness was complete.

'But you told me I could remain as prime minister, even if I lost the election ...'

Crouch was embarrassed by how reedy his voice sounded. He would try to pitch it lower.

'Quite so,' said McIntyre. 'I'm an officer and a man of his word. You will stay as PM –'

'Thank you –'

'- on two conditions. First, you'll do what we tell you. The crisis in the country is too serious to be dealt with by a single individual. You'll preside over a government of national unity, except that you won't take any decisions. Is that clear?'

Crouch sat perfectly still but his mind was racing. Don't give anything away, he kept saying to himself, don't show any emotion. McIntyre had forced him into a corner and now he had to find a means of escape. Should he save his skin or stand up for his principles? It took Crouch less than a nanosecond to find the answer to that question: for anyone placed in the position in which he now found himself, the first objective logically had to be survival and getting out of the room unscathed. He would think about standing up for his principles later – in the meantime, they could look after themselves.

'Throughout my long political career,' he began, but stopped himself as he saw that half the room was yawning and the other half rolling their eyes. 'I have always been guided by the national interest.'

This seemed to generate further amusement.

The Chief Marshal of the Air Force waded in. Flanked by two stern-looking female officers, he had a long thin face and an air of impatience.

'Tell me honestly, Prime Minister, do you really believe all that crap?'

His fellow officers fell about.

A florid-cheeked Rear Admiral decided to make a contribution.

'You're among friends, Crouch. I know it's not exactly second nature for you politicians, but why don't you speak honestly for once. Tell us what you really believe. Then we can judge if you're the right man to act as the figurehead we need in these troubled times. Just tell us the truth.'

There were all looking at him now. He knew he mustn't show any weakness. He searched for the right words.

Before he could open his mouth, General McIntyre delivered another blast.

'The second condition is that you remain inside Number Ten for the next twenty-four hours. Keep schtum. You must have no contact with the outside world – neither with your officials, nor the media, and certainly not with your revolting Russian tart –'

'- That's no way –'

'Don't interrupt.' McIntyre was red in the face and glowering. 'When the nation was facing its gravest peril, you spent your nights shagging an enemy agent.'

Doubtless the general was jealous of Crouch's sexual prowess. Which was a small matter of satisfaction, but didn't make him any less dangerous.

McIntyre recomposed himself, and banged his fist on the table.

'So that's the deal. We run the country and you stay out of the public eye. If you don't like it, we can easily find someone else. The home secretary, for example, is standing ready to do her duty if called. You're a spent force, Crouch. You're lucky to be alive, after all the damage you've done and your pathetic showing in the election. You're only useful to us because for the people who don't follow these things too closely – in other words, the vast majority of the population - you symbolise continuity. We need to keep your supporters onside – the few that remain – to prevent Barker getting anywhere near Downing Street. Most of them will say, "If that old arsehole Crouch is still in Number Ten, that means the rebels have lost", and they'll feel reassured. Do you accept?'

There was a long pause before Crouch replied. He had to sort out a couple of practical points first, before getting on to the high politics and questions of loyalty. It was a question of focussing on the priorities.

'Can I keep the car and the flat?'

General McIntyre peered over his glasses.

'Of course, if that's what's important to you. We get the power, you keep the trappings. That sounds like a sensible compromise - thank you for your understanding. You'll now be escorted back to your quarters, where you'll remain until we judge the time is right for you to re-emerge. You must have no contact with the cabinet secretary or the outside world. For your safety and wellbeing, the flat will be placed under armed guard. If you need anything, just let them know. You're dismissed.'

Two military policemen took up position behind Crouch's chair as he stood up. Each took one of his elbows and guided him towards the door leading into the tunnel.

'Everything's in place for tomorrow,' he heard McIntyre say. 'Barker's finished, and Crouch is under house arrest. The troops will take up position during the night. Tell the Palace they can call Barker now. Make sure they record his conversation with the King.'

The heavy metal door slammed shut behind him.

CHAPTER THIRTY-NINE

The waiting was getting on Matt's nerves. He had shut himself in his office to get a couple of hours' sleep on the sofa, but the myriad implications of his election victory continued to swirl around his head. In vain he tried to stop thinking about the millions of people whose lives would be directly affected by his every decision from now on. From his first seconds in office, he would have to demonstrate beyond any doubt that he was up to the job. His enemies would be watching and waiting for his first wrong move, and would show no pity. He couldn't afford the slightest slip-up. His body was exhausted but his mind wouldn't stand still. He felt shattered yet he had to show supreme self-confidence. He could see no rational explanation for Crouch's delay in handing over power.

At five o'clock in the afternoon, his nerves frayed and his impatience rising, Matt turned on the electric kettle and made himself a cup of tea. A whole day had passed, without any contact from either the Palace or Downing Street. The only news was that Crouch, despite Jenks's promise that he would be out by lunchtime, had refused to budge from Number Ten. Jenks must have either misread Crouch's reaction to his defeat, or his phone call to Matt had been a deliberate attempt to butter him up and play for time. Matt already felt let down, before he had even taken office, by the man who was supposed to become his most trusted adviser. Such ambivalence was typical of snotty-nosed civil servants like Jenks, who were congenitally incapable of coming off the fence. He wasn't going to put up with this outdated work culture of smarmy hypocrisy. These people thought they possessed a God-given licence to run the country in perpetuity. They didn't know it yet, but they would be in for a shock.

'What's going on?' Matt asked Jenks on the phone. 'You told me yesterday he'd be out within hours. Instead he's gone to ground like a frightened rabbit. Either your judgement's seriously impaired, or you didn't tell me the truth.'

'Mr Barker, I assure you, I would never – '

'Get this sorted, or your job's on the line. I'll give you and Crouch twenty-four hours, and then if necessary I'll occupy Downing Street by force. Yours will be the first head to roll.'

The official position was that Crouch was taking soundings from other parties in an attempt to build a new majority. The Downing Street spokeswoman added that the outgoing prime minister had the constitutional right and duty to examine all available options that could provide the country with stability and continuity. Matt knew that was nonsense – the numbers simply didn't stack up.

All kinds of unsubstantiated rumours circulated feverishly around Whitehall. The media were frantic. Crouch was having a nervous breakdown, or was negotiating another position. The nationalists had put a pistol to his head and were forcing him to stay in power. The President of the United States had told him that the survival of NATO depended on the ENP remaining in government. An eminent psychiatrist had claimed that Matt Barker's mental health issues made him unfit for office.

'You've got to cut through all this nonsense, and show your face,' said Sam. 'As the next Prime Minister, you must be the voice of reason that people can rely on. You should reassure them that you're ready to take power at any moment, and this absurd waiting game has to end.'

'I suppose you're right,' he said, and began to scribble down a few lines. A few minutes later, grim-faced but outwardly serene, Matt went down to face the hysterical hordes of hacks outside the Tufton Street office. He stood behind a makeshift wooden podium and delivered a brief statement.

'On a human level, one can understand why someone who has held the highest office in the land for several years wishes to cling to power. But the interests of one man count for nothing when the future of the entire country is at stake. The people's choice must be respected and the message from the voters was clear: the ENP lost the election and Mr Crouch can no longer remain as prime minister. I have no doubt whatsoever that the English people's innate sense of decency and fairness will prevail, and that Mr Crouch will accept this reality – the sooner the better, in the national interest. The idea that the country's democratic institutions can be held to ransom by one man is inconceivable. Justice will be done.'

Matt went back inside the building without taking any questions.

Two hours later, as the bells from Westminster Abbey were striking seven o'clock, Matt's patience was rewarded and he was politely summoned to the Palace.

'The country needs clarity,' said Timothy Fitzjohn. 'His Majesty will see you in an hour's time. I hope that's convenient.'

'Of course,' Matt replied, punching the air. Waves of energy swept through him and he felt like his old self again, as though he was floating onwards and upwards on a giant cushion of relief. The English might take their time about getting things right, but they always got there in the end. Muddling through and rising to the challenge were in their DNA.

After putting on a charcoal grey suit and white shirt, he accepted Sam's choice of a dark blue tie. He stood by the window, polishing his glasses, plunged in thought. It was still hard to take in; from the moment he went out of the front door, he would be swept along by what he called the paradox of power – the never-ending sequence of unforeseeable events, decisions and calamities that would be forever outside his control. It was too late to worry now. He patted down his hair, adjusted his tie in the mirror, and took Sam in his arms.

'There's my man!' said Sam, nestling against his chest while being careful not to crease or smudge his shirt. 'You look very distinguished and prime ministerial – just like Clark Kent!'

'A little more respect, if you don't mind,' said Matt. 'I'll let you know as soon as it's official.'

Outside, at the back entrance, Frank the driver was waiting by the car. He opened the rear side-door.

'All set, sir?' said Frank. 'Lovely evening for it.'

They drove off, between two unmarked cars in front and behind. Matt had been expecting a motorcycle escort, but presumably that would come later. He wondered what kissing hands with the King really meant – he'd better have an explanation ready for the next time he saw Sophie. In what felt like no time at all, the car swept past the small crowd that had gathered outside Buckingham Palace and through the gates. Matt stepped out and was greeted by Timothy Fitzjohn.

'Very good of you to come. I'm sorry it took a little longer than we expected,' said Fitzjohn, as he escorted Matt under the archway and into the inner forecourt. 'His Majesty is looking forward to meeting you. There's lots to talk about.'

'It's a great honour,' Matt mumbled. 'I never dreamed that one day – '

'You've deserved it. Democracy has a habit of coming up with surprises. You mustn't be nervous; the King will put you at your ease. He's very good at that, very direct. You'll see.'

In solemn silence, the two of them walked up the steps to the main entrance of the Palace and down what seemed like several miles of corridors. The small talk was over. After a few initial hiccups, the constitution was creaking into action. Power lay within his grasp.

CHAPTER FORTY

Inside the Palace, Matt was surprised to find everything so dark and stifling. Trying not to be put off by the ornate surroundings, epitomised by heavy-hanging crimson drapes and over-elaborate gilt cornices, Matt bowed to the King and accepted the invitation to sit down. He was determined to savour every minute of this historic encounter, which no doubt would be the first of many. He was even prepared to overlook the King's stuffiness and pomposity. Matt reckoned they both needed each other in the current circumstances. A good working relationship between the monarch and the prime minister was more essential than ever in these troubled times. After all the hardship and suffering, waging a class war was in nobody's interests. He would give the King the benefit of the doubt, and devote himself to working for the common good.

The monarch took a sip from a glass of water, and fiddled with the silk handkerchief in his breast pocket.

'Uncharted waters, it would appear,' he said. 'We've all got to work out what's best for the country. Sacrifices may be required, wouldn't you agree?'

Matt wondered who was in charge of polishing the King's black brogues, and how they made them shine so brightly. He didn't quite see the point of the question, but it would be discourteous not to reply.

'Indeed, Your Majesty,' he said.

'I'm advised that constitutional precedents don't tell us anything about electoral alliances. They only cover political parties, and the ability to command a majority in the Commons. We all have a duty to respect the constitution, which has served us so well over many centuries. So we're in a quandary, don't you think?'

Matt stiffened, as he switched off the faintly idiotic smile that he had intended as a mark of deference. If he'd understood correctly the way the conversation was heading, the man opposite him, for all his airs and graces and proclaimed interest in good causes, was about to suggest the unthinkable.

'With respect, Sir, who gave you this advice?'

The King's bottom lip twitched to the right.

'All people who, from long experience, know what's best for the country, including the chief of the defence staff, representing all the armed forces, and one or two business leaders and influential people in the media. People who, down the years, have proved their steadfast loyalty to me and to the nation - not fair-weather friends at all. The kind you can count on in a crisis. I have absolute confidence in their judgement.'

Matt shook his head, as if to empty it of the nonsense he was being forced to listen to. Bristling, he leaned forward.

'And what, may I ask, do these loyal friends of yours propose? What have they told you to do?'

'I was coming to that. They all agree that, given the critical situation in which we find ourselves, the best solution would be a government of national unity. I understand that you'd occupy one of the great offices of state.'

Matt's mind started racing. One of the corgis began yapping at his heels. The urge to kick it was almost overwhelming.

'I trust that would be acceptable?' the King went on.

A phone rang on the table next to where he was sitting.

'Yes, he's here now. Everything's under control. Just as we agreed.'

The King put the phone down, and placed his hands together, fingers extended, as if in prayer.

'Can I take it you'd accept? For the sake of the country, you understand. I would be most grateful.'

The sense of betrayal was like being kicked in the stomach. All his life Matt had respected the royal family and what they stood for. That the King should propose such a gross dereliction of duty was desperately disappointing. He had come to the Palace determined to see the King in the best possible light, and instead they were playing him for a fool. He couldn't let this pass.

'Tell me, in your so-called government of national unity, who would lead this coup d'état?'

The King's face had become more than usually florid. He started twisting the gold signet ring on the little finger of his left hand.

'I really can't say at this stage,' he finally let out.

That could only mean one thing.

'I'm still waiting for your reply,' the King went on, irrationally emboldened. 'Your approval is vital to our success. I hope I can count on your support.'

Unable to restrain himself any longer, Matt stood up, his eyes blazing.

'You're on their side, aren't you? Well, sorry George, you've made the wrong choice. You're with the crooks and clowns that have ruined and pillaged what remains of this country - you should be ashamed of yourself.'

'I don't appreciate your tone, Mr Barker. We're all servants of the constitution – '

'Let me tell you one more thing and then I'll leave. Listen carefully - your reaction to what I'm going to say will decide how you live the rest of your life.'

The King's facial tic went into overdrive. Matt walked over to the high-backed chair where the monarch was sitting. Looking down at him, Matt softly and calmly delivered his message.

'If you refuse to accept the result of the general election by asking me to form a government, your reign is over.'

The King laughed back in Matt's face.

'They're all against you, Mr Barker. You may have won an election, but no one of any influence in this country supports you. Your alliance is a ramshackle group of leftie friends, not a serious option for running the country. Any idiot can see that. The next prime minister has to be the leader of the largest party – that's what the nation expects and the constitution requires. You'll never make it to Number Ten – we've made sure of that.'

Matt clenched both fists. He resisted the temptation to grab the King by the lapels and bang his head against the mantelpiece. He mustn't give him the satisfaction of seeing him lose his self-control.

'You disappoint me, George, and you and your friends underestimate me. If you go against the people, you leave me with no other option.'

The King brought his hand up to his neck, as if he could already hear the swish and clunk of the falling guillotine.

Matt left the room without another word. As he ran for his life through the maze of deserted corridors, an alarm sounded. When he arrived downstairs at the main entrance, the two guardsmen outside their sentry boxes presented arms and let him pass unhindered through the gates. It must have been his imagination, but he could have sworn that one of them winked at him.

Seeing no sign of Frank or the silver Jaguar, he quickly texted Sam, before stopping to say a few words to the waiting press corps who had gathered in front of the statue of Queen Victoria.

'No decision has yet been taken on who should be asked to form the next government. I had a useful exchange of views with

His Majesty, and stressed the importance of respecting the result of the election. Later this evening I'll make a televised appeal on where I believe the country should go from here.'

Sam and Rob arrived right on cue. Together with a sizeable group of SOCA supporters, they all marched up The Mall, to catch the number 11 bus towards Shoreditch.

Hassan had everything ready to start filming when they arrived at The People's TV studio. With half an eye on the digital clock counting down the seconds, Matt finished debriefing Rob and Sam on what had happened at the Palace. In three minutes he would go on air to warn the people of the imminent putsch, and tell them to stand firm and defend their rights, whatever the cost.

'I wish we didn't have to do this, but there's no other way. We can't let down the millions of people who voted for us. This is our opponents' last desperate throw. People would never trust us again if we gave in without a fight. Are you with me?'

'Of course,' said Sam.

Rob stared at the floor.

'You should accept the offer to serve in the new government,' he said. 'Don't ask me why. Just be grateful for what you've achieved.'

Matt and Sam exchanged glances.

'You can't desert us now,' she said, 'after everything we've been through together, without giving any reasons. If there's something we should know, you've got to tell us.'

Rob wouldn't meet her gaze.

'What have they done to you?' Sam pressed him.

Rob looked up and stared straight through her.

'Trust me – I can't say any more,' he said. 'I've always been with you, but we can't go any further. I'm trying to save you.'

Sam threw herself on Rob, her clenched fists pummelling his chest.

'I can't believe this – what are you talking about? We can't possibly back off now.'

Rob roughly pushed her away.

'Let him go,' said Matt. 'Whoever's got to him, if he's lost his nerve, he's no use to us tonight. He'll recover soon enough.'

His face pallid, Rob picked up his briefcase and left the studio.

Matt shut his eyes and massaged his temples. Thirty seconds left. He was past caring and wouldn't be distracted. If Rob was a traitor, and there was evidence to prove it, they would have to get rid of him. This new discovery didn't bear thinking about – Matt would sort out the problem later. After doing some more breathing exercises, and a nod at the floor manager, Matt faced the camera to address the nation.

'This is an historic and decisive moment for us all. Five days ago, you voted to elect a parliament and a government. The election campaign was the most brutal and violent ever seen in this country, with tragic loss of life. Yet it produced a clear result. The Save Our Country Alliance won a narrow but indisputable majority in the House of Commons, with 340 seats. The English Nationalist Party won 290 seats. Logic, fairness and our constitution require that the Alliance should form the next government. The will of the people couldn't be clearer.'

'To my profound regret, the outgoing prime minister has refused to accept this result. In a desperate attempt to retain power, he and his corrupt cronies have persuaded the King to support a military coup d'état.'

'The former prime minister and the King may not realise it, but England is no longer a feudal country. They will not prevail. The King has forfeited his right to the throne. James Crouch will be arrested and charged with treason. He will of course be given a scrupulously fair trial.'

'I appeal to all of you who have the future of our country at heart to join me tomorrow in a march for freedom, to uphold our democratic rights. This is our country's chance for a fresh start, and a better life for you all. Let's seize it together.'

'Now get it out there,' said Matt to Sam. 'Use every platform you can find.'

Matt felt his phone vibrate. He saw it was Giles Penfold.

'Are you completely insane? Don't you realise you've just signed your death warrant? Your only chance is to disappear before they come for you, you've got to leave this minute, you understand, you mustn't wait a moment longer …'

Matt let him prattle on for a few more seconds, and then ended the call. Penfold and his like still hadn't realised that the old threats no longer worked. With the result of the election, the world had moved on, and the people Penfold used to work for were no longer in charge. Their authority was slipping away. If everything went according to plan, in less than twenty-four hours they would count for nothing.

Alone in the flat in Number Ten, curled up in bed in his paisley pyjamas and shivering with fear for his future, James Crouch couldn't get to sleep. He had never felt so low and ashamed of himself. By accepting the deal to stay in office without exercising power, he had seriously miscalculated, and lost all dignity and self-respect. He understood now that General McIntyre would never keep his side of the bargain, and would eventually throw him to the wolves. Valentina wasn't answering his calls, and he missed her terribly. He should never have let her go like that. The military policeman had locked his bedroom door – 'for your own safety, sir'. There was no way out. He wondered who would go and visit his elderly mother, wracked with Alzheimer's and arthritis, once they came to take him away. He knew that talking to him cheered her up, even if she made no sense, but from now on she would be on her own.

He imagined the knock on the door in the morning, at first light, the initial polite tap quickly followed by remorseless banging. He had been tossed on the mile-high scrap heap of pointless politicians whose shelf life was over and whose time had come and gone. He had started with nothing and worked his way up, yet his ultimate failure meant nobody would ever give him the slightest hint of praise or gratitude or recognition. The thought that he would end his life as a loser made him inconsolable.

CHAPTER FORTY-ONE

They entered Parliament Square as Big Ben struck twelve. Twenty tanks and armoured cars, splayed out in a semicircle, were parked outside the Houses of Parliament. A hundred hooded marksmen in military camouflage stood in a line by the Cromwell Green entrance, light machine guns at the ready. The military helicopters flow lower and lower, buzzing the crowd as it surged into the square. The chanting had stopped and the drums were no longer beating. From all sides, loudspeakers repeatedly blared out a warning that if the demonstrators didn't leave immediately, they would be evacuated by force. No one obeyed the command, as more and more people poured into the square.

Alone, with Sam a few paces behind him, Matt walked towards the marksmen. The loudspeakers fell quiet. Apart from the helicopters, now hovering above the river, and the screech of seagulls, a blanket of silence fell on the square. Matt came to a halt, ten yards in front of the soldiers. Then the order to fire was shouted out: perfectly synchronised, the marksmen raised their guns and took aim at the crowd, before firing a round in the air. Amid screams of panic, people started pushing in all directions. A minute elapsed, and then the order was repeated. The jostling first resumed, then ceased.

Matt steeled himself, imagining another crackle of gunfire and praying it wouldn't happen. Two more minutes passed without any further sound or movement in the square. The entire crowd collectively held its breath. All eyes were focussed on the row of marksmen and their weapons.

One by one, starting from the far end of the line, the soldiers slowly removed their hoods and laid their arms on the ground. Then they stood to attention, looking impassively straight ahead.

The tank crews jumped out of their vehicles, and also came to attention.

From different parts of the square, a few people started clapping. Suddenly, with an immense, ear-splitting roar, as one the crowd cheered its relief and gratitude. Matt found a tree to lean against and closed his eyes for a moment, his whole body trembling. He knew what he had to do. First, he texted Jenny to say it was safe for her and the children to come and join the celebrations. They were waiting for his call at McDonalds in Trafalgar Square, and now he wanted to have Sophie and Jack by his side.

Then it was time to show the world that power in England was changing hands. After asking Sam to come with him, he forced a way through the crowd to the main gate of the House of Commons, on the other side of the road. As the leader of the coalition that had won the election, it was his perfect right to enter Parliament. He had a word with the two policemen at the gate: without a second's hesitation, they shook his hand and let him through. He heard another roar from the crowd behind him, as his victorious entry into the Palace of Westminster was captured by a thousand cameras.

Inside the building, Matt solemnly made his way past the marble statues of imperial heroes to the central lobby, where he was greeted by the Serjeant-at-Arms, who was wearing his traditional court dress and black patent leather shoes. Matt was then escorted to the prime minister's office in the North Wing: he gingerly sat down at the centre of the long mahogany table. Sam took some more pictures and sent them to the main agencies. After he had asked the Serjeant-at-Arms to take one of him and Sam together, Matt stretched his legs under the table. Against all odds, they had done it. Tomorrow at the latest, he would enter Downing Street.

They returned to the waiting crowd in Parliament Square. As Sam took up position at the front of the crowd, Matt, light-headed and awash with happiness, leaped up the steps on to the makeshift stage that had been erected next to the statue of Winston Churchill. As he approached the podium, two special branch officers emerged from nowhere, staying close behind him. Matt bent down to adjust the height of the microphone. Looking across the heads of the jubilant crowd, he thought he recognised Sophie and Jack standing at the back with Jenny, and waved in their direction. He noticed that Sam was gesticulating excitedly, shouting something, but he couldn't make out what she was saying. A few paces behind her, Rob was talking into his phone, his hand over his mouth.

So many hard-won battles – not just against Crouch and the ENP, but also with himself and his insidious demons – had brought Matt to this moment. He raised his arms, looking around the crowd, smiling broadly, taking in the deafening cheers. His eyes searched for Sam, but she seemed to have disappeared.

'This victory is yours!' he began. The crowd roared its approval. 'Are you ready to take Downing Street?'

'Yes!' they all shouted, and the chanting broke out all over the square, louder and louder: 'Number Ten, Number Ten ...'

As he waited for the noise to die down, he looked up at the wide-open window on the fifth floor of Portcullis House, where he saw the glint of the sun on the long barrel of a sniper's gun.

'Just for your protection, sir,' said one of the men beside him.

Then Matt heard the crack of a single shot. His legs buckled and he saw Sam's blurred face as she fell on top of him. Her mouth was open and her eyes were shut, with blood spurting from the side of her neck.

CHAPTER FORTY-TWO

Dazed and desperate, Matt was led away from the platform, while the first aid team attended to Sam. They staunched the blood and put her on a drip, before carrying her on a stretcher to the waiting ambulance.

The hours waiting in the corridor at St Thomas's while they operated were the longest of his life. The thought that she had saved him and now might die was unbearable. He wished it had been the other way round.

After six hours, the surgeon came out of the theatre. He looked grim and exhausted.

'The operation went as well as could be expected. There's a good chance she'll pull through.'.

Matt sank on to a hospital chair, weak with relief, thanking the gods.

The next morning, before entering Downing Street at last, he brought a bunch of peonies to the hospital and sat next to her bed for an hour, holding her hand, talking softly to her from time to time and giving thanks. He would look after her and make sure she recovered. He promised they would spend the summer recess together, doing whatever she wanted. She could choose – they could lie in the sun somewhere under an umbrella pine or on a sandy beach, or fish for salmon from an old boat on a still loch, with no sound but the wind and the water rustling through the reeds. Or they could walk hand in hand over the hills, buy a dog, or potter about the Downing Street garden. Go to the opera or watch old movies in front of the fire. He would bring her breakfast in bed and lovingly cook her favourite meals. Whatever she wanted, he would give her. Always and forever.

As he was talking, every so often her eyes half-opened, and he felt a gentle pressure from her hand. Matt knew this was Sam's way of telling him to stop bullshitting and get back to work. In case he'd forgotten, he had a country to run.

Later that morning, when Matt finally arrived at Number Ten, he found that the real wielders of power had one last surprise in store for him.

As was the custom, before going inside, he stood in front of the shiny black door with the bronze number, posing for the photographers and TV crews. He was looking forward to meeting Christopher Jenks and the Downing Street staff, who by tradition would be lined up in the hallway to welcome him into his new home. When Matt judged the photo call was over, after a last wave to the media, he turned round and the door opened from the inside.

Amid the sound of affectionate cheers and clapping, to his astonishment Matt found himself face to face with Giles Penfold.

'Welcome to Number Ten, Prime Minister. I'm the new cabinet secretary. Jenks went off on gardening leave – his health wasn't too good - and they asked me to step in. We hope you'll be very happy here. I'm so pleased about the good news from the hospital. Now let me introduce you to your secretaries – I'm sure you'll find them a brilliant team.'

They never found the sniper.

Printed in Great Britain
by Amazon